FREEDOM'S
LAST STAND

THE RISE OF EVIL

RICHARD J. KELLY
JAMES MORAN

The Writer's Bloc, Inc. USA

"Freedom's Last Stand – The Rise of Evil" is a work
of fiction. Names, people, places, entities, events, and
incidents contained in this novel are either the product
of the Authors' imagination or are used fictitiously.

ACKNOWLEDGEMENTS

I would like to thank my best friend since I was three years old, Paul Liben. Without his inspiration, creativity, Biblical expertise, and editing abilities, Freedom's Last Stand would not have been possible. Special thanks to Father Frank Creamer, Ken B., Tony C., Vinny, Susan K., Big Al, Iron Mike, Maryanne T., Miss Wendy, Betsy G., and most of all my lovely wife Cathy, who put up with granting me all the time necessary to make FLS a reality.

-Rich Kelly

I will pour out my Spirit on all people.
Your sons and daughters will prophesy,
your old men will dream dreams,
your young men will see visions.
Even on my servants, both men and women,
I will pour out my Spirit in those days.
I will show wonders in the heavens
and on earth,
blood and fire and billows of smoke.
The sun will be turned to darkness
and the moon to blood
before the coming of the great and dreadful day of
the Lord.
And everyone who calls
on the name of the Lord will be saved.

—Joel 2:28-32

CHAPTER 1
IN A CITY THAT NEVER SLEEPS

"She's as beautiful as ever," he thought to himself.

He had taken the trip many times, but there was always something special about Lady Liberty at sunrise high above the glistening New York Harbor. This time was no different.

As he landed his helicopter on Liberty Island, Navy SEAL commander David Stein was greeted by his security detail and a large banner reading "Happy Birthday America! July 4, 2026." The banner was in place for the next day's big event at the Statue of Liberty commemorating the country's 250th birthday.

After boarding a 47-foot Coast Guard MLB, David was quickly transported to Battery Park where his ten-year-old Chevy SUV sat in an area that had been designated by the Secret Service as "off-limits" to the public. He began the drive home to Howard Beach near JFK Airport. Crossing over the Brooklyn Bridge, he glanced back over his shoulder and smiled at the bright orange glow of sunrise reflecting off the Freedom Tower. Before long, David was winding through city streets that told the story of his life.

Home for David was where St. Patrick and San Gennaro, NYPD and FDNY, meet. Houses remain in families for generations, and friends grow up together, sticking together for life. This was certainly true of David's friends, most of whom still lived on or near the block where they grew up. David's house was a tidy, two-story red brick home, with a neatly manicured lawn, and a modest backyard.

David's wife Sarah was the daughter of famed former federal prosecutor Mel Goodman. Sarah, a Messianic Jew, wore her faith on her sleeve, in contrast to her husband who was a confirmed agnostic. But David was proud of his wife in countless ways. Smart and savvy, sophisticated yet down-to-earth, witty and attractive, she was his alter ego and his equal.

As he stepped out of his SUV, David felt relieved to be home and was eager to change out of his dark blue aviator jumpsuit. He had a trim, well-defined build with chiseled features and a Mediterranean complexion. On his way to the front porch, he moved a small pink bicycle blocking the path to the door. For a moment, he reminisced about how many times his father moved his bicycle off the same path that led to the family home.

David gazed briefly at the mezuzah on the door frame and smiled. "This was Sarah's idea," he thought, as he reached into his pocket for his house keys.

Opening the door, David surprised Sarah, who was

dressed for work and getting their six-year-old daughter, Rebecca, ready for summer school.

As David kissed Sarah, Rebecca tugged David's sleeve and giggled. "Daddy! Daddy!"

He smiled at Sarah before bending down to hug Rebecca. "Are you all ready for the day, pumpkin?"

"Yes I am, Daddy. I've got my lunch, my bag, my clarinet, my…"

As Rebecca kept babbling, David turned to Sarah. "I'll take her to school."

"No honey, you need your rest. And leave the dishes; I'll get them later."

"Okay, but let me pick up Becca after school."

"Deal. Now go to bed."

"Sweetheart, I'm not the least bit tired."

Sarah smiled. "Just a suggestion."

She looked down at David's shoes and shook her head. "I also suggest that you throw those old shoes in the trash; they're falling apart."

"These are the most comfortable shoes I have."

Sarah looked at him skeptically. "You can't be serious. You've had them more than twenty years."

"Honey, not only are they comfortable, they're my 'good luck' shoes. Remember, I was wearing them the day we met."

"Well, maybe you can find a crazy cobbler who's willing to rebuild them. I have to run; see you later."

"Sarah, avoid the expressway; there was a five-car pile-up."

"I just heard that on 1010 WINS. Once again the Long Island Parking Lot is living up to its name. Bye hon, I love you."

"Love you, too."

✧

After dropping Becca off at school, Sarah began the difficult task of avoiding highway traffic while heading into the city. Work for Sarah was at a secure location in Manhattan where she directed government intelligence staff. It was Friday morning before the holiday weekend, and traffic was wild. She found success in taking the backroads, though travel time was still longer than usual. As she pulled into the parking lot, Sarah noticed that it was almost filled to capacity.

The guard in the booth stuck his head out the window. "Hey lady, there's no…. Oh, Ms. Stein, beautiful morning. There's one more spot left for your…company."

"Thanks, Tim."

"Running late today?"

"Yes, the traffic was worse than usual."

Sarah parked the white Volvo her father had given her as a birthday gift the previous year right next to a gold Ferrari with a Nevada license plate donning the letter "O."

Sarah was all too familiar with the owner of the Ferrari and couldn't help but shake her head. She was initially inclined to nick the Ferrari ever so slightly while opening her car door, but her conscience wouldn't permit it.

Sarah locked the Volvo and hurried along a concrete

walkway before darting up several stairs that led to an unassuming office building. The plaque to the left of the intercom near the entrance doors spelled out "Code Enforcement." Sarah caught a glimpse of her reflection in the mirrored entrance doors. She proceeded to neatly arrange her long brown hair behind her shoulders and affix the ID badge to her sleeveless tan blouse.

Once inside the lobby, Sarah entered an outdated 1940's Otis elevator and pulled out her pass-key, inserted it into the keyhole and turned it two clicks to the left. The elevator brought her five levels above the highest floor indicated on the panel. The doors opened up to a suite of high-tech state-of-the-art offices.

Approaching the security desk, Sarah observed Ben ogling a woman on the security monitor as she walked down the corridor. "Ben…..Ben."

He quickly swiveled around to face Sarah. "Ahh…. good morning, Ms. Stein."

"Ben, what are you looking at?"

"Ahh…Ms. Carlson just checked in. I was…uh… watching to make sure she got down the hallway, uh… safely."

"Yeah right, Ben."

"Have a great day, Ms. Stein."

"You too." Sarah shook her head as she walked away.

Sliding her I.D. badge through an electronic reader, she gained entrance to the secure area. Sarah was slim with an athletic build and a natural beauty making her appear younger than her years. Heading down the corridor, she suddenly came face-to-face with a colleague coming around the corner.

Sarah grudgingly acknowledged her co-worker. "Hello, Octavia."

"Good morning, Sarah," Octavia replied icily.

Octavia Carlson was an undercover agent, master of disguise, and one of the most successful field operatives the agency ever had. She was an agent who used all of her attributes to obtain intelligence, often for selfish gain.

"Octavia, you didn't happen to see Frank, did you?"

"Well, I saw him a couple of minutes ago; he seemed fit to be tied." Octavia winked salaciously, "If you know what I mean."

"And I'm sure you'd love to do the tying."

"And righteous Sarah will do the untying. How true to form, Miss Judgmental. FYI, Frank is working on the computer next to your office. I've noticed you've been spending a lot of time with him lately." Octavia smirked. "Now, if you'll excuse me, I'm flying to Dubai later today to do some… 'real' undercover work."

"You mean you're off to meet adoring fans at the world's biggest adult playground. No doubt you'll be working *under* the covers."

"Yes, it's a difficult assignment in the world's new financial capital."

"Tell that to Wall Street," Sarah shot back as Octavia walked away, her stiletto heels clicking like a metronome on the hard terrazzo floor.

Frank Robbins, the IT manager, appeared around the corner.

"She's lucky her position is so low-profile around New York, although it must be hard for Ms. Narcissist," Sarah said to Frank.

"Well, she is definitely aware of her movie-star looks." Frank and several other men in the corridor followed Octavia with their eyes.

"Unfortunately, her beauty is superficial," Sarah muttered. "So, what's up, Frank?"

"The project I've been developing for Octavia has hit a snag. We can't seem to get the radius beyond three feet. However, within that range, it's been a complete success. You can't see even a trace."

"Great, Frank. I'm sure you'll nail it down soon. So, what else is going on?"

"Director Campbell is up from Washington today. He wants us in his office, now."

"Right now?"

"He said to see him as soon as you arrive."

"Okay, Frank, let's get it over with."

Frank followed Sarah to the end of the long corridor and into a reception area. The Director's assistant nodded to them while she spoke into the phone. The door to Robert Campbell's corner office stood wide open.

Campbell, who was about sixty with thick salt-and-pepper hair and a large intimidating presence, sat at the head of a small conference table. Sarah couldn't help thinking that his perfectly cut pinstripe suit cost more than she made in a month. But that didn't bother her. What bothered her was the animated conversation Campbell appeared to be having with Octavia, who was seated on the Director's right.

The assistant hung up the phone. "Please go in; he's expecting you."

"Thanks, Helen," Frank said politely as he motioned for Sarah to lead the way.

Octavia saw them first, her dark blue eyes clearly saying "get lost" before the Director looked up.

"Good morning, Director," Frank exclaimed as they approached.

"Sarah, Frank, please sit down."

Frank took the seat at the foot of the table while Sarah sat as close to Frank as possible, trying not to look at Octavia.

"I just wanted to go over a few things with the three of you. I'll get right to the point. First, Sarah, you've been insisting for almost a year now that an attack on the homeland is coming. You've based your claims on some vague chatter and other intel that you managed to collect through several channels..."

Sarah was immediately perturbed by his tone and felt the need to cut in.

"Sir, with all due respect, the channels from which we received our intel have all proven to be reliable in the past."

"That's true, Sarah, and I appreciate your many accomplishments over the years. However, this agency cannot waste valuable time and resources barking up the wrong trees. We have many credible threats to pursue all around the world. I was just talking with agent Carlson about all of the progress she is making in Dubai where her extensive business and government connections are the perfect cover. Octavia has almost singlehandedly infiltrated the human trafficking and drug trade throughout the Middle East. As you know, the profits from these activities often end up funding terrorist attacks against the U.S. and its allies…"

Sarah jumped in again while continuing to avoid eye contact with Octavia. "Sir, there's no question that drug and human trafficking abroad are big problems, but that doesn't mean we shouldn't be on the highest alert here at home. Every law enforcement agency in the United States needs to know what we've been hearing."

Robert Campbell was not used to being interrupted. "Sarah, while you and Frank have been spending inordinate amounts of time working on your 'secret project,' Ms. Carlson has been getting tangible results on multiple fronts. She's an agent who is willing to use all of her available assets to achieve her goals." Looking directly at Sarah, he continued authoritatively. "That is why, Ms. Stein, starting Monday, you will be reporting to agent Carlson to assist her with the mission in Dubai."

Sarah couldn't believe her ears. "This can't be happening," she thought as she forced herself to look toward Octavia's end of the table. Octavia puckered her pouty lips when their eyes met.

"Sir, what about all of the projects I've been working

on? We still have loose ends in Venezuela, and we're finally starting to stabilize things in Nigeria." Sarah's tone was almost pleading, but she was too proud to beg.

"Ty Richardson will be transferring here from the London office. Frank will be his point-man and bring Ty up to speed with all of the areas you've been working on."

"Sir, respectfully, I need just a little more time. I know a domestic attack is imminent." With her emotions at the boiling point, Sarah managed to keep her voice on an even keel.

"Agent Stein, you have seventy-two hours to produce solid evidence that will support your claims. If the evidence is not on my desk by Monday at noon, you will report to agent Carlson in Dubai. Are we clear on this?"

Sarah looked down at the table and swallowed the lump in her throat. "Yes, sir," she quietly responded.

Director Campbell then turned his attention to Frank. "Okay. Now, Robbins, before the end of the day, I'd like an update on the shrouding project you've been working on for Octavia. I understand there have been some issues with the radius."

"That's right, sir. I don't think it will be ready for agent Carlson's pending field deployment, but I'm hopeful we can have it operational by mid-August."

"Good work, Frank. We'll talk further this afternoon. If there are no other pressing matters to discuss, I'll let the three of you get back to work."

Octavia got up first and put a hand on the Director's shoulder. "Great meeting, Bob. Call me if you're free for lunch."

"I don't have time today. Your flight to Dubai will be leaving from TEB at 7:30, hangar six. I'll be contacting you Sunday. Tomorrow I'll be attending the celebration with President Thompson."

"Please give my regards to our Commander-in-Chief. I would have loved to have been there but it's just not possible for a woman to be in two places at the same time, is it?" Octavia smiled at the Director as she strutted out of the office.

Sarah put a fist under her chin to keep her jaw from dropping. In all of her years with the agency, this was the first time she heard anyone address Robert Campbell as "Bob."

Sarah's eyes met Frank's as they stood up. Without speaking, they said to each other, "we need to talk."

Frank nodded to the Director before he and Sarah headed for the door. "Just a moment, agent Stein. I'd like a word with you."

Sarah turned around as Frank slipped out of the office. "Sir?"

The Director approached and moved in closely before speaking in a low voice filled with concern. "Sarah, you're one of the best agents I've ever worked with. But lately it seems you've lost focus. Has the stress of the job become too much for you?"

"No, sir. Don't worry...I can handle it."

"That's what I thought. It just occurred to me that you haven't taken any time off in ages. If you need to put in for a week or two before you're re-assigned, I'll approve it."

"Thanks, but I actually relax more when I'm working. Maybe in September."

"It's your call. And I hope I'll see you on Liberty Island tomorrow for the country's 250th birthday."

Sarah paused for a moment and felt a rush of anxiety as she walked out of the Director's office. "Yes," Sarah whispered to herself, "Two, hundred…and fifty."

She didn't get far before running into Frank. "Sarah, could we speak in your office?"

Frank's voice brought Sarah back into the moment. "Sure. When's a good time?"

"Now?"

"Frank, I have a meeting with senior staff in an hour and then a conference call with Jakarta."

"This should only take a few minutes," Frank assured her.

"Okay, if you think it's urgent."

Ushering Frank into her office, Sarah gestured for him to sit down as she sunk slowly into her high-back chair. Sarah's office had several large windows and on a sunny day it was brightly illuminated. But on that day, storm clouds were gathering overhead and it seemed unusually dark and foreboding.

She looked Frank in the eye. "Is it what I think it is?"

"Sarah, it's worse."

"How bad?"

"Chatter everywhere. Excited chatter, like something's about to happen."

"What are they saying?"

"Sounds like they're saying 'take her out.'"

"Are you sure about the translation? Are we understanding this properly?"

"Yes, we believe the translation of these few words is accurate. We think we know exactly what they're saying. They're saying other things that I'm still deciphering, but I'm confident that we hear 'take her out.'"

"So, does that mean an assassination attempt or an attack could be coming soon?"

"Seems very possible."

"Do you think it's enough to convince Campbell? The last thing I need is to be transferring to Dubai. And working for Octavia! Of all people!"

"I know. Look, Sarah, the chatter is getting more intense by the hour. First thing Monday morning, I will take everything we have to the Director and press him as hard as I can. I think I can make a pretty strong case that an attack is imminent."

"Thanks, Frank. I appreciate anything you can do."

For months, Frank had been alerting Sarah to the growing evidence that terrorists were ready to strike a major American target. Sarah had tried to warn anyone who would listen. Although the translations of the chatter were evident to her, things had been quiet on the security front for quite some time, and few in the intelligence community were willing to acknowledge the seriousness of the potential threat. Even her husband David seemed unwilling to concede the serious risk of an attack.

"Let's call Katy," Sarah said to Frank as she pressed a button on her phone.

Katy Thompson was the nation's First Lady and had also been Sarah's roommate in college. Katy was the one person in Washington who might understand the importance of Sarah's concern.

Upstairs in the West Wing, Katy's iPhone rang. "Hey, Sarah, what's the latest?"

"We have additional evidence of a possible strike. Frank Robbins is with me on speaker if you want to hear more."

"Okay, what do you have?"

"Hello, Mrs. Thompson, it's an honor. What we're hearing is more chatter, animated chatter, as well as serious conversations. Among the translations, there seems to be one key phrase."

"What phrase, Frank?"

"It appears they're saying, 'take her out.'"

"Take out whom?" Katy asked. "Do you know who the target might be?"

"No, but we're working on it."

"How long have they been saying it, Frank?"

"For about a month, Mrs. Thompson."

"Sounds like an assassination plot. Who could it be? What do you think, Sarah? Could it be the queen? We're hosting her next Wednesday."

"That could be, Katy. Aren't you also having the prime minister of France over on Tuesday?"

"Yes."

"And the foreign minister of Colombia to discuss trade?"

"Yes, the President is scheduled to host her this Monday."

"And the prime minister of India — the one with the doctorate from Oxford?"

"Friday, a week from today."

"All women."

"Well, what can I say, Sarah. We rule, right? How does it feel to be ruled, Frank?"

"Oh, Sarah is a *benevolent* despot, Mrs. Thompson. I have no complaints."

"Seriously, Frank, thanks for the update. You're a patriot. Sarah, I've got to go now. Dan will be back from Camp David at any moment, and he'll want dinner."

"Yeah, right. Your servants will make him dinner."

Sarah paused for a moment.

"Does Dan believe us?"

"Well...NSC, Defense and State have not confirmed your suspicions, so he is not treating Frank's information with any urgency."

"Let *me* talk to him."

"That's *my* job, Sarah. We're going to talk tonight. It's our anniversary and I'm going to make him listen. Otherwise, his night might be lonely — if you know what I mean."

"You go, girl. I'll be praying for you. Call me later."

"Will do."

"And by the way, happy anniversary."

"Thanks. Bye, bye."

Frank looked at Sarah and took a deep breath. "Do you want to do it now?"

He motioned for Sarah to follow him out into the corridor. "What, Frank?"

"You know." Frank used his finger to draw an angelic circle in the air above his head.

"Oh, yes."

"It shouldn't take long," Frank added. "We're near the end of this."

"Okay. Let's do it."

Sarah and Frank walked down the corridor and retreated into a sound-proof tech lab. The sign above the door read, "LEVEL 5 PERSONNEL ONLY."

Surrounded by cutting-edge communications and information systems, they walked toward the center of the room as the sliding door automatically closed behind them.

Thirty minutes later, they emerged from the lab.

Frank handed Sarah a device that looked like an ordinary iPhone.

"The project is complete. HALO is fully operational."

"Frank, do you have the charger?"

"There is no charger."

"Then how does it maintain its power?"

He whispered in Sarah's ear, "nuclear battery."

"Nuclear battery!?"

"Shhhhhh."

"Frank, is this safe?"

"Totally. It's built to the latest safety standards. It has a half-life of one hundred years."

Sarah's eyes opened wide. "A hundred years?" Frank

nodded. "Thanks for the details, Frank. I just hope this will never be needed."

"I'm sure it won't. But just in case…"

"God forbid."

"Amen to that."

Returning to her office with Frank, Sarah looked out the windows at the dark sky and torrential rain. "You know, Frank, we live in troubling times, increasing natural disasters, raging wars. So many seem to care only about themselves. They ignore the lessons of the Scriptures, even the possibility that a God exists."

"We do live in tough times, Sarah, but we are prepared. That's what we do here."

Sarah nodded while thinking to herself, "I love Frank, but he just doesn't understand."

"Frank, would you tell Doris to cancel the staff meeting and the conference calls? I think it can all wait until Monday."

"Sarah, are you leaving now?"

"In about a half hour. Do you want to come with us tomorrow for the celebration? I can get a great seat for you on Liberty Island."

"Tomorrow's Saturday. Don't you usually observe the Sabbath?"

"I do, but I will make a rare exception for America's 250th birthday." Sarah pointed toward the ceiling and smiled at Frank. "I hope the 'Boss' understands."

"I'd love to come, but my folks are having a holiday cookout. So, if I'm ever able to finish the work I was planning to do this weekend, I should probably see their new place. They just bought a house up in Westchester."

"Frank, I almost forgot. They're in Scarsdale now."

"Your hometown."

"Yes, and you'd better drop in and say 'hi' to my dad the next time you're up there. Well, if I don't see you, have a great Fourth."

"You, too. And, by the way, please explain our project to David as soon as possible." Staring intently at the iPhone, Sarah momentarily froze. "Are you okay?"

"Uh, sure. And thanks. I'll...I'll be sure to explain it to David."

She opened the office door while trying to give Frank her most confident look.

"Great, I'll see you Monday. Goodnight, Sarah."

"Goodnight, Frank."

Frank looked earnestly at Sarah while she clutched HALO in her left hand. "Oh, by the way, just don't drop it!"

Sarah tried to laugh as she closed the office door in his face.

As soon as she sat down at her desk, she felt an unexpected wave of exhaustion overtake her. She put her head down on the desk. Shutting her eyes for a moment, she soon fell asleep.

"I'm trapped!" The metallic odor was stronger than usual, the oxygen almost gone. "Please help me!! I can barely breathe! Help me David! I can't move. I must

see you and Becca one more time! There's so much more to say!!" She was pleading for God's help, asking Him for a way out of her darkened tomb.

Sarah awoke suddenly and took a deep breath as she swiveled around in the chair.

Looking out the office windows, she was glad to see the rain had stopped and the sky had mostly cleared.

The nightmares were intensifying. Each time, Sarah would experience increasing feelings of fear and dread, as if she were trapped alone in a mysterious unknown darkness.

What did it all mean, if anything? She thought she should finally tell David about her recurring dream, but once again the timing wasn't right. David was preoccupied with security for Saturday's big event on Liberty Island. Just telling him about HALO would be all that he could handle.

She removed her pistol from the desk drawer, placing it in her handbag before heading to the elevator. Shaken a bit from her dream, Sarah entered the elevator and pressed the L button. Just before the doors completely closed, a black open-toed stiletto wedged into the gap.

"Room for one more?" Octavia glided into the elevator. Her sultry figure was enhanced by a tight black leather dress that exposed her long shapely legs through a slit stretching up to her hip.

"Octavia, I thought you were on your way to Dubai." Sarah took in Octavia's strikingly provocative pose, the choker with a black onyx stone adorning her neck, perfectly manicured red nails, and sensuous scent of her perfume. "Are you going out for the night?"

Ignoring Sarah's question, Octavia leaned back against the elevator wall.

"So, what are you and David doing tonight? Or should I ask, what are you not doing?" Octavia smiled wickedly.

"That's none of your business."

"Well, maybe I'll make *him* my business. And Sarah.... exactly how long has it been?"

"Stay out of my personal life."

Walking seductively across the elevator, wetting her lips, Octavia leaned her body in against Sarah.

"When you're working for me, honey, you'll do exactly what I want you to do."

"Don't touch me, and don't test me." Sarah shoved Octavia away, forcing her against the wall.

The elevator doors opened. Sarah stepped quickly into the lobby.

Octavia whispered to herself as she watched Sarah head out to the parking lot, "See you at the celebration tomorrow, bitch."

On her trip home, Sarah reflected on the encounter with Octavia, but that was the least of her problems. She was growing more concerned about the nightmare she had been experiencing over and over again. Sarah always thought it was brought on by a prophetic experience she had as a young girl, but this time she assumed it was in some way connected to fears brought on by the recent chatter.

The phrase "take her out" continued to haunt Sarah's thoughts. She sensed that something dark lay ahead.

The early evening of July 3rd turned out to be typically hot and humid as window air conditioners hummed throughout Queens. Sarah drove past children playing in open fire hydrants and lining up at ice cream trucks that seemed to be on almost every block.

In the family room, David was stretched out on the couch with his feet atop the coffee table. Sarah would not approve of his "darn old shoes" on the furniture. He listened as Rebecca recounted her day at school and the fun she had playing T-ball in gym class. After hearing the play-by-play rundown of Becca's game, David grabbed his favorite New York Mets cap from the shelf behind him. The cap sat next to the framed picture of Gil Hodges that David's father put there after the Amazing Mets won their first World Series in 1969.

He placed the cap proudly on Rebecca's head. "Daddy, when are we going to Citi Field to see the Mets?"

David glanced at the ever-present laminated Mets schedule on the coffee table. "Your grandfather said he'll get you tickets for any game after the All-Star break, pumpkin." Rebecca smiled ear-to-ear as David playfully twisted her cap sideways.

Hearing an approaching car, David looked out the

window. "Here comes Mommy." He took his feet off the table as the Volvo pulled into the driveway.

Sarah entered the house with a troubled look on her face. Alex, Rebecca's calico cat, slipped inside just before Sarah closed the door. Rebecca had found Alex rummaging through the trash cans in the driveway almost a year earlier and insisted on keeping him.

"Hi, Mommy!"

As David stood up, Rebecca ran to Sarah and gave her a hug before picking up Alex. "Hi, sweetheart."

"Mommy, I learned in school that only one in three thousand calico cats is a boy." Alex purred loudly as Rebecca stroked his fur.

For a moment Sarah forgot about her hectic day at the office. "Oh, that's very interesting, Becca. Speaking of Alex, I think it's time for his dinner." Rebecca lowered Alex back to the floor.

"I'll feed him right now, Mommy." Rebecca quickly scampered off to the kitchen following Alex.

David, noticing Sarah's flat affect, put his arm around her. "Honey, is everything okay?"

"Well, not exactly."

"More chatter at work?"

"Yes, let's go into the office and talk."

David gently guided Sarah into their small home office at the back of the house. "So, what's going on?"

Sarah told David about the concerns she and Frank had been having about potential attacks.

"Sarah, you've done all you can. You've taken this all the way to the First Lady. She's going to try one more time to convince the President. What else can you do? It's time to let it go."

Sarah stared at him sullenly before walking over to the window, looking outside for a few moments.

She spun around and looked sharply at David. "You don't believe me, do you?"

She was happy that he no longer traveled around the globe on dangerous missions, but she felt that being away from the front lines seemed to have dulled his ability to recognize terrorist threats. She secretly thought that David had lost his edge.

David did not entirely believe in the magnitude of Sarah's concerns but he knew that he had to temper his response. "Of course I believe you. The President and his national security team have not verified its source, and they don't believe it's a high-level threat."

He gently put his hand under her chin, slowly lifting her head up. "Sweetheart, you did all you could do."

Sarah looked wide-eyed into the distance as they embraced. She wanted to believe that everything would be alright but in her heart she knew that tribulation was at hand.

As Friday night Shabbat approached, Rebecca stood at Sarah's side and watched her mother light two candles on the dining room table, eighteen minutes before sunset.

Sarah passed her hands over the candles several times before covering her eyes and reciting a blessing.

"Blessed are You, Lord our God, Sovereign of the universe, Who has sanctified us with His commandments and commanded us to light the lights of Shabbat. Amen."

Sarah opened her eyes, raised a four-ounce glass of wine in her right hand and proceeded to recite the Kiddush.

She knew David would not appear until the traditional hand wash and challah bread rituals were complete. But he had kept one very important promise that he made to Sarah long ago; David bought only Kosher food when he went shopping. It brought back memories of his upbringing and the Kosher deli his parents owned and operated.

"It's time to serve you two ladies a very special dinner."

Wearing an orange-and-blue New York Mets apron with matching oven mitts, David entered the dining room as if on cue, carrying the vegetarian lasagna he made from scratch.

"My girls' favorite food."

"Daddy, you are the best cook! And I love your pasketti too!"

"That's 'spaghetti,' honey."

"That's what I said Daddy, pasketti." Sarah and David laughed as Rebecca began to happily wolf down the lasagna while sauce surrounded her mouth.

After dinner, David and Sarah were cleaning up the dining room. "I saw Octavia in the elevator tonight as I was leaving work."

"I thought she'd be halfway to Dubai by now. What did she have to say?"

Sarah chuckled, wondering if she should tell David everything about the elevator run-in. "Not much."

"That's unusual for her. She always has a racy comment to make."

Sarah considered telling David about her possible reassignment to Dubai but decided it could wait until after Saturday's big event. "That's for sure," she murmured.

"What's that, hon?"

"Oh, nothing."

CHAPTER 2
BOYS' NIGHT OUT

FOLLOWING DINNER, SARAH's spirit was uplifted. She went into the den to call her best friend, Debbie, who was married to Scott Miller, David's lifelong friend.

Growing up in the same neighborhood together, David and Scott were as inseparable as brothers. They went to the same public schools and played on the same sports teams. They were two Jewish kids surrounded by a sea of mostly Irish and Italian friends – Robby and Mike, Johnny and Carl, Terrence and Sloan, Rick, Paul and Joe.

Growing up in the 1990's meant Nirvana, computers, and video games. But it also meant the iconic punch ball, stoop ball, and every imaginable game one could play with a Spalding or a tennis ball and sometimes a makeshift bat. They sustained their own world where the sights, sounds, and images of the city's magical past remained present in their lives.

By the time high school graduation arrived, there had been a parting of sorts. David had already graduated early at 16 and headed to Harvard. Joe went to West Point. Scott stayed in the neighborhood with the guys and commuted to Queens College, where he met his wife Debbie, while also working at his father's trucking company.

But the parting was temporary. Graduating in just three years at age 19, David did the unexpected for a Harvard alum. He returned to the neighborhood and joined NYPD. His original plan was to go on to Harvard Law School. But after his parents were killed in an armed robbery at their deli, David felt compelled to join the force. Scott also joined NYPD while most of their other friends were already with FDNY. That was before David met Sarah, who persuaded him to join the SEALS. Scott did likewise. They ended up on the same team, going on missions throughout the world.

The Miller home was a few doors away from David and Sarah. A big bear of a man and mostly muscle, Scott was a sober, often serious SEAL. But with a booming voice and a legendary laugh like the Joker in Batman, Scott could suddenly morph into the life of the party, electrifying everyone. Part hero and part court jester, he was a bundle of cartoon characters rolled into one.

Debbie was very much his counterpart. Both were visceral, gregarious, down-to-earth New Yorkers, verbalizing every twist and turn of their daily lives. And like all of their friends, both were intensely loyal to people and places.

"Deb, the phone's ringing."

"I know, I know. That's Sarah; I'll get it. Scott, take out the garbage. I'd do it myself but I just had my nails done.

"And I know you've been chewing that tobacco again."

Scott slipped the Skoal canister deep into his pocket.

Swatting it with his huge right hand, he lifted the trash bag that sat just inside the kitchen. He shot Debbie a sideways glance before heading outside.

"Shabbat Shalom, best friend."

"Coast clear, Debbie?"

"Yup, he's outside but not for long. So quickly, let's confirm tomorrow." Scott stepped back inside the house.

"What are you whispering about?"

"Oh, nothing; just girl talk."

"Then I don't want to know."

"So why ask?"

Scott let out a booming laugh. "Good one, Deb. Anyway, I'm gonna take a quick shower."

"Okay, see ya. Sarah, are you still there? Do you know what tonight is?"

"Oh, that's right, Debbie...boys' night out. The monthly gathering at Tony's Bar and Grille."

"No surprise there."

"But there *is* a surprise tonight. My dad will be showing up at Tony's and then he'll be sleeping over at our house."

"Sarah, that's so great! Please, tell him I said 'hello.'"

"Okay, see you tomorrow. And remember, we're going shopping, right?"

"Yes. Shopping's the word. Hey, I hope you're going to wear your new dress on Liberty Island. It's such a classic!"

"We'll see. I'll try it on again as soon as David leaves the house. Night, Deb."

"Sleep tight."

David entered the family room where Sarah was helping Rebecca with her math homework. "Sarah, do you know what tonight is?"

"Yes, Debbie just reminded me. It's boys' night out."

"And I'm going to try to forget about everything and have a good time."

Sarah nodded, letting out a sigh. "Well, you have a good time for both of us, honey. I'm going to take a nap."

David leaned over to kiss Sarah on the forehead as Rebecca giggled behind him. He gave his daughter a bigger hug than usual before leaving the house.

"Love you, pumpkin."

"Love you too, Daddy."

∽

A fixture in the neighborhood for nearly half a century, Tony's was a guy's place featuring burgers and beer and a pool table in the back.

Pulling up to Tony's, David saw familiar vehicles occupying the small parking lot. From Harleys to Ford pick-ups and classic Vettes, his friends had arrived and taken over. Getting out of his car, he heard Springsteen's "Glory Days" blasting from the bar.

"Hey, look, it's Harvard boy, slummin' with the grunts."

David whirled around to see his old friend Don approaching. "Hey, Donny, how are you, man?"

"Good. I can't complain. Hey, there's the other SEAL right behind you. Hey Scotty, what's been happening, bro?"

"I could tell you, but then I'd have to kill you!" Scott burst out laughing.

Don put up his hands in mock surrender. "Man, I miss that crazy laugh!"

Scott caught their friend Rick trying to sneak up behind them. "Look! It's Rick the Red, King of Ireland! What's cooking at FDNY?"

"Lots of changes at the top, Scotty boy. I say, 'If it ain't broke, don't fix it,' but if they keep fixing what isn't, it will really need fixing."

"I hear ya, Ricky. Almost as bad as starting a fire and then putting it out like you're a hero."

"Yeah, tell me about it," Rick said, shaking Scott's hand.

"Scotty, speaking of fixin' things, what's the story with that busted light in the front corner of the parking lot? The thing's been blinking and buzzing for the last ten years. I told Tony I'd pay to fix it a hundred times."

"I think Tony figures it's like a lighthouse beacon, leading everyone here. Besides, this lot's got plenty of light. The place is lit up like Citi Field."

Rick stared at the flickering light for a moment. "Ya know what Scotty, maybe Tony's got a point."

"Buddy, forget the light; let's grab some beers."

Scott spotted three more familiar faces approaching from across the parking lot. "Hey there's Rafa, Robby, and Iron Mike! Nice of you boys to show up. What are you doing?! Wait, don't answer or Johnny over there might have to read you your rights!"

Scott led the charge as the guys filed into the bar.

An hour later, Tony's was packed. The dark paneling that had covered the walls since 1973 was barely visible due to the crowd.

The front door swung open. "Okay, all of you have the right to remain silent...."

"Hey, there's Pops!" David yelled as Mel Goodman walked in, surprising everyone.

The whole place erupted in applause.

Led by David, they raised their beers and began to chant. "Pop! Pop! Pop! Pop!"

Mel was easily the best dressed man in Tony's. His dark Brioni suit complemented his lean six-foot frame. With thick grey-streaked dark hair, Mel still had a commanding presence at sixty-eight but usually wore an engaging smile. David often told him he looked like a Jewish George Clooney.

Mel put up his hands to acknowledge the chants before working his way through the crowd as the guys jockeyed to shake his hand or pat him on the shoulder. After the noise died down, he sat up on the bar and surveyed the sea of NYPD and FDNY caps with an interspersing of Mets, Jets and Giants hats.

"Pop, I didn't know you were coming," David said as he approached Mel.

"Just got in from Manhattan."

Mel then began to address the crowd. "Gentlemen, it's great to be with New York's Bravest and Finest and other heroes whose occupations need no mention."

Someone yelled out, "Yeah!" and the whole place erupted in applause.

Mel winked at Tony behind the bar. "Tony, please tell me these guys have been acting their age."

Tony's thick black mustache curled upwards. "Sorry, Mel, I took an oath when I opened this joint; I cannot tell a lie."

"In that case, just get me a beer." Tony slid a tall Heineken bottle down the bar. "Thanks Tony."

Mel turned to the crowd. "Tonight, I want to toast every one of you for being heroes who save lives and keep New York going."

Someone began a chant. "Ooh! Ooh! Ooh! Ooh!"

"Everybody raise your glasses. Tomorrow is our country's 250th birthday, but tonight, I want to remember the heroes of America's darkest morning.

"And so, let me offer a toast...to the heroes of 9/11, to all of you who were there that day, nearly 25 years ago. Despite all the horror that happened, you rescued more than 28,000 out of 31,000 people in those towers after the planes hit. While everyone else was running out of the towers, you were running into them, trying to save as many lives as possible." With that, everyone in the crowd raised their drinks.

"And I'm not going to stop there. I also want to toast all you do, every day. How your courage, your incorruptibility, and your self-sacrifice shine through. Let me say how honored I am to know each and every one of you personally and to call all of you...my friends. Okay, drink up guys! The next round's on me!"

"Pop! Pop! Pop!," responded several guys in the crowd.

"And also the round after that!"

Mel stepped down from the bar and gave several of the guys powerful handshakes and bear hugs.

He approached David and embraced him as well. "Thank you, son."

"Any time, Pops. I love you."

"And I love you too, son...I'll never forget."

A moment later, the big front door of the bar swung open with a loud thud. The strong lights from the parking lot that would normally shine through the open entrance were mostly blocked out. Mel looked up and smiled as the place fell completely silent.

"Well, if it isn't the General himself! Jeez Joe, you sure know how to darken a doorway! You make the Rock look like a pebble."

Joe Biggs turned slightly as he maneuvered his bulk through the entrance. At 6'7" and weighing well over 350 lbs., Joe was undoubtedly the largest man ever to set foot in Tony's Grille. He nodded slightly toward the bar.

"Mel," Joe said in his deep voice with a hint of southern drawl.

Joe lived in Savannah until the seventh grade, when his family moved to Queens. He was an ex-Army officer and later a professional wrestler. "General Joe" was his stage name and it stuck with the people he grew up with.

The guys used to call him "Amazon Man." The name was quickly dropped when it became clear that using it could be suicidal. Several of the men cautiously acknowledged Joe with their eyes as he made his way to the bar.

Sitting at the bar, Robby and Rick laughed as they pointed at Joe's Mickey Mouse watch. "Hey Joe! Where'd you get the sharp watch?! From a Cracker Jack box?!!" Robby yelled loudly enough for everyone to hear.

"Yeah, does it glow in the dark?!" Rick cackled, barely able to get the words out.

Joe's face turned to stone as he reached Robby and Rick on their barstools.

Using his massive hands, Joe picked up both men by their belts and dangled them in the air. "Hey Joe, we love Mickey Mouse," Robby stammered.

"Can you get us watches too?" Rick blurted out.

Joe grinned. "That's what I thought." He slowly lowered the guys back down onto their barstools. "Hey Tony, their dinner's on me, but they're not getting any watches."

"No problem, General, I mean Joe, I mean General Joe," Robby said carefully.

"Enjoy your dinner, boys," Joe said before moving on.

Rick and Robby looked at each other as they wiped the sweat from their brows. Robby whispered, "I learned a lesson tonight, Rick."

"What was that?"

"Don't make fun of Mickey Mouse."

Rick gave Robby's upper arm a friendly punch before chugging his beer.

Tony had Joe's usual platter waiting for him at the far end of the bar, a huge surf & turf spread with all of the fixings that would normally feed a family of five. The noise level gradually returned to normal after Joe took a seat.

Turning away from David, Mel spotted Mike and put a fatherly arm around his shoulders.

"Let's talk, Michael. I heard your wife was sick. Same as my Edith was, may she rest in peace."

"Edith was a great lady, Mel. I can't believe she's been gone nearly five years. She was like a second mother for all of us."

"That she was. So, Lorraine was able to beat her breast cancer?"

"Looks like she's out of the woods. She's much better than last year, thank God," Mike said as he crossed himself.

"But you had an insurance problem."

"Yeah, the insurance company didn't exactly come through for us. We owe plenty." Mike looked down at the floor, trying to hide his worry.

"That's what I heard, Michael."

"Yeah, but it's okay. Lorraine and I can handle this. We work hard and we always land on our feet. It's like the Bible says, 'The Lord helps those who help themselves.'"

Mel shook his head. "Michael, I don't think that's in the Bible."

"Seriously? Then where did it come from?"

"I don't know. According to Sarah, the good book says that God helps those who help others."

"Oh man, now I feel like a fool. But like I said, the insurance company gave us the runaround, but it's okay."

"No, Mike, it's not okay. Open your hand." Mel placed an envelope in Mike's palm.

"What...what is this??"

"Open it."

Mike looked at Mel before carefully opening the envelope with his finger. "A...a check...wow! Oh no, Mel. Oh no, that's too...I can't accept that."

"I insist you do."

"Oh, man. This is like a miracle." Mike squeezed the small crucifix that hung from his neck.

"Michael, as David Ben-Gurion once said, 'In Israel, in order to be a realist, you must believe in miracles.'"

"I'm definitely a realist, Pop." Mike fumbled with the envelope, looking at his hands. "But I don't know what to say."

"Don't say anything. Just put that in your pocket and tell Lorraine I said 'hi.'"

"I sure will."

"But you do owe me one thing."

"Anything you want, Mel. What is it?"

"A rematch on the pool table."

Mike smiled. "You got it, anytime."

"You were lucky when you beat me last time. I'll kick your butt next time. By the way, I get first break."

"Ha! Okay, Pop, tell me when and we'll do it. You're

the best." Mike gave Mel a parting pat on the back before heading to the bar.

A moment later, Mel felt a tug at the bottom of his shirt. He turned around to see Rebecca smiling up at him while Sarah stood behind her. "Hey! It's my two favorite gals! What are you doing here on guys' night?" Mel laughed as he gave Rebecca a hug.

"Sorry, Dad. We just popped in for a minute. Becca heard Joe was in town and she insisted on thanking him for the birthday present he sent her."

"Is that so, young lady?"

"That's right, Grandpa. This Minnie Mouse watch is so cool!" Rebecca extended her arm so Mel could get a good look at the watch.

"It certainly is cool, cupcake, and I'm sure Joe can't wait to see you." Mel pointed to where Joe's bulk was being supported by two barstools. Rebecca immediately took off toward Joe.

"Dad, I'm glad you can stay over tonight. Becca is going to be so happy."

"I wish I could do it more often, Sarah. Maybe soon, when I retire."

"That would be great."

They watched as Rebecca approached Joe, her tiny hand reaching up to tap his massive arm. Joe put down the huge turkey leg he was about to take a bite from and looked to his side.

"Hi, Uncle Joe!"

"Well, well, if it isn't Miss Becca!"

Joe reached down with one arm and scooped Rebecca up into his lap. Rebecca giggled with delight.

"Now how's my special girl?"

"I'm here to thank you for my Mini Mouse watch. It got here June 14th, right on my birthday. It's so cute!"

"You are very welcome. A special watch for a special girl.

"Now, listen up Becca. If you ever need me, you can just push that little button on the side of your watch and my Mickey Mouse watch will light up." As Joe pointed to the watch on his left wrist, Rebecca's eyes lit up. "And, my little Mini Mouse, I'll know exactly where you're at."

"No way! Joe, you are the coolest uncle!" Rebecca pushed the button; a florescent green light lit up the face of her watch. A few seconds later, the face of Joe's Mickey Mouse also lit up green.

"Thank you so much!" Rebecca reached up, hugged Joe around the neck and kissed his cheek.

Joe blushed. "Just wish I could see y'all more often. I hope you're here for dinner. Tony will make anything you want."

Rebecca frowned. "I wish I could stay but Mommy said we have to go home."

"In that case, you better run along, Becca. I don't want to get in trouble with Miss Sarah."

"You could never be in trouble, Uncle Joe."

"I'd like to think so, but one never knows."

Rebecca gave Joe another peck on the cheek before climbing down from the barstool.

"Bye, Uncle Joe."

"Bye-Bye, Becca."

After Sarah and Rebecca left, Mel immediately locked eyes with Carl. "Hey, Carl! What's happening, big guy?"

"Mel, great to see you! I've been working hard, trying to keep New York safe for democracy." Carl smiled as he looked around at the crowd. "It was good to see Joe made it tonight. What's it been? At least six months?"

"Yeah, I hear he's real busy lately."

"Mel, what does Joe do exactly? He never said where he's been working since he stopped wrestling."

"He's a contractor."

"Contractor? What, like pouring concrete?"

"He does whatever Uncle Sam needs him to do. That's all I know. He can't really talk about it. Hey, I heard you're doing detective work like my son-in-law did."

"That's right, Mel. I made detective in January."

"Mazel tov. You like it?"

"Well, you get to see lots of bad stuff. People are crazy these days, or maybe 'insane' is the right word."

"But you've always said that, Carl."

"I know. Honestly, it's much worse now. Criminals are worse. The bad elements in society keep pushing the envelope. Children killing children. Children killing their parents. Wives taking out contracts on their husbands, and husbands on their wives, not just to kill them, but to slice and dice them. I'm seeing more human trafficking and even child abduction. It seems like there's a dark spirit unleashed that is pure evil."

"But besides that, the world is basically okay, right Carl?"

Mel and Carl both chuckled for a moment.

"Seriously, Pop, something is happening out there. It's like the city, or maybe the whole country, is speeding down the L.I.E. in a car with no brakes."

"That's what my daughter says. I don't know if David agrees."

"Well, Sarah's right and David's wrong."

David, standing a few feet away, whirled around.

"What? Me, wrong?"

"Yeah, you," Carl said with half a smile. "Excuse me, guys. I just caught sight of Ricky the Red over by the pool table. I need to bust his chops a little!"

Mel and David laughed as Carl headed for the back of the bar.

"So, what else is new in your world, David?"

"Nothing's new, Pop. Sarah's still worried about the chatter she's been hearing."

"Well, I believe her concern about an attack might be overstated this time."

"I agree."

"Just try and reassure her."

"I tried but it's not working very well."

"I gave Sarah my own opinion, based on decades of experience."

"And?"

"No effect. She prays now even more than she used to."

"I know."

"So how are the arrangements for tomorrow?"

"Nailed down."

"You and Scott are heading it up?"

"Yes, with help from NYPD and the Coast Guard, and of course, the Secret Service."

"You want to take a drive out there and check it out?"

"Now?"

"Yeah, now."

"Okay, but I can't stay out too late. I've got an early start tomorrow."

"Got it. Whose car?"

"Yours, but I'll drive, Pop."

"I know you like driving my Mercedes, but you really should get your own one of these days."

"With what?"

"I told you I'd buy you one."

"I appreciate it, but I love my Chevy."

"Too proud to say 'yes?'"

David smiled sheepishly at Mel as they pushed their way out Tony's front door. "Let's go."

CHAPTER 3
THE LAST NIGHT

THE TRAFFIC WAS surprisingly light for a Friday evening as they drove across the 59th Street Bridge. Mel and David reached Battery Park in less than an hour and found a parking spot near its northern perimeter. Because they arrived in Mel's car rather than David's, they could not park inside the secure zone, since the vehicle had not been cleared by the Secret Service.

They left the Mercedes on Battery Place and entered the park on foot. Mel glanced at David.

"Aren't there any guards here?"

"No, Pop, the guards are ahead of us, near the museum."

At the seawall, just past the city's Holocaust museum and not far from the southern tip of Manhattan, a group of Homeland Security personnel was stationed.

It was a gorgeous night, suddenly clear, crisp and cool for an early July evening, as a cold front pushed the humid city air out to sea. The water of New York Harbor glistened under the stars and full moon.

"Remember when we all came down here?"

"I do, David. Unforgettable. You, Sarah and I. It was before Rebecca was born. I wish you would see Yad Vashem. I haven't been there since Sarah was 12."

"Yeah, I hear Israel's Holocaust museum is incredible."

"But you can't see it...unless you go to Israel."

"I know. Sarah keeps asking me about going."

"Do you think you'll go someday?"

"Maybe."

"Tell you what. Let's go to Israel next year. You, Sarah, Rebecca...and her grandpa."

"You?"

"Yeah, me. Deal?"

"Alright, Pops, next year in Jerusalem – the whole family."

Mel laughed good-naturedly. "I'll believe that when I see it, David, but now I've got you on record."

Mel and David approached the security detail where Mel was immediately recognized.

"Mel Goodman, what an honor!" exclaimed one of the officers, as he firmly shook hands with the former U.S. Attorney for the Southern District of New York.

"Mr. Goodman, you were the best federal prosecutor New York ever had."

Mel glanced at the name just below the officer's badge. "Officer Grattan, the honor is mine. You men keep us and our country safe." Mel motioned toward David. "And let me introduce my son-in-law, David Stein."

"Pleased to meet you," the head officer said.

"Pleased to meet you as well," David replied. "I'll be leading the security detail for Liberty Island tomorrow. So you and your men are on the overnight?"

"Yes, we'll be relieved at 0400."

"Any security concerns tonight?"

"No, nothing, Mr. Stein. All is quiet."

"Good, tell the next shift we'll be here at 0700 sharp."

"Yes, sir."

"You gentlemen have a good night."

"We will, sir."

Mel and David departed and began walking along the water's edge. "So, Pop, how's business?"

"We're doing well. Security's a booming field. I make more money in one year than I did in all the years I was a prosecutor. But you know what?"

"You miss prosecuting."

"I don't miss the politics of it."

Mel stopped walking and squared his shoulders toward David, looking at him intently. "Here's what I miss. I miss going after bad guys, working with the cops, talking with the feds, fighting for justice. I miss locking up some of the worst people on earth."

David felt the passion in Mel's voice. "You sound like me, or maybe I'm starting to sound like you."

"You miss being out there on missions."

"Yeah I do, and I know Scotty does, too. We reminisce a lot."

"Well, you have a lot to reminisce about. You were two of the best SEAL leaders the country ever had. Think about it. For more than twenty years, you two had your hands in almost every critical mission. You were there when they got OBL."

"I'll never forget it. Scott broke his leg two weeks before, so he was off the field. But he heard and saw it all."

"So we both miss our former work, son. The difference is that I received honor and glory for the job I did. But you didn't. Nobody knew when you were on your exploits. That Homeland Security team knew me, but they didn't know you from Adam."

Mel put an arm around David's shoulders.

"They didn't know that standing next to me was one of the greatest warriors ever."

"Well, Pop, I appreciate that."

"Ready to go, son?"

"Yeah, I have to be here again in a few hours. Let's go."

They nodded farewell to the DHS team and walked through Battery Park until they reached the street and Mel's Mercedes. After they got in and pulled away from the curb, Mel glanced through the side-view mirror and saw a van driving slowly alongside the park's perimeter. Knowing the area was often a make-out spot for young people, Mel was not concerned.

"What are you looking at?"

"Oh, nothing. Probably just some college kids."

It was almost completely dark as moonlight had replaced the sun while Mel and David drove away. The van that Mel had spotted came to a stop behind the Holocaust museum. A moment later, a royal blue, open

T-top Corvette pulled up on the access road, close to where the security guards were positioned.

Emerging slowly from the Vette was a statuesque long-haired blonde whose hour-glass figure was tightly wrapped in a gold-sequined mini-dress with a low-cut scoop neck. Her gold stiletto heels clicked on the sidewalk as she strutted into the secure, cordoned-off area. She caught the eyes of the entire security detail before sashaying toward the water.

Officer Grattan cleared the lump in his throat. "May I help you, ma'am?" he said as the other officers stood frozen.

"I'm so glad you're here, officer. I seem to be a bit lost. With all the traffic, I decided to take a shortcut through the city, and somehow ended up here. I'm looking for the FDR Drive."

The alluring blonde seemed not only confused but a bit vulnerable as her hair blew across her face.

Striking a seductive pose, the woman asked, "So, are you all here because of tomorrow's *big* event?"

Officer Grattan tried to stay composed. "Yes, ma'am, that's right."

The woman dropped her purse. "Oh…excuse me." She turned around and bent down slowly to retrieve it.

The men looked at each other and raised their eyebrows after examining her voluptuous figure. Straightening up slowly and tossing back her long hair while still facing the water, the woman gestured to the Statue of Liberty in the distance.

"Look at her, Lady Liberty. Isn't she beautiful?"

"Oh, she certainly is," replied one of the guards as he remained captivated by the woman's beauty.

Forgetting their priorities, the guards turned their backs to the Holocaust museum and joined her in gazing beyond the shoreline at the Statue.

Turning around quickly, the woman faced the men. The expression on her face turned ice-cold.

"Are you boys familiar with Proverbs 24:24?"

The members of the security team looked at each other, bewildered by her question and change of tone.

At that moment, behind the museum, several figures quietly emerged from the van and ambushed the detail.

Using silencers, they shot each of the security officers in the back of the head, killing five.

Officer Grattan fell to the ground but continued to move.

Spotting his movement, the woman sat on his back. As blood ran down the side of his face, he looked back at her in bewilderment. Pulling his head up by the hair, she stared coldly into his eyes.

"You didn't answer my question! Proverbs 24:24 says, 'Be silent when you are tempted to flatter a wicked woman.'" She smiled and kissed him sensually on the lips before snapping his neck, instantly killing him.

The woman stood up and checked her nails. "Clean up this mess. I have a reservation at Provocateur."

As soon as David and Mel returned to the Stein home in Queens, Mel went upstairs to check on Rebecca. Opening her bedroom door, he saw she was asleep. Downstairs he said goodnight to David and retired to the small in-law suite in the basement.

While David made his usual rounds checking locks and turning off lights throughout the house, he found Sarah using the computer in the den. "Honey, you're still awake?"

"Yeah, I couldn't sleep. By the way, Debbie called and said Scott will meet you here tomorrow at 6:00 am. Debbie and I are going shopping. Dad will stay with Becca."

"Going shopping on Shabbat? That's not like you. By the way, your father and I just got back from a little excursion to lower Manhattan."

"Anything interesting?"

"We met some guys from DHS who treated your father like a rock star."

David paused for a moment and smiled at Sarah. "So, what's this 'secret project' you're doing with Frank?"

"How did you know?"

David confidently stepped closer to Sarah. "Remember, I am in the intel business too."

Sarah smirked. "That's good to know."

David pulled up a chair. Sitting shoulder to shoulder with Sarah, he took a look at the computer screen. "So, what's the big secret that you can't tell your husband?"

"Do you have clearance?"

David laughed. "Has there been more chatter tonight?" Sarah nodded. "Have you identified the source?"

"It's from a source that you wouldn't imagine."

Sarah quickly closed her laptop and swiveled her chair to face David, taking his hands in hers. "David, before you go to bed, I want to show you something."

Sarah opened the desk drawer, removing the iPhone device Frank Robbins had given her earlier. "This looks like an ordinary iPhone, but it contains top-level security information. God forbid, but if something ever happens to me, this becomes everything. You must promise me you'll access it."

"What are you talking about?"

"Just hear me out, David. If something happens to me, for any reason, you have in this device everything that Frank and I have worked on. If or when the time comes, ask Frank for the activation code and then follow the instructions on it...all the way."

"Honey, nothing is going to happen to you."

"If you love me, then you will assure me."

"Sarah, if you want me to make a promise about something that isn't going to happen, okay. I promise."

"Thank you, darling."

David could feel that Sarah was upset about their intense conversation. "You know, you look as beautiful as the day I met you."

"Do you really mean that?"

David leaned over and stared into her eyes. "You know I do."

Sarah got up and headed for the hall. Looking back at David she softly said, "Wait here."

As David watched Sarah bounce up the stairs, a

quizzical expression crossed his face. After waiting more than a few minutes, he went to the kitchen to finish cleaning up.

Just as he put away the last of the dishes, he heard the creaking of wooden stairs as Sarah came down from the second floor. The kitchen door opened.

"Honey, are you ready to…" David was unable to finish his sentence. Sarah stood across the kitchen wearing the lingerie he had given her last year on Valentine's Day. "Wow! I haven't seen that in a while."

"I know, it's been too long."

David threw the dish rags on the counter. For a moment, he was entranced by her beauty. He took her in with his eyes as he moved closer, then gently put his hands around her waist.

Sarah whispered into David's chest, "Honey, life can be so consuming. Sometimes we forget…about us."

"I'm starting to remember, real quick."

"I love you, David."

"I love you, too."

As they kissed passionately, David reached to turn off the kitchen light. He lifted Sarah into his arms and carried her up the stairs.

"Oh, the slings and arrows…" Sarah uttered.

"…of outrageous fortune," David finished.

"Do you remember the first time we said that?"

"How can I forget? It seems like yesterday."

Carrying Sarah over the bedroom threshold, David closed the door behind them.

CHAPTER 4
JULY 4, 2026

"*Beep beep beep beep, beep beep beep beep, beep beep beep beep.*"

David reached over to turn off the alarm on his night table. The digital clock displayed 4:30 am. He looked over at Sarah, who moaned and pulled the covers up around her chin.

After a quick shower, he donned his uniform. Putting on his watch, he saw Sarah eyeing him in the mirror.

"Come here, honey."

David sat on the edge of the bed. Leaning in, Sarah pulled him closer and locked him in a kiss.

"I love you."

"I love you, Sarah. Hey, I took your advice. I'm not wearing those old shoes today."

A car horn blared loudly in front of the house. "That's Scott. I've got to go."

David got up and headed for the bedroom door.

"Be safe, honey."

"Okay, I'll see you tonight."

David's footsteps landed heavily as he rushed down the stairs.

A wave of fear swept over Sarah. Turning her face into the pillow, she began to cry.

A few hours later, Sarah called Debbie.

Leaving her worries behind about the intel she and Frank had been receiving, Sarah was back in good spirits as she reflected on Friday's dinner and her night with David.

"Hey, Deb, Katy Thompson just texted me to confirm. She even arranged to get us a ride to Liberty with Dan on Marine One!"

"President Thompson? No way! That's awesome! We can surprise the boys when they get there."

∽

Stopped at a light, Scott looked over at David in the passenger seat. "Well, looks like you had a good night."

A little unnerved that Scott could read him so easily, David put on his best poker face. "Yeah, it was great to see all the guys at Tony's, then I took a ride with Mel."

"Come on, buddy, I'm talking about what went down after hours."

"I was out cold as soon as I hit the sack."

"So, that's your story; I assume you're sticking with it."

"You assume correctly. Hey Scottie, what do you say we take the gals out for a double tonight?"

The light turned green; Scott stepped on the gas.

"Man, Debbie would love that. Maybe someplace nice, with a view of the fireworks?"

"Sounds like a plan — a great ending to a great day."

As David and Scott crossed the Brooklyn Bridge, they caught a glimpse of Lady Liberty before the buildings of lower Manhattan obscured the view. Arriving at Battery Park, they parked the car and walked toward the dock on the Hudson. They could feel the warmth against their backs as the sun rose over the East River.

"I think that's it," Scott said, pointing at an approaching boat.

"Yeah, that's DHS."

"You mean the 4 a.m. team?"

"Yup."

"Do you have any concerns about today?"

"No, Mel and I checked out the crew and the scene last night. Should be as smooth as a cruise on the Circle Line. Let's go, Scotty."

Boarding the craft, they greeted the six-man Coast Guard crew and shook hands with them. "Good morning, gentlemen," David said. "Any incidents last night?"

"Nothing reported from the night detail, sir, and all-clear since we arrived."

As David was about to check the boat for safety, one of the crew called out to him, "Commander Stein, the boat has already been inspected from bow to stern. We are prepared and ready to go."

"Thanks, men." David took the helm and throttled up.

As the boat moved away from the dock, he noticed the engines straining and the stern sitting lower in the water than usual. "We appear a little bottom-heavy."

"Just some extra equipment in the aft compartment, sir," one of the men replied.

As the vessel gained speed and headed toward Liberty Island, Scott joined David at the helm.

Scott peered at David and noticed a pensive look on his friend's face. He had seen that same look before when the two of them were on dicey combat missions. David's built-in radar was picking up something that put him on alert. He turned to the crew and called out to them.

"I'm surprised you guys got here by 6 a.m. despite the holiday traffic."

"Arrived at 5:45, sir."

"So what happened to 0400?" Scott whispered.

"Yeah, tell me about it," David said under his breath.

David and Scott glanced at each other, confirming their unspoken concern.

✍

On Liberty Island, the presidential helicopter had landed, carrying the President, First Lady and their staff, along with Sarah and Debbie. Exiting Marine One, they were surrounded by Secret Service personnel who escorted Daniel Thompson to the presidential podium as the Columbia University marching band played "Hail to the Chief."

"Is this amazing or what?" Debbie gushed as she viewed the cheering crowd and the various versions of

U.S. flags from the last 250 years flapping in the breeze. The Secret Service escorted Sarah and Debbie to a prime viewing spot near the First Lady. "The boys will be so surprised to see us!"

"Katy, you did it! You rock!" Sarah said as she and Debbie took their assigned places.

Katy looked approvingly at Sarah's pink outfit, it hadn't stood out on the crowded Marine One. "Maybe I 'rock' a little, but you look more like the First Lady than I do. I love that retro Oleg Cassini. All you need is the pill box hat!"

Sarah smiled. "I don't know if I'd want to go quite that far."

Anticipating David's arrival, Sarah excitedly looked out toward the Hudson to see if she could spot his boat.

Stepping up to the podium, the President received several rounds of applause before addressing the throngs of people assembled on the lawn, many of whom were waving the Stars and Stripes.

"Today, on July 4th, we celebrate the birthday of the greatest nation in the world."

Raising his right arm, he gazed up at Lady Liberty. "As I stand before you on this memorable day, I can assure you of one thing: As this Lady stands proud, strong and free, so does America.

"For another 250 years and beyond, Lady Liberty will continue to stand as a pillar of freedom for the United States and the world…"

As the President continued his speech, Sarah noticed

several Secret Service agents locked in animated discussion among themselves. Sarah turned to the agent closest to her.

"What's going on?"

"Agent Stein, we just got word from Teeterboro. The six Coast Guardsmen in Battery Park for the 4 am shift were found dead in a hangar at the airport. A Coast Guard helicopter appears unaccounted for."

"Oh my God, that's David's detail..." Sarah said under her breath before frantically phoning her husband's number.

❦

Frank sat for a few seconds, staring in shock at his computer.

He believed he had finally decoded the message but hoped against all odds that there was a mistake.

He immediately called Sarah.

When the call went to voicemail, he quickly began texting:

"Sarah, the chatter is NOT 'Take her out,' it's 'Take her *down*, a gift from France.' They want to bring down the Statue of Liberty!!! That's the target — and it looks like it's happening today!!!!"

As she was receiving Frank's text, Sarah heard her phone ring.

"Sarah?"

"David, where are you?"

"I'm on the Coast Guard boat with Scott."

"David, that's NOT the Coast Guard detail! The Coast

Guard crew, the one that's supposed to be on your boat, was found dead at Teeterboro."

"Where are you, Sarah?"

"I'm on Liberty Island. I just received a text from Frank. He cracked the code! There's going to be an attack on the Statue of Liberty! Today!"

David immediately cut off the call.

"David? David?!!" Sarah yelled into her silent phone.

⌁

David whispered to Scott at the helm, "The 0400 detail is dead. Our wives are on Liberty."

"I thought they went shopping," Scott whispered back louder than he intended.

"That's what they said last night."

Recovering from his momentary shock, Scott nodded to David.

David glanced back.

Both men drew their guns, whirled around, and pointed them toward the back of the boat.

"Put your hands over your heads!" David yelled at the imposters in the rear of the vessel.

They all did as they were told before Scott carefully approached and disarmed each man, throwing their guns overboard.

In the western sky above Liberty State Park, a helicopter flew rapidly toward the boat.

David signaled the chopper to approach.

"I assume that incoming bird is genuine Coast Guard," Scott said quietly to David.

David confronted what appeared to be the group's leader and pointed his gun at him. "This little adventure is just about over for you."

The man glared back at David. "No David, it's over for you. Sorry to ruin your day, but my friends and I have other plans for your country's celebration."

David wanted to inspect the aft cargo area to see what the extra weight consisted of, but there was no time.

The chopper descended swiftly toward the boat. The midday sun glinted off the barrel of a 50 caliber gun mounted on the side of the open helicopter. David knew that kind of firepower could quickly kill everyone aboard.

Scott and David were not about to wait and see if the approaching chopper was flown by friend or foe. If friendly, the terrorists on the boat had no way out. If unfriendly, the two SEALS had only one way out.

The leader of the "crew" took a few steps toward David and Scott. "Game-over, Stein!"

The helicopter descended further off their starboard side. David knew the boat would provide better cover if it slowed down. He slammed the throttle into neutral before tapping three fingers against his left hip. Three seconds later, Scott followed David head-first over the gunwale on the port side. They could hear 50 caliber rounds clipping the boat as they dove deeply into New York Harbor.

At a depth of about ten feet, Scott thanked God for his Kevlar vest as a bullet slammed into the right side of his rib cage. He would have a nasty bruise, maybe even a broken rib or two, but he would live. He'd survived far worse things in his many years with the Navy.

The two SEALS understood that bullets do not travel well in water. The trick was to go deep enough to be out of range but not so deep as to prematurely run out of oxygen.

Although he couldn't see him, Scott sensed that David was nearby and had stopped descending. Scott leveled off too, believing in David's instincts and trusting they had reached a safe depth. They could just make out the engine noise as the boat picked up speed again, circling above them before moving on.

Approximately four minutes later, Scott felt David's hand signal on his shoulder. Helicopter or not, they knew from their SEAL training — it was time to surface or risk drowning.

∾

"David! David!" Sarah shouted as David's voicemail picked up for the fifth time in a row.

Rushing to the head of the Secret Service detail, she told the agent that a full-blown terrorist attack seemed imminent. Agents began to quietly scan Liberty Island and the attendees of the July 4th celebration but found no signs of danger.

President Thompson, who was still addressing the crowd, was signaled by an agent to wrap up his speech quickly. Sarah ran to the seawall and looked in the direction where she thought David's boat would be approaching.

❧

In control of the vessel, the terrorists sped full-throttle toward Liberty Island. As the boat accelerated, the helicopter above lowered down hoists to bring up the crew, four of whom made it into the chopper. The remaining two began to follow after tying off the wheel to keep the unmanned vessel on course.

Rising to the surface, David and Scott had their guns ready. Surging out of the water, they spotted the distant chopper and opened fire.

Bullets ripped through the two remaining Coast Guard imposters; they fell off the hoists and crashed into the water. The helicopter quickly left the area, disappearing over Jersey City.

"Scotty, what do you think they packed the boat with? Maybe C-4?"

"I don't know, buddy, but whatever it was, there sure was a whole lot of it."

As the unmanned craft sped toward Liberty Island with nothing but open water ahead, David and Scott paused for a moment. Watching helplessly, they began to swim to the island as fast as possible.

❧

Secret Service agents on the island received a confirmed intelligence report warning of a severe threat to the tri-state area and that the President might be a target. They were already on heightened alert after hearing gunfire from out in the harbor. Most of the civilians in the crowd seemed to think the gunshots were some sort of fireworks related to the Fourth of July.

An agent spotted the approaching boat through his binoculars. "Get POTUS on Marine One! Now!"

A group of agents surrounded the President and rushed him toward the helicopter. "Where's my wife?!"

"Mr. President, we have a detail across the island. They will be bringing her any moment."

Observing the commotion with Debbie, Sarah gazed up at the Statue of Liberty and thought to herself:

"Take her down."

Turning to look across the harbor, she spotted what looked like David's boat speeding toward the island from about two hundred yards out.

All around the island, a whirlwind of activity ensued. Having witnessed the President being hustled toward his helicopter, the crowd of spectators realized something terrible was happening. The island quickly erupted in chaos.

Sarah felt a strong hand squeeze her upper arm. She turned to see Robert Campbell. His face said it all but after a tense moment, he finally got the words out. "Sarah, I can't tell you how sorry I am. Not believing you was the biggest mistake I've ever made."

His words were no solace as three Secret Service agents approached and tried to help them through the crowd toward Marine One.

◈

As David and Scott swam furiously toward Liberty Island, they watched in horror as the boat made impact. An enormous blast reverberated through the water followed by several smaller explosions. A ball of fire, smoke and debris erupted over the island.

Looking up, they saw an unfathomable sight:

The Statue of Liberty began swaying side to side.

Many in the crowd ran for their lives while some froze, staring in shock at Lady Liberty. A horrible screeching sound of bending and twisting metal bellowed across the harbor. Her torch cracked and broke off, crashing into the fleeing crowd below. The rest of Lady Liberty toppled from her foundation, falling face-first into the water. Screams filled the air as dozens of spectators were crushed beneath the crown.

When David and Scott got close to land, they were increasingly hampered by floating body parts and debris. Finally reaching the shore, they saw the dead and dying all over the island. Frantically, they cried out for their wives while searching for them among the carnage and rubble.

Their exhaustive search turned up a few dozen survivors. Among the wounded they found First Lady Katy Thompson, who appeared to have serious injuries and was subsequently air-lifted to Westchester Medical Center.

But David and Scott found no trace of their wives. That grim reality hit home when they heard techs from the Medical Examiner's office talking about the many bodies closest to the explosion that were pulverized or disfigured beyond recognition.

After almost ten hours of assisting first responders with the massive rescue effort, Scott and David collapsed on a stone bench that was relatively unscathed. With the loves of their lives gone, the two best friends tried to contain their grief as they stared out at the distant Verrazano Bridge.

❧

At dusk, the two friends drove home in a thick mental fog, with neither one saying a word. They passed dozens of emergency vehicles heading the opposite way toward lower Manhattan. On the car radio, 1010-WINS was reporting on the Liberty Island disaster without commercial breaks.

They were halfway across the Brooklyn Bridge when an already-shaken WINS reporter gasped and went silent for a moment.

"We have earth-shattering news out of Jerusalem... Sources are telling us that the Dome of the Rock, a Muslim shrine that has stood on the Temple Mount since the year 691, has exploded. We don't know yet what caused the blast, only that a cloud of thick black smoke can be seen above the sight. Stay with 1010-WINS for more on this huge developing story."

David looked at Scott and turned the radio off.

Standing on his front porch in his grimy damp uniform, David had no idea what he would tell Rebecca.

"Sarah knew it," he said to himself. "She knew something was coming. Nobody would listen, including me, and now she's gone."

David stared at the mezuzah for what felt like an eternity. He used to love coming home. For the first time in memory, David entered his house with a feeling of dread.

Looking at the stairs to the second floor where he had just carried Sarah up the night before, David saw Rebecca.

Hearing him, she cried out, "Daddy!"

Mel appeared at the top of the stairs, took Rebecca's hand, and led her down to David. The three of them cried and hugged tightly together.

Just as David was thinking about what he might say to Rebecca, there was a knock at the front door.

Could it be Sarah??!! He looked out hopefully from the front window.

"Frank!" David yelled as he opened the door. Both men fought back tears as they quickly embraced.

"David, I need to talk to you right away."

Frank and Mel exchanged glances. Mel knew that Frank would not be here for business unless it was unavoidable.

David put his hands out. "Frank, please, not now."

Frank stepped up to David. "Hear me out. Sarah would want you to hear this." David agreed and asked Mel to take Rebecca to her room.

Frank followed David upstairs to the master bedroom. David sat on the corner of the bed and put his head in his hands. Still covered by the dirt and debris of devastation, he stared at the floor before looking up at Frank. "What is it?" David asked in a barely audible voice.

"Do you have the device that Sarah showed you?"

"What difference does it make?"

"I need to tell you something...Sarah needs to tell you something."

"Frank, Sarah's gone."

Frank took a deep breath. "I know, but she still needs to tell you something."

Reaching into his nightstand, David pulled out a camo-leather case containing the device that looked like an ordinary iPhone.

"Sarah knew something was coming and I believed it because her instincts have always been right. She spent the last year gathering intel, and making plans in case an event like today happened. She prepared this just for you, for the only man she loved, the only man she thought could carry out this mission."

"What mission?"

"Enter the code, David, and let Sarah tell you."

David thought of the night before the attack, the night Sarah showed him the device and tried to convince him how important it was. Turning it on, David peered at the key pad.

"Okay, Frank, what's the code?"

"It's the answer to a question."

"What's the question?"

"What was the month, day and year you and Sarah met?"

Fighting back tears, David shut his eyes, as if the pain washing over him had finally become unbearable.

Opening his eyes, he sighed and entered the numbers: **9-11-2001**

CHAPTER 5
SEPTEMBER 11, 2001

DAVID WALKED UP the steps out of the subway during the early-morning rush hour; his feet were aching badly. Scott breezed past him. "What's wrong, man? You're moving like a snail again."

"Scotty, it's these damn shoes. They're too tight."

"Yeah, you've been complaining about them for like three months now."

"I can't take it anymore. I'm going to stop at Charlie's and get some new treads before work."

Scott looked up at the sky. "Hallelujah! It's about time. I'm sick of hearing you whine about your feet."

On the crowded sidewalk, the alluring aroma of hot pretzel vending carts wafted around them.

"Scotty, you get the coffee and pick up a dozen bagels with cream cheese. I'll meet you at roll call."

David hurried around the corner to the shoe store. The owner was sweeping the floor when David entered. "Hey Charlie."

"Officer David Stein. Are you here to buy something this time? Or you still just looking?" Charlie shook his head as he held the end of the broom.

"My feet are killing me."

"I've been telling you for months you need new shoes. Take a seat; I got just what you need."

"So you have New Balance or Nike?"

"I'm giving you the shoes that all great cops wear."

Charlie pushed the track ladder to the end of the shelves along the right side of the store. Quickly stepping up three rungs, he reached the top shelf and came back down with a shoebox. Kneeling in front of David, he removed David's old shoes before tossing them into a trash can. "Those are garbage."

Charlie opened the box, took out the shoes and held them up proudly. "These are The Hammer."

"The Hammer?"

"The Hammer. Treat them right and they'll last you fifty years."

"Fifty years?"

Charlie smiled. "Well, at least 25."

David slipped his feet into the shoes and laced them up before walking around the store, smiling and nodding approvingly.

"Nice and soft on the inside, like a hammer on the outside. If you gotta knock out a guy or kick in a door, The Hammer won't let you down. Just ask any of New York's Finest."

David reached for his wallet. "Nice Charlie, nice. How much?"

"For you, Officer Stein, it's on me."

"No Charlie, let me pay you."

"Hey, it's okay, anything for the men in blue." Charlie continued sweeping in the back of the store.

"Thanks Charlie, have a good day."

David looked at the price tag on the shoebox, pulled three twenties out of his wallet, and placed them on the counter as he left the store.

"David!"

David looked in the window and smiled at Charlie before walking away.

⁊

David was at his desk sipping coffee, just about to bite into an everything bagel with cream cheese when the phone rang.

"First Precinct. Officer Stein."

"David, it's Robby."

"Where are you, man?"

"I'm at the World Trade Center with Mike; a plane just hit the North Tower."

"I know. I heard it was a small plane. Is NYPD with you? How about Scotty?"

"Yeah, NYPD is out in force. So is FDNY."

"Listen, Robby, I'm coming down there. Hang tough, man."

As David sprinted to his patrol car, he spotted one of his lifelong friends and fellow officers.

"Yo, Johnny, can I borrow your Mag? I'm going to the Towers."

"Sure, take it. You're gonna need it; I hear there's not much visibility in there."

～

Weaving quickly through the streets of Lower Manhattan, David chirped the siren at crowds of people frozen in place as they watched the smoke billowing from the towers. David parked as close to the World Trade Center as he could get. Two blocks from his car, he spotted Scott in a crowd of NYPD officers of all ranks.

"Scotty, talk to me."

"A second plane just hit the south tower…this was no accident. The buildings are already crawling with rescue personnel."

"I'm going in anyway."

"Man, be careful. Both towers could be unstable."

David rushed to the stricken south tower as throngs of people poured out of the lobby. Entering from the large plaza, David heard Robby's voice in a stairwell, directing people on their way down. "Okay, folks, keep moving this way! You're all going to be fine!"

David rushed up the stairs, weaving through the streams of people until he reached his friend.

"Hey, Dave! I can't get to the floors above us but we're getting people out at a pretty good clip!"

"We just have to do what we can."

Robby spotted an elderly woman leaning against the landing wall, trying to catch her breath. "Hey, lady, are you alright? Donny, relieve me," Robby said to a fellow fire fighter as he rushed toward the woman. Robby put an oxygen mask over her face, then lifted her into his arms and began carrying her down the stairs.

"You're so sweet," she whispered through the mask.

"Just doing my job, ma'am. Okay, everybody, keep coming! Follow me downstairs. You're all doing great; just keep moving!" Robby yelled as the stream of people headed toward the ground floor and out of the building.

Outside, Robby handed the elderly woman over to a paramedic, then raced back up the stairs.

Weakened by the explosion and fire, the stairwell began to partially collapse.

Near the 50th floor, Robby fell into a gaping hole. Trying to pull himself up, he was hampered by falling debris and sank deeper, becoming trapped. Mike, his friend and fellow firefighter, came up behind him from the lower floors.

"Mike, get out of here!"

"No dice, buddy! I got you, bro!"

"Save yourself and get out of here!"

"Not without you! Grab my hand!"

"If I do, you could fall through!"

"Do it! Grab my hand!"

Robby grabbed Mike's hand. More of the stairs gave

way, trapping Mike as well. A few floors above them, they heard David running down the stairs.

"Robby! Mike! Where are you guys!? Can you hear me?"

"David! We're stuck beneath the landing!"

"Where are you?"

"We're down here, somewhere between 49 and 50! I think!"

"Where? I don't see you!"

"Keep coming. Follow my voice!"

"Okay, keep talking. I think I'm about three flights above you!"

When David reached the gap in the stairs, he grabbed a beam with one hand and held the Mag Lite with the other. As he extended the long flashlight, Robby got a hand on it and pulled himself out to a stable part of the floor. The floor began sinking beneath Mike.

"David, hold my ankles and I'll reach down for Mike."

David grabbed Robby's feet; Robby reached in and took hold of Mike's hands. Using all of his strength, he managed to pull Mike out.

The building began to creak and sway as the three men bolted down the remaining stairs and safely out of the south tower.

Mike and Robby joined the other fire fighters who were helping evacuate the wounded to St. Paul's Church. David located a makeshift NYPD command post on Murray Street.

David saw Scott at the command post.

"David, thank God you're alright!"

"Somehow I'm in one piece, Scotty. What's with the other tower?"

"Looks like we evacuated everyone who could be saved."

"I'm going in; there must still be people in there."

"It's too dangerous!!"

"One more sweep of the building, buddy!"

David raced past the giant bronze sphere toward the north tower as paper rained down on the Austin J. Tobin Plaza. He climbed the stairs, three steps at a time, finding debris strewn about on most of the lower floors. There was no sign of life, only liquid slowly trickling down the stairs. The odor of jet fuel permeated his nostrils.

But when he reached the 76th floor, he heard moaning coming from above.

At that moment, his radio squawked; Scott was calling from outside the building.

"David, man, get out of there! The building's unstable!"

"I can't! I hear someone on 77!"

"I don't want you to die in there!"

"If I leave, that person's going to die!"

"Robby's going nuts outside! If you don't come out of there in five minutes, I think he's crazy enough to go in after you."

"Tell him to sit tight!"

David ran up one more flight and kicked open the door to the corridor. Floor 77 had sustained heavy damage; many of the walls had buckled.

The moaning got louder. David hurried to his left,

aiming the flashlight around the corner where the light fell on a young woman who appeared to be trapped. A large piece of an I-beam and concrete had fallen on her right leg and soot covered her face.

"NYPD. Are you okay, ma'am?"

"Officer! My leg is caught!" she groaned. "I can't move."

David wedged the butt end of the MagLite between the floor and the chunk of concrete to make just enough room for his hands to get underneath. "Hang on, you're going to be okay. When I tell you to pull your leg out, do it!"

Using all of his strength, David lifted the heavy slab. "Now!"

The woman slowly stood up, leaning against the wall for support. He pushed the Mag out of the way with his foot before dropping the slab.

"Here, hold the flashlight; put some light on your right knee."

He bent down to get a closer look. The knee was swollen and bruised but looked to be intact.

"I think I can walk."

She took three wobbly steps before falling into David's left side. He picked her up in his arms and made reassuring eye contact.

"It's okay. I can carry you. You're not going 77 flights on that knee. When we're out of here, we'll have the paramedics look at it."

David carefully dodged rubble as he carried the woman toward the stairwell for the long downward climb.

As David made his way down the stairs with the young woman in his arms, he noticed an unusual necklace she was wearing. It was the Star of David and in the center was a small lamb.

She squeezed the necklace as the building shook and the sound of bending metal reverberated around them.

"Hold onto that necklace. We need all the help we can get."

Between the 34th and 33rd floors, David saw several stair treads missing above the landing. "Put your left arm around my neck and aim the flashlight with your right hand at the gap in the stairs."

The young woman gasped. "We'll never make it over that! There's at least five steps missing!"

"Just hold on tight."

Taking a running start, David gained momentum and prepared to leap.

The woman's fingers dug into his left trapezius muscle just as they got airborne. His feet slammed down onto the landing. Managing to keep his balance as momentum thrust him toward the wall, he spun to his right and braced himself as his left shoulder blade bore the brunt of the impact. The MagLite slipped from the woman's hand and disappeared into the deep hole.

"Oh! Officer, are you okay?"

"I don't think I broke anything."

"Sorry about your flashlight. Ohhhhh…the slings and arrows….," she lamented.

"…of outrageous fortune…."

He finished the line for her as he continued to race down the stairs.

"Where does a policeman learn Shakespeare?" she asked, trying not to laugh.

"A little school about two hundred miles north of here, in Cambridge."

"Harvard?? I went there, too!"

Looking at him, she thought for a moment.

"I'll tell you what. If you get me out of here alive, I'll take you to see Hamlet…it's playing on Broadway."

"It's a deal."

"It's a date."

As they approached the 11th floor, a tall dark man in a black suit and tie, wearing sunglasses, quickly and methodically walked past them as he headed up the stairs.

David stopped and turned around. "Sir! Don't go up there! It's not safe!"

The man glanced back at David and the woman. He gave them a wispy smile but never broke stride as he continued to climb undaunted.

With the woman still in his arms, David resumed running down.

"Must be CIA or FBI. Maybe he knows something we don't. But we still have to get out of here!"

The two finally reached the rubble-strewn ground floor, in what used to be the majestic lobby of the north tower.

Exiting the building, they confronted a surreal scene — lower Manhattan now looked like a war zone.

David saw something falling at the western end of the plaza. "Don't look," he said as he tried to turn the woman away. Out of the corner of his eye he saw a body slam onto the concrete.

"Look at what?"

"Something you shouldn't see."

The tower rumbled as the upper floors began to collapse.

David looked back in horror as the antenna atop the north tower began to sink. He hurried across the plaza as fast as he could while carrying the young woman in his arms. Through the dust he saw a firefighter coming toward him from the edge of the road.

"Robby??!!"

"David! Come on! We gotta take Fulton over to Broadway! There's a safe spot in front of Trinity!"

Robby got behind David and kept a hand on his shoulder as he pushed him east down Fulton Street.

None of them said another word until David lowered the woman onto the steps in front of St. Paul's Chapel.

"David! You two need to cover up! That north tower is coming down!" Robby yelled before moving on to help others.

David sat down and quickly removed his shirt. He pulled the young woman into him as closely as possible, covering them both. With their grimy faces pressed together forehead to forehead, he could feel her warm breath against his cheek. For the first time since his parents were killed, for some reason, he felt completely alive. Even amidst the devastation surrounding them, the pounding that he felt in his heart was not due to the tragedy that was happening outside the shirt, but what was happening beneath it.

The entire area became enveloped in a dark cloud. It sounded and felt like a speeding locomotive was coming toward them as thick grey dust ran down the city streets and filled the air. David pulled the woman tighter.

"Are we going to make it?" Her voice trembled in a whisper.

Gazing into her eyes, David replied softly with assurance. "Yes, we are going to make it."

The protection of David's shirt could not totally prevent the ash from covering them. David pulled the woman even closer. He wasn't sure how much time had passed while he and the woman continued to huddle under his shirt. It could have been ten minutes or it could have been an hour before they heard a voice through a distant megaphone giving the "all-clear."

Robby tapped David on the shoulder before slipping a towel and two water bottles under the shirt.

"Here you go, brother," Robby said before running to help other first responders.

David slowly pulled his shirt off of their heads. The dust had not entirely settled, but the area was brighter as a pink cloud began to light up the sky. The inside of the church had apparently been set up as some kind of triage area.

They looked on as EMS personnel transported injured people through the front doors.

David twisted open one of the water bottles and gently poured it over the woman's face. With his hands, he carefully cleaned her eyes, her nose, and her mouth. In the light of day, she was much more beautiful than he first realized. She sat up, took the bottle from David's hands, and poured it over his face, cleaning his eyes, his nose, and his mouth.

She looked at David and whispered one word to herself.

"Elijah."

"Excuse me, ma'am?"

"Oh…no…nothing officer."

Amidst the death, dust and chaos, for those few moments, time stood still. They could see only each other.

"By the way, I never asked you your name."

"I'm Sarah."

"Hi Sarah, I'm David."

David leaned down toward her and paused for a moment, their lips nearly touching. Continuing to gaze into each others' eyes, they suddenly joined in a passionate kiss. From that moment on, David and Sarah somehow knew they would never part.

∽

"David."

David looked up and saw a life-sized holographic image of Sarah speaking to him from across the bedroom.

"*David, I hope someday we will watch this together, perhaps on our 50th wedding anniversary,*" she smiled. "*Both of us laughing at my doomsday assumptions. But darling, if you are watching this without me, that means it is all true. I am no longer here.*"

Astonished by what he saw, David stood up and slowly approached her flawless, life-size projection.

"*For a long time, Frank and I have been working on advanced hologram technology and have loaded it onto the device you hold in your hand. You can call it 'Halo.' If you can see me now, we have succeeded.*"

"*We have been monitoring terrorist activity and gathering intel for more than a year. If you are watching this alone, terrorism has likely struck again. Based on our work, I have included instructions on what you must do, for our daughter's sake, for the sake of our country and the world.*"

"*Darling, I know you are overcome with grief, but if you love me, you must be strong.*"

As David stood mesmerized, he felt Frank's hand on his shoulder.

"*You must heed the instructions; you must fulfill the mission. Let Dad take care of Rebecca while you're away from home. Lorraine – Mike's wife – can help him.*"

"*I love you, David. Death will not separate us. I'm still alive in the Lord.*"

Sarah's image slowly faded away as HALO shut down.

Stunned and in shock, David turned to Frank.

"How could this be happening?"

The door to the bedroom burst open; Rebecca entered, followed by Mel. They embraced David and wept.

"I thought I heard Mommy," Rebecca said.

"Mommy has gone away," her father replied.

"Will I see Mommy again?" Rebecca asked as her eyes filled with tears.

David struggled for an answer. "Yes, you will see Mommy again, someday."

Rebecca seemed to accept her father's assurance.

Mel, sensing that David wanted to be alone, took Rebecca's hand and led her out of the room. "Come along, sweetheart."

"Frank, I really need to be by myself right now."

Frank nodded before leaving the bedroom.

David curled up on Sarah's side of the bed. Grabbing her pillow, he could still smell her. "I'm sorry, I'm so sorry, I should have listened to you. We all should have listened to you." He buried his face in the pillow, sobbing uncontrollably.

"Beep beep beep beep, beep beep beep beep, beep beep beep beep."

"Honey, get the alarm," David whispered, reaching across the bed to put his arm around Sarah, but no one was there.

Waking from what he momentarily thought was just a bad dream, the grim reality sank in.

Sarah was gone.

Getting out of bed and ignoring the alarm, he slowly

staggered to the bathroom. Splashing water on his face, he picked up the razor for his usual morning shave as his eyes fell on Sarah's toothbrush. He threw the razor in the trash. Looking in the mirror at his bloodshot eyes, David knew he would never be the same.

He heard a knock outside the bedroom. David opened the door to see Frank holding a cup of coffee. Mel stood behind Frank wearing a stoic expression. "I thought you could use this." Frank handed David the cup. "I need to explain to you and Mel how the HALO device works."

"Yeah, okay, Frank, if we have to."

David took a sip of coffee before activating HALO.

Mel gasped in disbelief when his daughter appeared in front of him. "My God, what is this?"

The holographic image of Sarah began to speak.

"David, it's time to begin your mission. You must fund it privately. Tell Dad to reach out to Ronald Siegel the financier. Do not delay. You need to reassemble your entire SEAL team. You and Scott should start contacting the men today.

"Have everybody meet at JFK. Siegel will provide your team with a jet. I have spoken with him and he will help with whatever else you need.

"Your immediate mission will be to seek, find, and destroy those responsible for any recent attacks on our homeland.

"Your first stop will be Jakarta. The person you will meet is someone you and Scott already know — a 'friendly' named Singh. His mother was from Taiwan, his father was from India and he's been a valuable source of intel. His contact information is on HALO.

"Once you land in Jakarta, two unmarked buses will be scheduled to arrive. You and your men will board the buses. The drivers will get out and Gladiator can drive one and Scotty the other. If the men who deliver the buses don't offer to leave, beware…and do what you have to do. If the drivers get out, they will assume control of the plane, from refueling to maintenance testing, until you're finished with Singh.

"And you must make sure that Singh is really Singh. Question him; ask him 'what's the good word?' If he says 'foghorn,' he is Singh. If not, he is an imposter and you have to kill him. You will be using HALO to receive my instructions throughout the mission. HALO will respond only to your voice or Frank's. I'll be able to converse almost as if I'm with you, and I wish I were."

David thought, "I wish you were, too."

"Take Frank and Scotty with you wherever you go. That's it for now; I'll talk with you in Jakarta."

Sarah paused for a moment, looking into David's eyes as if she were there. "I love you always."

All three watched her image fade away.

Mel sighed. "We have work to do," he said, turning to David and Frank. "I'll take Rebecca home to Scarsdale with me and I'll meet with Ronald tomorrow."

"Okay," David nodded solemnly to Mel.

It nearly devastated David to think he would be away from Rebecca, but he knew what he had to do.

∽

David and Mel continued to mourn Sarah's loss but stayed busy as David and his select group of SEALs prepared to leave their families behind.

Over the next several days, the world was repeatedly shocked as numerous reports of terrorism came in from all continents. By the Saturday following the attack on Liberty Island, David and Scott had their SEAL team assembled in New York, and Mel had received the necessary funding for the mission.

The night before leaving, David was home alone. He sat on the edge of his bed staring at Sarah's image in silence for hours.

Finally, he snapped out of his trance and turned off HALO.

Laying back on the bed, he stared into the darkness.

"I will find them — and I will kill them."

CHAPTER 6
LEAVING AMERICA

IT WAS JUST past sunrise on July 12th when David's SUV pulled into the Siegel Corporation private hangar at JFK. He was unloading his gear as the rest of the SEAL team started to arrive for boarding. For the first time in a week, David was able to barely crack a smile.

Among the SEALs was Chad "Gladiator" Perry, who would be the pilot.

Chad was a trust fund kid and scholar-athlete who prepped at Deerfield and St. Albans. Standing 6'2" with piercing blue eyes like Ray Liota and a military bearing, he was a quiet blend of brain and brawn, righteous idealism and worldly wit, with a cool, unflappable exterior. Chad was a master aviator, combat tactician and an expert in counter-intelligence.

Decades before Chad was born, a St. Albans headmaster famously told parents of his students that his first job was to get their kids into Heaven, not Harvard. He would have been proud of Mr. Perry: He was accepted at Princeton, but Heaven was invariably first in his heart and mind.

To Chad, David was like an older brother, his loyalty to David exceeded only by fealty to his God and his parents. Next to Scotty, Chad was David's most valued SEAL.

"Gladiator, good to see you," David said as Chad approached.

"Good morning, Skip."

The youngest of David's original SEAL team, Gladiator came on board in the second decade after 9/11. He distinguished himself as a legendary sniper with the patience of Job and the ability to mark and 'drop' an enemy target from well over a mile away.

"Chad Perry."

Chad looked over his shoulder to see his old friend.

"Scott Miller."

The two embraced.

"There is no joy in our meeting today, but it's good to see you, brother."

"And you as well."

"I'm sorry for your loss," Chad said as he looked at David and Scott.

Patting him on the back, Scott said, "Well, we're going after the vermin. That's why we're all here."

David looked around the hangar and saw that the men had their gear packed. "I think we're ready to board."

This was the SEAL team that hunted bad guys across the globe, from Berlin to Baghdad, Cairo to Khartoum, Amman to Kabul, Bangkok to Mumbai. From al Qaeda and ISIS to MS-13, pirates to pushers, human traffickers to regular army units serving tyrants and torturers, they tracked them down and wiped them out.

Many well-wishers, including family and friends, arrived to bid the men farewell. Mel, Rebecca, and General Joe were among those who gathered around David and Scott.

Joe extended his massive right hand to David. Alex, Rebecca's cat, slept soundly, curled up and purring in the crook of Joe's left arm.

"Dave, I wanted to go with you but Washington has me on hold."

"Understood. I'm just grateful for whatever time you can spend with Mel and Becca while I'm gone."

"Me too."

Fighting back tears, Mel looked down at Rebecca as he held her hand. "Cupcake, say goodbye to your father."

"Bye, Daddy!"

Rebecca hugged David. "Sweetheart, you be good to Grandpa while I'm gone."

"I will. I love you, Daddy!"

"I love you too, Becca. Remember, Mommy is always with you."

Rebecca reached up and tugged David's shirt, bringing his ear down to her mouth before whispering.

"I know Mommy's still here, Daddy. I heard her voice the other night in your room."

David nodded and smiled as he looked into Rebecca's eyes.

"It's good to see you smile," Mel said before he and Rebecca had one last, long embrace with David.

"Stay safe: you're my son."

"I will, Dad."

David stared at the ground quietly for a few seconds, then faintly asked, "Have they found Sarah?"

"No, son, there are still hundreds missing. The forensic units believe that some bodies, due to the magnitude of the explosion, will never be located or identified."

David rubbed his eyes. Hesitating for a moment, Mel spoke solemnly.

"But David," he said with a lump in his throat, "they found this."

Mel reached into his pocket and pulled out a small evidence envelope. He slowly removed a ring and held it up between his thumb and forefinger.

David stared at the ring intensely before slowly taking hold of it.

He put Sarah's wedding ring onto his left pinkie finger, next to his own ring.

Looking at Mel, David's face turned to stone.

Mel grit his teeth. "Avenge my daughter."

Mel took Rebecca's hand and led her back to the car. She turned around and waved before getting into the backseat.

David mouthed "I love you."

Rebecca smiled and did the same.

As David watched them leave, Scott stood beside him and put his hand on David's shoulder.

*

"Okay, is everybody on board?" David asked as Frank and the SEALs took their seats on the plane.

"They're all here, Skip," Scott said.

David secured the cabin door, then stood in the aisle at the front of the plane and called his men to attention. David's serious tone quickly silenced the background chatter.

"Gentlemen, the mission we are about to embark on is not about any personal vendetta. If anyone has a reason to have one, it would be Scott and me. Our mission is to locate and kill the terrorists, while gathering any intel they might have on future attacks. This mission, this battle, is for our lives, our families, our country, and those in the world who will choose to defend freedom. We do not know when this mission will end, or if all of us, or any of us, will return. But there's one thing we do know…we must fulfill this mission.

David scanned the rows of seats, making eye contact with every SEAL individually.

"Men, there is no choice."

David looked back into the open cockpit and gave Chad a thumbs-up. "Okay, Gladiator, let's see what this bird can do."

Chad's voice came over the speakers. "Guys, please prepare for takeoff. Winds are out of the southeast at twelve miles per hour with scattered showers. We should experience slight turbulence before we rise above the clouds."

David sat next to Frank, who had a window seat in the first row. Frank nervously watched as the ground crew pushed the aircraft out of the hangar.

They began to taxi onto the runway. Many of the men looked out the windows to get a final glimpse at family and friends, fearing they might never see them again. Chad pushed the throttle forward. Soon the plane was barreling down the runway and into the air.

"Crank it, Scotty," yelled Danny, one of the oldest members of the team.

Scott punched the code into the satellite music system. Hearing the first few notes of their favorite combat song, the SEAL team knew it was time for business. Phil Collins's "In the Air Tonight" blasted from the sound system as the plane ascended through the clouds above Long Island and out over the Atlantic Ocean.

The trip from New York to Indonesia lasted 14 hours. For the first seven hours, the men slept soundly. Later in the flight, some of the SEALS took the opportunity to examine the military satellite communications and weapons systems.

News started streaming in from the limited number of networks that were able to broadcast following the mass destruction and global cyber-attacks.

Initial reports confirmed their worst fears:

CNN reported, "Breaking news! Sunday, July 12, 2026…the world will never be the same. As of this hour, multiple targets in cities across the nation have been hit with what law enforcement agencies are calling 'major explosive devices.'

"We can report now that Boston, New York, Washington, Miami, Chicago, Houston, Seattle, San Francisco, Los Angeles and San Diego have all been struck. Including the deadly attack on Liberty Island, casualties in America are said to be at least in the tens of thousands."

Many of the SEALS looked at each other in disbelief as they grew more concerned for their loved ones at home.

"In related news, unnamed sources have confirmed that the New York Stock Exchange is not fully operational and that many of the securities normally traded in New York will be listed in Dubai until the repairs to the NYSE are completed.

"This just in: It has been reported that the governor of Greater Babylon has been killed. I repeat, the head of state of Greater Babylon has apparently just been assassinated. We will report back with further details as they emerge."

"Sounds like the start of Armageddon," Scott mumbled as his thoughts continued to swirl around the loss of Debbie.

Although he had faith in Sarah's mission and David's command, he was torn about leaving behind his friends and family in America. Scott kept his concerns to himself, and tried to focus on the mission ahead.

Less than an hour later came more alarming news during the flight, this time from Europe:

"We can now confirm that just outside the Vatican, the Pope has been assassinated by a suicide bomber as earlier reports suggested. Repeat, the Pope has been assassinated outside the Vatican while praying and giving blessings to crowds of people already distraught due to the eruption of worldwide terrorism. We can also confirm that the prime minister of Italy, Alfonse Genero, has been airlifted to Rome after being shot and is in critical condition... Wait...we are now reporting...Prime Minister Genero has been pronounced dead after arriving in Rome. Italian media outlets are reporting that Foreign Minister Anno Corinthia will likely be named interim Prime Minister. In response to the rioting in cities across the world over the recent bombing that destroyed the Dome of the Rock in Jerusalem, Mr. Corinthia has been meeting with Mideast leaders this week while trying to form a commission of inquiry into the atrocity for which no one has claimed responsibility. And...what? Can you confirm that? Yes, I'm told that as we speak, Joseph Herrmann, the head of the European Union, has just been killed in a car bombing outside his hotel in Florence, Italy.

"Also breaking now, unbelievably, we have yet another death of a major dignitary to report. In New York, Lin Chang, the UN Secretary General, has allegedly committed suicide by jumping onto the promenade near the Hudson River from his twenty-third-floor apartment in Battery Park City. Repeat, the Secretary General of the United Nations has apparently committed suicide. Nearby on Liberty Island, search and rescue teams continue their recovery efforts. President Thompson's body is among the hundreds still missing from the celebration of America's 250th birthday."

"Shut it off," David said to Scott, pointing to the TV. "Gentlemen! We are at war; the world is at war."

∽

As the plane began its descent into Jakarta, Chad's voice came over the PA system in the cabin. "The tower has cleared our approach. Prepare for what should be a smooth landing."

Scott awoke and noticed David still asleep next to him. "David. David, we're landing."

Scott nudged David in the side. David raised his head and opened his eyes.

"Man, you were out cold. You probably hadn't slept in over a week."

"Sleep won't come easy until all these terrorists are dead."

"I'm afraid you're right, brother."

Through light wind and rain, Chad glided the plane down safely onto the runway. As they taxied to a stop in a hangar, the SEALs began to gather their gear. Two buses approached on the tarmac just as Sarah had planned. Boarding stairs were rolled up to the cabin door. Chad stepped out of the cockpit.

"David, I'm going to check out those buses and drivers. We don't want any surprises."

"Gladiator, it should be fine. Sarah planned this whole thing."

"David, I'm going to check out those buses and drivers."

Chad gave David a smirk before opening the hatch.

"Good idea." David smiled as he watched Chad head down the stairs.

⟡

Deep beneath the howling desert winds, in a clandestine underground compound in Syria, the tech commander for an international terrorist ring scrutinized the computer-hacking operation. The atmosphere in the room was stressful. The tension could be cut with a knife.

"These petty little attacks we've been orchestrating have successfully caused world chaos, but it's not giving us the dominance we need to achieve our leader's goals. We must have those weapons!"

"I'm working on it, Commander. We're very close," Thor, the senior technician, responded carefully.

The commander leaned down and spoke softly and menacingly alongside Thor's face.

"Get it done."

Sweating profusely, Thor wiped the fog off his bifocals, taking his eyes away from the computer for a moment. He knew if he didn't complete the task, the consequences would be severe. The other eight techs in the room had their eyes locked on the screens in front of them, trying to ignore the confrontation between Thor and the commander.

Several minutes later, Thor leaned back in his chair and took a deep breath of relief.

"Commander, we have the codes; we have control."

The operation center's heavy doors slid open. Colonel Nigel Coles entered, his shoes pounding on the hard steel floor as he approached the men who quickly stood up at attention.

"Commander, did we achieve our goals?"

"Thor was a little late, but he was successful."

The colonel extended his hand to Thor; the two men shook.

"Congratulations, Thor."

The colonel stared into Thor's eyes for a few moments of uncomfortable silence.

"But, you were late!"

He pulled out a pistol and took aim at Thor's head.

"No, Colonel…"

Smiling broadly, the colonel pulled the trigger.

Thor closed his eyes in relief after the weapon made a harmless "click."

"Good job boys, but if you're late again…the clip will not be empty."

They all exhaled deeply as the colonel left the room, waving his gun and laughing to himself.

The road to Singh's place was filled with potholes and old cobblestones, winding endlessly through tight neighborhoods of small outdoor markets, shacks and other hovels connected by a seemingly infinite number of clotheslines. Seeing that westerners were passing by, dozens of barefoot children in tattered clothing lined the sidewalks with their hands cupped.

"Uang! Uang!" The children pleaded, yelling toward the buses as pungent odors, blaring music and exotic chants wafted from several shops.

"There's the building," David said, pointing to an old brick walk-up numbered 5086.

The run-down facade matched that of the other buildings in the dreary impoverished neighborhood. After the buses came to a stop, the SEALs filed out. David selected a dozen to go inside with him, including Scott and Frank, while the rest of the team formed a stealth perimeter around the building. David led the way into a small lobby and up the narrow, wooden, creaking steps. They located a door on the second floor with a number "9" on it.

Scott and David stood on either side of the doorway and tapped their pistols on the door three times. The door opened quickly; a heavy-set, gruff old man with a long handlebar mustache, wearing a chartreuse turban, emerged.

Seeing several guns pointed at his head, he yelled, "Oh my! Oh my!" David put his hand over the man's mouth and pushed him against the open door. "Relax, pal, I've got one question for you." The man's eyes bulged in terror. "What's the good word?"

"Mummm, mummm, mummm."

Scott leaned in and whispered behind David. "We could probably hear him better if you take your hand off his mouth."

David smiled and removed his hand.

"Foghorn! Foghorn! Foghorn!"

David signaled his men to enter the apartment.

Catching his breath, Singh was incredulous.

"What kind of greeting is that, David?! Don't you recognize me?"

"Singh, it has been well over a decade; you've got a few more grey hairs and a few more pounds since we last met."

"Thanks a lot."

"Sorry, brother."

The two men embraced.

Walking David into his apartment, Singh said, "Please come, eat, drink, sit down, relax, sleep. My rumah is your rumah!"

Singh took David aside; his tone became serious. "David, my condolences on your loss. Sarah was quite an operative…the best."

"Thank you, Singh. I appreciate that."

"Now, we must find out who's behind all of the horrors, but all my communication systems went down just a few minutes before you arrived."

"Well Singh, we've got just the man to help," David pointed at Frank.

"Singh, meet Frank Robbins."

Singh walked over to Frank, his burly body wrapping Frank in a huge bear hug.

"So this is Frank! I've heard your voice and Sarah's many times. A pleasure to meet you, young man."

Crushed beneath the weight of Singh's hug, Frank had just enough oxygen to squeak out a reply. "A pleasure to meet you in person, Singh. Sarah thought the world of you."

"And of you as well, Frank."

After finally being released, Frank caught his breath. "So, how long have they been down?"

"Network operations have been sporadic since Liberty Island. Not only were they killing people, it appears they launched a major cyber-attack that has affected our systems. You're welcome to try repairing it. Come with me."

Singh ushered Frank into a room filled with several work stations and servers.

"This is an exact replica of our operations center in New York," Frank exclaimed. "It's the same layout, with the same equipment as our office where Sarah and I worked."

"Yes Frank, and we've stored every bit of intel and analysis you and Sarah captured." Singh gestured with his hand toward the equipment. "It's all yours, Frank. I'll close the door so you can concentrate. If you require food and drink, my wife, Kemala, will prepare something."

"Thanks, Singh. If I need anything, I'll let you know."

Singh joined David and his men in the other room.

"Singh, I believe you knew Gladiator only by voice, until today."

"Of course. It's an honor, Mr. Perry."

"It is good to meet you in person, sir," Chad said as he shook Singh's hand.

"You know, Gladiator, I was once a marksman too, but now my eyes are no longer what they used to be."

David's radio made a fuzzy sound before a voice broke through.

"Skip, are you guys okay in there?"

"So far, so good, Kenny. Anything happening outside?"

"Not much. Hank, Danny and Willie are working their way up that rise 250 yards back. I figure it couldn't hurt to check it out."

"Alright Ken, keep me posted."

"Will do, Skip."

Moments later, Frank emerged from the computer room.

"Did you get anything, Frank?" David asked.

"I need everybody inside."

As the men filed in, they watched Frank working feverishly.

"It appears the terrorists who are behind this are trying to seize the nuclear arsenals of several nations, launch them against others, and eliminate any potential override of their control," Frank lamented. "Look! They're entering launch codes for missiles in Russia!"

Watching top-secret nuclear launch codes flash on his screen, Frank realized the enemy was quickly gaining access to the world's most dangerous weapons. The room fell silent; every man wore a worried look on his face.

David walked over to Frank. "Can you stop them?"

"I'm trying, Skip. The Russian missiles will launch in 47 seconds."

"Can you identify the targets?"

"Israel."

"What are the other targets, Frank?"

"All of the Russian missiles are programmed to hit coordinates in Israel."

"Frank! We have only 33 seconds!"

"I know!" David watched over Frank's shoulder as the launch clock counted down. Tension filled the room. All eyes were wide open. Some of the men nervously clasped their hands together as if praying…11 – 10 – 9 – 8 –

"Frank!"

7 – 6 – 5 – 4 – 3 –2 - 1 – 0…

The room fell quiet for what seemed like an eternity. Then the word "DISARMED" appeared on Frank's screen.

Wiping the sweat from his forehead, Frank let out a deep sigh. "Oh my God."

"Exactly," said Chad.

The feeling of relief was short-lived. More "ACCESS GRANTED" warnings appeared on Frank's screen.

"Frank, what else can you do to stop this?"

"Two things, David. I've created a virus that will slow them down before they seize another country's arsenal. Then, we can control the ICBMs ourselves."

"How many silos are they attempting to seize?"

"All launch sites in Europe, except for Britain. I think I can control the U.K. missiles before they do."

"You stopped them once; you'll stop them again."

"Thanks for the vote of confidence, Skip. We're about to find out…Yes! Yes! Our virus is blocking them! We've got the British nukes, and we'll have a lot more soon."

"Great work, Frank," David said staring at the monitor. "Does that cover all the missiles worldwide?"

"There's one obscure silo in India but I doubt the terrorists are aware of that location. I'll check it out." Just as Frank spoke, his screen began to blink red. *"LAUNCH ALERT, LAUNCH ALERT, LAUNCH ALERT."*

"Frank, what the heck is going on??!!"

"They've gotten control of the Indian missile!" Frank looked back at David. "And it launched!"

"What's the target?"

"The coordinates have it headed for..." Frank swallowed hard and double-checked the computer. "... Jerusalem."

David looked at Chad, "Gladiator, get Steve Dobson on the line!"

A few seconds later, David yelled at Steve's image on Chad's satellite phone. "Steve! Jerusalem's got some serious incoming. Looks like impact in 17 minutes!!"

"I know! We're aware of the threat. Iron Dome is ready. We'll fire as soon as the missile is in range."

"Steve, this is no Scud," Frank said quietly. "Can the Iron Dome handle a big ICBM?"

"We'll see in about two minutes. Warning sirens are blaring across the country. Our civilians know the drill but there wasn't much advance notice with this one."

"Is there anything we can do? Can you detonate it mid-air, Frank?"

"I'm afraid there's nothing."

Chad stood up and spoke to the group. "I know of

one thing we can do..." All eyes were expectantly aimed at Chad. "...Pray." The room was eerily still as the missile remained on course for Jerusalem.

Anticipating devastating news, David stood silently in the middle of the room.

The flashing 'RED-ALERT' on Frank's screen was suddenly replaced by a green-and-blue message: THREAT DISABLED.

Frank double-checked radar images; the missile's flight path ended over the Indian Ocean. "Steve, can you get a visual to confirm that Iron Dome has shot down the missile?"

"Negative, Iron Dome has not fired. The incoming missile is off my screen, too, but there's no evidence of mid-air detonation or impact."

"Then where is it? What would bring it down in mid-flight? Guidance malfunction?"

When Steve didn't answer, Chad spoke up. "Frank, there are things even more powerful than the Iron Dome."

"Our systems are now frozen...but it looks like theirs are too. We've lost control of all the arsenals."

"And the terrorists, Frank?" wondered Chad.

"The launch systems aren't working for anyone; they're totally shut down."

Singh looked at Frank. "So we're back to the beginning?"

"Essentially yes," answered a bewildered Frank. "Your systems are fully restored, but all parties are locked out of having any control of nuclear weapons."

"Frank, find out what happened. Nuclear missiles don't just disappear."

"I'm on it, Skip." Thinking for a moment, Frank swiveled his chair around and faced David. "Why do you think Singh's network crashed right before we got here?"

David paused for a moment, staring wide-eyed at Frank. "It means they know we're here."

Frank's stomach sank. David had no reply. Silence filled the room.

Suddenly, David heard an eerily familiar whistling sound just before his radio erupted. "Incoming!!! RPG's!!!!..." He tackled Frank to the floor as the rest of the SEALs instinctively hit the deck. In an instant, the room exploded into a deafening burst of thick smoke and flames. Heavy gunfire followed the blast, ripping apart what remained of the room's equipment.

The sound of return-fire echoed through the massive hole in the side of the building. Fewer and fewer rounds whizzed through the room as the SEALs who fought outside drew enemy fire. Feeling Frank's heart beat uncontrollably, David began to question the wisdom of bringing an office tech out to the front lines.

Sensing that the dust had begun to settle, Scott opened his eyes. The power had been knocked out, plunging the room into near darkness. David keyed his radio. "Kenny! Talk to me!"

"We've got heavily armed combatants at two o'clock; we picked off the vermin who launched the RPGs but the rest are dug in on top of the ridge. Gladiator might have the elevation to take out some of 'em." Chad nodded at Scott, pointing toward the end of his rifle case protruding from under a mangled desk. Chad crawled across the floor and pulled out the rifle case. The others remained flat on the floor as bullets continued to fly through the room intermittently.

David dusted off his radio. "Kenny, were any of you guys hit?"

"Pete took a clean through and through in the upper leg; we all have cover but we're pinned down."

"Hang in there. Gladiator's setting up."

Chad selected a gap in the bricks to shoot from. Flat on his stomach with the sniper rifle a foot off the floor, he quickly took out six hostiles before any of them could react. He hit five more out of a group of seven that tried to flee. The attackers went into full retreat, taking cover behind rusty pick-up trucks as they ran.

A moaning sound came from the far side of the room. David craned his neck to get a look at the big pile of debris that had been forced against the wall opposite the blast. Singh's face was visible near the bottom of the pile. David crawled over to Singh and began to carefully remove the rubble. "Oh my! Oh my! David! I thought I was dead!"

"Can you move?"

"Yes, yes, I think so."

There was a lull in the gunfire outside. "Skip."

David grabbed his radio. "Kenny, what's the deal?"

"All clear, the fighters are either on the run or dead."

"Good work, bro."

David helped Singh to his feet as the rest of the men stood up. "Anyone hurt?"

"They're all good," Scott said. "Now, let's get out of here." The men filed out of the room, leaving David alone.

"I'll be down in a minute," David called after Scott. David removed HALO from his pocket and said one word. "Sarah."

In the midst of the rubble, Sarah's surreal figure appeared… "David darling, if you're seeing me, you've made it to Jakarta, and you've met Singh. Well done. I'm sure you had your hands full thwarting terrorist plans for nuclear destruction."

David thought, 'how did she know that?'

"You're probably wondering how I knew that." David couldn't help but smile. "Now it's time to fly to India, cross the Bay of Bengal and land in Mumbai. There you will visit with another 'friendly' named Raja. You've never met him, but I have several times, when I was in field operations.

"All of Raja's information is on HALO. Several trucks will meet you at the airport. Again, watch the drivers. They'll complete maintenance on the plane. Gladiator and Scott can drive the trucks. Make sure that Raja is indeed Raja. When you get to his place, ask him, 'where is the government?' If he answers, 'on his shoulders,' he is Raja — if not, kill him. Be safe, follow my instructions, and all should go well." Sarah's image paused for a moment, appearing to look into David's eyes, as if she were there. She softly said, "I love you."

"I love you, too," he whispered as Sarah slowly vanished.

❦

Making his way down the rubble-strewn stairs, David caught up with Frank. "Did you ever find anything on those cyber attacks?"

"Nothing Skip, but all nuclear weapons systems around the world remain shut down."

"Okay men, for whatever reason, the world is safe... for the moment. Gentlemen, back to the airport and on to India. Let's roll."

David embraced Singh. "David, I'm confident you'll make it the rest of the way on your mission." Singh lowered his voice to a whisper. "Your wife just saved the human race, you know." Singh started to walk away, then turned around. "Quite a woman."

"Singh, do you need any help getting out of here?"

"Don't worry. Other than our apartment being destroyed, Kemala and I will be okay. She is waiting in our escape tunnel." Looking out at the street, Singh put a hand on David's shoulder. "Be careful, my friend...you are being watched. Even Sarah could not predict today's attack."

"David, we're ready to move out," Chad called from the bus.

"Farewell, my friend," Singh said as he watched David leave the building.

David gave Singh a thumbs-up before jumping onto the stairs of the moving bus.

❦

"We have to fix this. We have control over nothing; we've been stopped," the senior technician said to Thor as the distant sound of pounding heels could once again be heard approaching. The steel doors opened. Colonel Nigel stepped inside.

"Well, I have not heard any happy reports of nuclear devastation, anywhere in the world! What the hell is going on here?!!"

Thor nervously answered as all of the men stood up at attention. "Ahh...we were successful at launching a missile at Israel, but it, it disappeared."

"Oh, it just disappeared? Like in thin air? Amazing, so what do you think happened to it?" Smiling bitterly and stroking his chin, Nigel began to theorize. "Maybe it got intercepted by aliens." As Nigel paced back and forth in front of the men, his expression gradually turned serious. He moved close to Thor and leaned into his face. "That's one piss-poor excuse; you'd better have another explanation."

One of the other technicians stepped forward. "Colonel, a virus developed out of nowhere and disabled our control of..."

Nigel put a finger to his lips. "Shhhh....Out of nowhere? Okay, we can work this out. Just get back to it and do your job." Relieved, the men sat down and resumed their efforts. As the colonel was about to leave the room, he abruptly stopped and turned around before the doors opened. "Oh Thor, by the way, do you remember what I said about the next time you fail?"

Thor looked around at his nervous associates as he squeaked out a reply. "You said the clip will be full?"

The colonel smiled as he approached Thor. "Is that what I said?"

Thor nodded meekly.

"Damn Thor! You're right, that is exactly what I said." The colonel whipped out his pistol and quickly shot dead all eight of Thor's men as they sat at their computer terminals. Thor looked around in horror at the carnage. Nigel stepped behind Thor, pressing the barrel of the gun to his head. Sweating, Thor closed his eyes.

Nigel smiled and pulled the trigger – 'click.' "Damn! I must have run out of bullets!" Thor opened his eyes; Nigel put an arm around him. "Thor, buddy, it's your lucky day!"

The colonel casually waved his pistol around the room as he headed for the door. "Dispose of this garbage and get me some people who know what they're doing!" Nigel stopped in the doorway and smiled at Thor. "And by the way, get back to work."

CHAPTER 7
MUMBAI AND BEYOND

THE TURBULENT SIX-HOUR flight to Mumbai was relatively calm after the stress of narrowly avoiding nuclear devastation. Soon after they landed, a convoy of six military trucks arrived to transport David and his men.

The drive through the dark night from the makeshift airfield in the middle of nowhere was about ten miles along desolate dirt roads. As they approached town, the only light came from the occasional cooking fires that could be seen burning in the shacks they passed. Raja's place was located in an archaic stone building on a dead-end street. At four stories, it was the tallest structure in the area. Before approaching, Scott and Chad observed the building from an alley behind the old Oliver Hotel. Deciding the area was safe, they returned to the convoy.

David picked the same group of twelve SEALs to go with him that he had selected to enter Singh's apartment. "Raja should be on the fourth floor, guys. Gladiator,

Scotty, and Frank come with me. The rest of you stay on the third floor. Be ready if things hit the fan."

David, Scott and Chad had their guns drawn. As David led the way up the stairs, Frank brought up the rear, looking at his tablet. They were just turning on the landing between floors when they heard the "ch-chunk" of a shotgun being racked on the fourth floor. "Get back!" David yelled, pushing on Chad's shoulder. Chad, Scott, and Frank backed down the stairs. David held up a small antenna mirror to look around the corner of the landing. The barrel of a twelve-gauge shotgun was sticking out near the top of the railing; a cloud of smoke wafted toward the ceiling. "Listen up! You're surrounded! Put down your gun and slide it against the outside wall where I can see it!"

"How can I know to trust you?" A man replied in broken English.

"You don't have much choice."

"Okay, I will do what you said." The shotgun slid across the upper landing. A tall, thin man wearing a dusty and worn turban and a narrow mustache stepped into view, he took a long drag on his cigarette. "Who are you? Indiana Jones?"

"If I was, I would have shot you already."

The orange tip of the man's cigarette glowed brightly as he took a heavy drag. "You have a point. So, how can I help you?"

"That depends on your answer to my question." David climbed the stairs. Nose to nose with the man with the barrel of his pistol pressed into the man's ribcage, he asked, "Where's the government?"

"Where it should be...on his shoulders..." David lowered his gun. "So it's you...David." Raja shook David's hand.

"I don't know who's more relieved, you or I."

"Trust me David, I'm much more relieved." Raja smirked.

"So how can you help us, Raja?"

"David, show me what intel you have and I'll tell you everything you need."

"Well, first let us inside."

Raja dropped his cigarette on the floor and crushed it with the heel of his boot. "Come in." He ushered them through the door. The place had been converted into a command center. "Come right in and let's talk," Raja gestured, as David was followed by Scott, Frank and Chad. What had once been a living room with wood plank floors and white plaster walls, now contained a long conference table surrounded by a dozen chairs. Old wooden file cabinets lined the walls. The hotel could be seen through large windows at the far end of the room.

David looked around. "Looks like this place hasn't been touched since 1952."

Raja smiled faintly. "What...were you expecting the Ritz Carlton? Frank, let me see what you have."

"Okay, here are the terror cells we uncovered back in Jakarta."

Raja looked over the computer diagrams and maps

Frank had laid out on the table. "I know all of these places. I've got people, supplies and arms not far from every one of these points."

David was impressed. "All of them?"

"Yes, from western India to Pakistan and all the way to Israel."

"How were you able to coordinate all of this?"

"Simple...Sarah."

For the next hour, Raja helped Frank connect each cell location with the people and supplies Raja and Sarah had prepositioned.

David acknowledged Raja when they were done. "Thank you, for everything."

"No, thank you for Sarah's wisdom."

David looked at Chad. "Okay, time to move. Get on the trucks, guys."

Raja pulled David aside. "David, there is only one place you must avoid."

"Where is that?"

"The desert on either side of the Syrian - Jordanian border. It's a dangerous wasteland, and the cells that control the area are heavily armed."

"Don't worry Raja; we don't plan to cross the desert on foot."

"One more thing, David."

"What's that?"

"Be careful. It's rumored there's *a beeg* price on your head."

"Do you know how much?"

"Enough for many men to have interest in killing you. I think it's time for you to get out of here."

David's eyes widened. "Agreed."

❧

After a smooth landing in Islamabad, the SEALs journeyed westward, first with trucks, then by horseback to the infamous no-man's land along the Pakistan-Afghanistan border. It was a region SEAL teams were all too familiar with.

"We rest here until nightfall," David said, seeing that the men were tired. "The enemy should be to our west/northwest. In the meantime, let's keep a low profile. We own the night and will overtake them." The men bunked down to catch some much-needed rest.

Once the sun had set over the rugged terrain of the Himalayan foothills, David and his men were on the move. Using night-vision goggles, they traveled northwest quickly and quietly, creeping like foxes through the Margalla hills. Five hundred yards out, they spotted a small rise of smoke coming from the far side of the Tilla Charouni peak. "Okay guys, we gotta move on that smoke signal. Tie up the horses; we'll approach on foot."

David split the team into four groups. As the terrorists were occupied with their evening meal, they were stunned by the incoming shoulder rockets and sniper fire. The group of about fifty enemy combatants was quickly overwhelmed. It was the last meal any of them would have.

The SEALs continued across the Afghanistan border into deeper and more dangerous terrain.

About two miles in from the border, David spotted distant movement. He stopped and put up his hand. "Gladiator, check this out."

Chad adjusted his binoculars. "It looks like they've taken prisoners. Look to the left."

A terrorist combatant was herding three men at gunpoint, forcing them toward the opening of a cave while another was beating them with a bullwhip.

"You got this, Gladiator?"

"Butter on bread, Skip. I'll need my long range," Chad said before taking out his Barrett M82 sniper rifle. Chad's expression humbled; his eyes closed for a moment to pray. He opened his eyes, took position and peered through the telescopic sight. "Too close."

David looked at him. "You're over a mile away."

"I mean, the captors are too close to the captives." Gladiator looked through the sight again. "What the......? That guy's nuts."

Chad watched as one of the captives broke free, knocking out two of the terrorists with blows to the head. He tackled a third, twisting his head and breaking his neck with his bare hands. The other two captives fled but were pursued and gunned down. One of the terrorists aimed a revolver at the surviving prisoner, who had nowhere to run. He pressed the barrel against the prisoner's head before pulling back the hammer with his thumb. "You killed my friends, now I kill you! Ila al-liqa!" the terrorist yelled at the prisoner.

Training his sight on the enemy, Chad whispered, "Farewell," before calmly pulling the trigger.

In less than a split second, the bullet tore through the terrorist's head, dropping him to the ground before he was able to get off a shot. Gladiator picked off the six remaining combatants as they scattered for their lives. "All clear Skip, I'm gonna pack up."

The team cautiously approached the remains of the enemy camp where they found the lone prisoner wiping blood spatter and human debris from his shirt. "Who the heck are you?" David stared at the sole survivor, a grizzled man with a short greyish beard and wild blue eyes.

"Flynn's the name," he answered with a thick brogue.

"Where are you from?"

"Father was Irish, mum Scottish. Born and raised in Glasgow. Worked in British intel. Became a mercenary. They captured me yesterday. I killed them today."

"I didn't ask for your life's story, but nice work, Flynn."

"So who the hell are you? Janey Mac?" growled Flynn.

"David Stein, United States Navy SEAL. Pleased to meet you." David extended his hand. Through his tight grip, David could feel Flynn's tremendous strength as his knuckles popped. "And this is Gladiator, the man who saved your life."

"Nice shot, laddy. I guess I owe you one."

"Just doing my job, friend. Welcome aboard."

"Who says I'm your friend? And who says I'm aboard?"

Chad shrugged. "Your choice, Flynn. But we have plenty of supplies, including food. We could use a man like you."

Flynn stared at Chad for a moment. "Ah, let me think about it...where's the food?"

David looked at Scott. "Get this man something to eat."

Flynn smirked. "Thanks, mate. Killing terrorists has built up me appetite."

～

The next day, as the men moved toward the western end of Afghanistan, heading for Iran, things were surprisingly calm. "Dave, I've got one question for you," Scott said as they passed poppy fields that stretched far off into the distance.

"Shoot."

"Where are these terrorists coming from?"

"What do you mean, Scotty?"

"I mean, I thought we had taken care of terrorism long ago in these parts."

"Well, as far as we knew, we did."

"So, who brought terrorism back?"

"I wish I knew."

CHAPTER 8
CORINTHIA'S WORLD

THE SEAL TEAM reached a small base camp, one of several that Sarah and Raja had prepared along the route. As David drank coffee from a canteen, Chad called to him while staring at his tablet, "Hey David, check this out!"

A news anchor was announcing the start of a speech by Anno Corinthia, Italy's charismatic Prime Minister, at the newly relocated United Nations. After the catastrophic attack in New York, the United Nations was moved to Rome. As Corinthia strode to the podium, the delegates gave him a standing ovation.

"Ladies and gentlemen, fellow citizens of the world, the recent assassinations of national and world leaders have left us with a terrible vacuum in the battle against our terrorist enemies. I am honored to confirm that the European Union has chosen me to be its new leader and that I accept the choice that you have made to elect me as Secretary General of this august body." The hall erupted in sustained applause that lasted several minutes.

Corinthia continued:

"Let me be clear. The same force that causes terrorism has caused every war that humanity has ever fought. That force is us – it is our division into nations, cultures and religions, all competing against each other. There is one and only one way to stop the terrorists who are now warring against us. It is for us to unite. We must become one. One world, one people, one humanity. We must rid ourselves of all that divides us. That is how we defeat the terrorists, and that is how we finally bring peace to humanity. Are you with me on this?" he asked the assemblage.

"Yes!" They shouted in unison.

"Some would say it's impossible. I say that anything is possible if we come together. Will you help me bring us together?"

"Yes!"

"For 80 years, since its founding, the United Nations has lacked the ability to enforce our vision of unity and peace against the propagators of division and war. Will you help me to give us – you and I – that ability?"

"Yes!"

"Thank you. I accept the great responsibilities you have bestowed upon me. Together we will defeat terrorism and unite the world." Corinthia stepped down from the podium to a new round of tumultuous applause.

Scott shook his head after listening to Corinthia's speech. "I don't get it, Skip. He said nothing – just a bunch of lies about uniting the world...why all the...?"

"You mean all the adulation, Scotty? I don't think those were lies."

"Seriously?"

"I think he literally wants to unite the world, and everybody in that room knew it. He wants to transform the UN from an ineffective club of blowhards and squabbling nations into the vehicle for a one-world government. That's why they were cheering."

"They believe that one guy can do it...I mean, the whole one-world stuff?"

"Yeah, they do, Scotty."

"Do you think he can do it?"

"It looks like he's capable of anything, and that should worry all of us."

As he caught a final glimpse of Corinthia's image on the broadcast, David was struck by a sense that there was something oddly familiar about the man, but he just couldn't remember what. "We need to know more about this guy. Scotty, why don't you do some digging into Mr. Corinthia's past."

After leaving the UN building in Rome, Anno Corinthia entered his limousine and sped off to his headquarters not far from his official residence near the Tiber. Arriving, he passed through a maze of portals and a succession of secure doors that opened automatically, leading to a chamber where he and his closest confidants met.

Corinthia entered the office and sunk into an ornate

chair that resembled a monarch's throne. The secretary's voice came over the intercom. "He's here, Mr. Corinthia."

"Send him in." A door opened at the far end of the office. "Well, here comes my favorite, shall I say, 'faithful ward.'"

"Greetings," Marcus Wodan whispered in a low, eerie voice as he bowed.

"No need to bow Marcus....at least not yet."

"Where is our operational man?"

"He will be here momentarily." They heard the heavy pounding of boots before the door opened again. In walked Colonel Nigel Coles, a UK-born American and former Green Beret. Nigel, a highly sought-after mercenary, was a master of psychological warfare. He enjoyed pushing the buttons of his enemies and provoking them into making mistakes they would never have thought possible. At 48, he had rugged good looks, standing a lean 6'4", his 5 o'clock shadow and short thick wavy black hair had recently developed a hint of grey. "Welcome, Colonel."

"Excellent speech, Mr. Corinthia. It seemed the people were pleased with what you said. Hell, I almost believed every damn word you were saying."

Corinthia shook his head and smiled. "You're unique Nigel; that's why I hired you. Keep in mind, I hired you; you did not hire me."

Smiling, Nigel approached Corinthia and put a hand on his back. "I do respect where the money comes from. After your magnificent speech, looks like you got the whole world in your hands, Anno."

Wodan looked at Nigel in disgust as he dared to touch Prime Minister Corinthia and disrespectfully address him by his first name. Nigel caught the look on Wodan's face. "What's your problem, weasel?"

Wodan knew better than to respond. He quickly abandoned any inclination to confront Nigel.

Corinthia grinned. "I do indeed have the world in my hands. People appreciate a leader who puts out fires and brings unity and peace...even if that leader himself must occasionally start a few." Corinthia pointed toward Nigel. "And you, my friend, are going to start more than a few for me."

"Damn straight, Anno. But we have an emerging problem. There's a band of outlaws that's extinguishing fires without my...oh sorry, *your* approval."

"Indeed. I am very familiar with these mercenaries, especially their leader, David Stein. I have anticipated his involvement since the day I met him long ago. But do not worry. I have taken out a special...insurance policy to cover the Stein problem if he becomes more, how shall I say...successful." Corinthia looked at Nigel. "Just make sure of one thing, that Stein never makes it to Israel alive."

Nigel grinned broadly. "Like taking candy from a baby!"

The doors to the chamber swung open; the scent of exotic perfume suddenly filled the room. A striking, statuesque woman, wearing long black satin gloves and a skin-tight black leather cat suit entered. Long black hair extending to her hips, she was the essence of erotic beauty and sexuality, with a strong sense of darkness encompassing her seductive presence.

Nigel eyed the woman up and down. "Damn Anno! I like your choice in secretaries! You sure know how to pick 'em!"

For a moment, the woman lost her composure. She gave Nigel a disgusted look before arching an annoyed eyebrow at Corinthia. "Anno, who is this snake that slithered into your office?"

"Well, let me intro...duce myself. Commander Nigel Coles, at your service." Nigel wiggled his eyebrows and licked his lips.

The woman glared at the colonel. "Put your tongue back in your mouth, snake."

"I'll gladly put the tongue away, but I can't control that pesky snake." The woman's eyes widened in anger.

Corinthia jumped in to re-set the tone. "So good of you to come, Octavia. Marcus and Colonel Coles, meet the new Queen of Greater Babylon." As Octavia extended her hand, Wodan bent down and kissed it.

"I'd prefer to be called 'Empress.'"

Nigel looked at Corinthia and rolled his eyes.

Nigel moved closer to Octavia, continuing to examine her up and down. "I guess I'm next in line for a kiss."

She looked at Nigel with disdain. "Anno, has the colonel had his rabies shot?"

Corinthia tried to stop the banter. "Empress, you'll be working closely with the colonel. He will provide you with anything you need."

"That's right honey! Anything at all! I'll be rounding up your stock in trade. I know what you like."

"Nigel, the Empress rules the richest piece of real estate on earth, Dubai. The question is, what can Her Highness give us?"

"Anno, my dear, the answer is simple. Nigel will supply my, hmm…goods, and I will give you a piece of my pie."

"And what is your pie?"

"What else but the world? All the riches you could ever need, diamonds, gold, money, whatever your heart desires."

Smiling, Corinthia approached her. "We have a deal."

Octavia glared at Corinthia. "I am the Empress. Why would you expect me to collaborate with this Nigel creature?"

"Because he is the best at getting you what you want."

Grinning ear-to-ear, Nigel bowed slightly. "I love a woman who's a challenge."

Shaking her head, Octavia sneered wickedly at Nigel before turning to Corinthia. "Anno, I must leave immediately. I will take the snake, but I'm holding you responsible for his performance."

"The snake may slither but he won't bite." Corinthia continued. "I'll be waiting for my piece of pie."

Nigel strutted close to Octavia and whispered, "Who said I won't bite?"

"Come along, snake, and keep your venom to yourself."

Wodan and Corinthia watched as Octavia glided out of the office with Nigel following closely. Nigel looked back at Corinthia and playfully chomped his teeth, mouthing a "Thank You." The doors closed behind them. Corinthia smiled at Wodan. "Master, it looks like Octavia has met her match."

Corinthia nodded. "Perhaps...one never knows."

"Does she tempt you?"

"Marcus, she obviously tempts Nigel, but nothing tempts me. While Nigel is busy gathering Octavia's 'herd,' I have a mission for you."

"What is it, Master?"

"There is something in Scotland that I must have, Marcus. Something ancient, something...eternal." As Corinthia leaned closer to Wodan, his voice took on an evil density. "You will find it for me."

"Yes, I know what it is you seek."

CHAPTER 9
OCTAVIA

BOARDING A LEAR jet with Nigel for her return to Babylon, Octavia pondered the recent past, including her meteoric rise to power as mistress of the world's wealthiest city. Peering through the window of the plane, her mind wandered off to thoughts of Sharif. It had only been a year since she met the dashing young prince while visiting Dubai.

Sharif was from a prominent family related to the Saudi royals. Harvard educated, he was a reformer with a big heart, a shrewd mind, and idealistic dreams. He was a leader of a new generation of Middle Easterners that demanded human rights and democracy from old autocracies clinging to ancient ways. Witnessing Dubai's continuing rise to the heights of wealth, and becoming a fully independent state with its own Emir, Sharif had a global vision of bringing its prosperity to the poorest of the world's people.

Octavia recalled her first encounter with Sharif

while attending a session of the ruling council, which he addressed as a guest speaker.

As Sharif approached the podium, she had been instantly drawn to his physical presence and charisma. Octavia could not keep her eyes off him.

"Friends, I am as proud as anyone of all we have accomplished. My father is elated by our progress. But I'm here to tell you that now is the time to do more. It is the time for greater freedom and more human rights. We can be an example, to reach out with compassion to the poor, the needy, the hopeless, across this peninsula and throughout the world. Brothers, change is coming. It is coming to our doorstep. We must not fear it or oppose it. We must embrace it. We must take the lead in it. That is our aim, that is our dream, that is our vision, and I hope... you will make it yours today."

The members of the council rose to applaud, led by other young leaders who embraced Sharif's vision. Even the Emir grudgingly applauded, as did Octavia. As the crowd dispersed, Sharif turned and came face to face with Octavia.

"Prince, that was inspiring."

Enchanted by her beauty, he gazed at Octavia in silence. "Why, thank you."

"By the way, I'm Octavia Carlson."

"Octavia Carlson?" Sharif stroked the tight well-groomed beard on his handsome face. He took a deep breath as he composed himself. "Are you by chance from the renowned Carlson family in America?"

"I am."

"My father often spoke highly of your father and your family."

"How did your father know them?" Octavia probed seductively.

"Our fathers partnered in several energy investments, over, I think it was twenty years ago, or so. I remember as a child, my father was quite upset hearing of your family's passing."

"Thank you, it has been twenty-five years since the tragedy."

Sharif bowed slightly. "My condolences." Their eyes met as urgent passion flared between them.

"So Ms. Carlson, what brings you to Dubai?"

She smiled and twirled a lock of hair around her index finger like a schoolgirl. "Business of course, and by the way, I'm also a strong supporter of your…ambitious plans."

Sharif was intrigued. "We must talk, Ms. Carlson. How long will you be in Dubai?"

"Until tomorrow evening."

"How about meeting for lunch tomorrow in my office? It's right down the block."

Batting her eyelashes, she tossed her long hair over her shoulder. "I would love to. I'm staying close by, at the Ritz."

"What would you like for lunch?"

"What do you have, Prince?"

"Anything that suits your appetite."

"Anything? Now that's hard to fathom."

"Well, if it's food you want, yes, anything."

"You're very perceptive, Prince."

"I'm told I listen well," Sharif smiled.

"What else do you do well?"

"If you have an appetite for, say, horseback riding, we have some of the finest stallions on the Peninsula."

"That would be lovely."

"It was a pleasure meeting you, Ms. Carlson."

Gently biting her lower lip, she looked him up and down. "Call me 'Octavia.'"

"And please, call me 'Sharif.'" She offered her hand; he kissed it.

"A gentleman."

"A lady."

"Goodnight, Sharif."

"Goodnight, Octavia. Until tomorrow."

Nigel stepped out of the galley holding two champagne glasses. "Your Highness, a toast to our new relationship." Nigel grinned as he handed a glass to Octavia. She sat in one of two luxurious recliners that made up the entirety of the plane's front row.

"How civil of you," she sneered.

"Looks like you'll have time to share all your dirty little secrets with Uncle Nigel, since we'll be neighbors for the flight." He made a move to sit next to her.

"Take your little pea shooter and go to the rear cabin, or Mustafa will use you for target practice."

Nigel turned around to see Octavia's guard holding a large assault rifle.

He smiled broadly. "Woman! You are really starting to turn me on! If you need me, I'll be in the Mile-High Club." Nigel raised his glass before heading toward the back of the plane.

∽

Octavia's thoughts returned to the encounter with Sharif like it was yesterday. She recalled dining with him; it was a sumptuous candlelit feast fit for a queen. But most of all, she reminisced over the romantic ambiance and the words they spoke to each other.

"Sharif, have you ever met Anno Corinthia?"

"Italy's prime minister?"

"Why, yes."

"I've never met him, but I have heard him speak. He sounds like an altruistic leader."

"Oh yes, he is."

"We need him to speak out; he knows Shahim."

"Dubai's Emir?"

"Yes Octavia. Shahim respects and will talk to him. And maybe Corinthia can convince him to honor the rights of the people. But remember, the Emir is set in his ways."

"Yes, and I have seen and heard how stubborn Shahim is. He has rolled back reform. Just look at the women here, Sharif. He makes them dress like old dowagers, unlike his father. And I'm supposed to do likewise so I don't attract anyone's attention."

"I don't think that's possible."

"What do you mean?"

"You attracted *my* attention."

Octavia paused for a moment, gently biting her lower lip before looking into Sharif's eyes.

"And you Sharif have…whetted my…appetite."

"I'm glad."

"Can we leave here and talk alone at The Ritz?"

"I suppose we could do that." They left together. Octavia slipped her hand through Sharif's arm as they walked in the moonlight toward her hotel.

Entering her suite, she pointed toward the bar. "Please, Prince, make yourself at home, and prepare drinks of your choice." She gazed back at him. "I must change into something more comfortable. I'll be back in a moment."

As Sharif stood at the bar he felt the raging of flesh against spirit. He was not sure he could conquer temptation if she freely offered herself to him. The bedroom door opened across the suite with a slight click.

"I hope I didn't leave you alone too long."

Sharif turned from the bar with drinks in hand. Octavia stood across the room dressed in a long red silk gown. She glided over to the couch. Sharif joined her and handed her a drink. They sat down and simultaneously put their drinks on the coffee table. Unable to resist each other, they began to caress and kiss. After several minutes that seemed like hours, Sharif gently took Octavia's hands in his own and slightly backed away.

"I can't…"

"My Prince, you're a sheik. You must have had many women."

Looking deeply into her eyes, Sharif gently shook his head. "I can't do that sort of thing…not anymore."

"Why, my Prince?"

"I don't think you'd understand."

"But Prince, I want to understand."

He gripped her hands. "I'm a follower."

"A follower? A follower of whom?"

"Octavia, I am a follower of the Son."

Shaking her head, she looked at him in disbelief. "The sun in the sky??"

"No, Octavia…the Son of God."

She stared at Sharif for a long moment. Frustrated with being rejected, she jumped off the couch and steamed over to the bar, pouring herself another drink. "Sharif, I can compete with other women, but how do you expect me to compete with your so-called God?"

"You don't have to compete with him because he's your God, too."

"So, my Prince," she seductively strutted in front of Sharif, "you're giving up this…." motioning her hands around the curves of her body, "…for a dead God?"

"No, not for a dead God, Octavia, but for a living God. There's something brewing in the world. Something catastrophic, something evil that has to be defeated. I have to be a part of fighting it. I don't fully understand it yet but I can't do this sort of thing anymore. I really must go."

"When will I see you again?"

"I don't know, but we will meet again."

"I want you, Sharif. I want you as my Prince, and no God is going to keep me from getting you." Sharif stood and walked toward Octavia, looking into her deep brown eyes.

"It doesn't have to be like that." Sharif put his hands on her shoulders and kissed her forehead. "We will meet soon, and we will ride horses together on the beach. What we desire is still possible, but we must do this the right way."

"And what, may I ask, is the 'right way?'"

"The right way, is God's way." Sharif desperately searched her eyes for a sign of hope that she understood. "Don't you have any faith?"

Her once beautiful brown eyes turned black with anger. "Yes, I have faith; I have faith in myself."

Still tempted by her beauty, Sharif knew he had to flee. "You have bewitched me and I will see you again, my queen." He hurried to the door without looking back, escaping from the room, untarnished.

Standing alone in disbelief that anyone could reject her, Octavia let out a heinous scream as she hurled her cocktail glass against the closed door of her suite, shattering it into pieces.

Sharif's rejection of her made the need for his conquest even greater. She would not stop until he became her possession.

∽

The months flew quickly following her encounter with Sharif. While still working undercover, Octavia traveled to Dubai frequently. She became an omnipresent figure and celebrity, investing large amounts of money in Dubai and putting her name on everything. However, her real fortune was being made secretly.

Octavia could thank Sharif for her rise to power. He had graciously yielded the public stage to Octavia, recognizing the value of her charm, poise, and raw appeal. And Octavia made the most of it.

Sustaining what amounted to a ruthless political campaign against Shahim, she made everything from his advanced age to modernization an issue. From the abolishment of clothing restrictions to the holding of elections, she proclaimed that Dubai needed reform befitting a world-class city. The only initiative of Shahim that she supported was his union with Iraq to form a new state, which some were beginning to call Greater Babylon or simply Babylon.

Octavia knew that eventually, Shahim would move against her. One day, the old autocrat did, arresting her and threatening to impose the death penalty for insurrection. Shahim was persuaded by Corinthia to deport her instead. Following her exile, Octavia headed back to America for sanctuary.

Octavia owned many assets but none more valuable than the heart and mind of Sharif. Outraged by her exile, Sharif and his reformers led massive demonstrations against the Emir and his government, demanding that she be allowed to return and that fair elections take place.

Then came the Liberty Island attack, the outbreak of world-wide terrorism, and with Corinthia's covert help, Shahim's assassination.

Following the Emir's death, Octavia concealed herself in a lead-covered basket on a cargo plane bound for Dubai. When she felt the wind lift the wings of the plane into the air, she knew she was safely headed back. With Sharif now appointed as Greater Babylon's interim governor, Octavia believed that nothing could stop her and she would reign forever as Empress. Her popularity in Dubai soared, and Sharif, who had no ambition to rule, remained thoroughly infatuated with her. Sharif resigned and appointed Octavia as governor of Babylon.

In the weeks that followed, Sharif became troubled by Shahim's murder as rumors swirled about Corinthia's role in it. He was also disturbed by Octavia's refusal to hold an election and the rapid depletion of the national treasury through her extravagant spending. She achieved a cult-like status among the people and called for a referendum designating her Empress of Babylon, abandoning Sharif's movement for freedom and reform.

Several months into Octavia's reign, one of Sharif's allies played right into her hands. At a public appearance, with Sharif by her side, the man rushed toward Octavia. Yelling "death to the tyrant," he tried to stab her but was stopped by Sharif's quick intervention. The attempt on

Octavia's life made Sharif feel more protective of her. After the incident, he barely left her side, but eventually Sharif had to leave Dubai to attend a commerce seminar in Rome.

When he returned, he learned that the man who had tried to kill Octavia had been executed. Rumors persisted that Octavia had him tortured for days before his death, a charge she hotly denied.

Sharif knew of her great wealth, exceeding even that of his own family. What he did not know was how she attained it. He did not know that she had squandered the Carlson family fortune. Sharif was completely unaware of Octavia's darkest secret. He was in Culture Village having dinner with two friends at the Palazzo Versace Hotel, when he heard screams from an adjacent alley.

Sharif and his friends ran outside, where they saw a man holding a knife to a young girl's throat. The girl stood trembling in bare feet, her disheveled light brown hair partially hiding her face.

"You ran away again!" the man yelled. "This time you die!"

Sharif approached. "Drop the knife!"

The man looked up in shock, instantly recognizing Sharif.

"My prince...Sharif!"

"If I am your prince, drop the knife, now. And don't run." The man slowly let the knife fall from his hand onto the ground. Turning to the girl, Sharif said, "Don't be afraid; you're safe now. Nobody is going to harm you." Then Sharif faced the man. "What is this about?!"

"I was unemployed, my Prince. Then someone told me I could make big money...with this girl."

"You're a pimp?"

"Only for a few months."

"What is your name?"

"Bekhir."

"Bekhir, I will deal with you in a moment, but first I must speak to the girl." Sharif rolled up the girl's sleeve, wincing at the track marks.

"How old are you?" Sharif asked as she pushed her hair away from her face. She glanced at him before staring at the ground.

"Fifteen, Sir."

Sharif stifled the urge to strangle Bekhir. He knew that if this girl with the innocent dimpled face and big blue eyes were his own daughter, Bekhir would already be lying dead in the alley. The sadness in those eyes confirmed that she had experienced things no girl ever should.

"What's your name?" Sharif asked softly.

"Alice," she answered in a quivering voice while visibly shaking.

"Where are you from, Alice?"

"Scotland."

"How did you get here?"

The girl could not hold eye contact with Sharif as her eyes darted from side to side. "They, they kidnapped me while I was walking home from school and they brought me here. I was put on an airplane, with a hood over my head."

Sharif removed his kaftan and placed it around her shoulders. Alice looked up at Sharif with a tentative smile.

"Does your family know you're alive?"

"I, I don't know, Sir. I want to go home." She choked back tears.

"How long have you been here?"

"A few months, I think."

Sharif turned to Bekhir. "And you, Bekhir, you've been involved in this treachery for how long?!"

Bekhir looked away. "A few months too, my prince; I am so ashamed."

"Who's running this abomination?"

"I don't know. All I know is that it's very big."

"I will have you arrested, and under the old laws, I could have your hands cut off."

Bekhir dropped to his knees, sobbing uncontrollably. "No, no please my Prince. They threatened to kill my wife and my children, I didn't have a choice....I, I have made a terrible mistake. I'll do whatever you want. Please, I beg your forgiveness."

Pacing back and forth, Sharif looked down at Bekhir. "You will not be arrested, on one condition."

"Anything, my prince, anything."

"You must take me to those responsible for what has been done to this girl."

"If they find out I led you there, they will kill my family."

"Bekhir, I will protect you and your family...you have my word." Bekhir looked around nervously but did not answer. Sharif stepped closer to Bekhir and extended a hand; Bekhir took it. The prince lifted Bekhir off of his knees. "I said, you have my word."

"Okay my Prince, but you and your friends will need guns. You must be heavily armed when you meet the people who run this horrible operation."

"I will call the police instead."

"No, no, the police are all bought off."

"If that's the case, I'll handle it myself. Just lead me to the filth who have been selling girls."

Sharif kneeled in front of Alice and held her hands. "I will make sure you get back to Scotland tomorrow but I do need your help to save other girls. Will you come with us to Bekhir's bosses? We will keep you safe but we must pretend we are selling you. We are going to break this terrible ring wide-open but we need you."

"Yes, Your Highness, I want to help. Thank you... thank you."

"Please, call me 'Sharif.'"

Sharif immediately called six trusted Blackwater contractors and quickly put together a plan. Sharif, Bekhir, and Alice got into a black van that pulled up to the hotel less than an hour later. They soon reached the compound where Bekhir said the trafficking bosses were based.

It was a large three-story U-shaped building with a stone courtyard behind ten-foot high iron gates. A fountain at the center of the courtyard could be heard gently gurgling on that still night. Bekhir tightened the silencer before pressing a button on the gatepost. A door swung open at the center of the building. Two beefy men emerged.

"Bekhir!" one of them bellowed. "Have you brought us another girl?" A metallic 'click' sounded as the gate was unlocked remotely.

"No, I brought you this!" Bekhir pulled out a gun and shot the two security guards.

Hearing the muffled shots, several other men emerged from inside. Sharif and the others fired at the group, taking them all down.

"Let's go in!" Sharif yelled to the Blackwater men.

Inside there were girls everywhere in what looked like the former lobby of an old luxury hotel, with marble floors, Roman columns and arches. Sharif was appalled when he saw some girls who looked as young as twelve. Hearing the gunshots, most of the girls scattered in fear, hiding in the many rooms where "business" was conducted.

Sharif and the Blackwaters, followed by Bekhir, ambushed a group of six men playing poker in a room at the far end of the main corridor. Sharif kicked open the door. "Who among you is running this operation?" Five of the six men dropped their cards and reached for their guns. Sharif shot all five before putting his gun to the head of the sixth man.

"He's upstairs!" the man yelled.

"What's his name?"

"Jock Hardley. He's an American."

Sharif and the others carefully made their way back to the main stairway near the entrance, taking cover behind several wide columns.

"Jock! This is Prince Sharif! Come down now! You're surrounded! There's no way out!"

After nearly a minute of tense silence, a door near the top of the steps opened. A tall stocky blond guy emerged with a girl in front of him. He violently pulled back the girl's long hair and held a knife to her throat. Sharif and the others aimed their guns at the man.

"Drop the knife, let her go, and we'll talk."

"Prince Sharif, drop your guns or I'll slit her throat."

"We'll kill you first."

Jock pressed harder on the knife; a small amount of blood dripped down the girl's neck. "You don't know what you're messing with, Prince. We own the cops, courts, and the government."

Sharif smiled. "Jock, I am the government."

Hesitating for a moment, Jock knew Sharif was right.

"This is your last chance. Put down the knife and let her go. Tell me, who are the masterminds behind this operation and we will work something out."

Jock pointed at Bekhir.

"He's as good as dead for leading you here. So am I, and my family as well, if I tell you what you want."

He paused for a moment before dropping the knife to the ground and nudging the girl forward. She ran down the stairs in bare feet.

"Jock, now tell me, who's the man behind this?"

Jock pulled a cigarette and a book of matches out of his shirt pocket. He lit up and took a drag before heading down the stairs, chuckling bitterly.

"It's not a man…"

Jock stopped in the middle of the staircase, flicked his cigarette, and watched it bounce off the bottom step, landing at Sharif's feet.

In a flash, Jock pulled a gun from an ankle holster and held it against his own head.

"…It's a woman."

Jock squeezed the trigger, instantly killing himself.

᧔

The next morning, Sharif met with Octavia.

"I have bad news and good news," he said.

"Tell me both."

"The bad news is, there is a huge sex slavery ring operating right here in Dubai. And the good news is, we have busted it wide open."

"What are you talking about?" she asked agitatedly.

"Last night, my men and I rescued dozens of girls who worked as sex slaves in the darkest corners of Dubai's luxury hotels and illicit brothels."

Octavia could not hide her displeasure. "Why does a prince engage in such trivial pursuits?"

"The exploitation of young women and girls is not trivial, Octavia."

"You should not have acted on your own! It's much too dangerous! You are a prince!" Octavia fumed. "Why would you want to be a vigilante and take the law into your own hands? That's why we have a police force."

"Octavia, the police are being paid to look the other way."

"And how do you know that?"

"A man named Bekhir Kherani told me. This was confirmed by Jock Hardley, who was running one of the brothels. Before Jock blew his brains out, I asked him, 'what man is running this operation?'" Sharif silently approached Octavia, putting his hands on his hips. "He told me it was *not* a man."

"What?" The uneasy look on Octavia's face spoke volumes.

"He said…it was a woman. Only someone with the right connections could run such a large human-trafficking operation and not get caught." Sharif stepped closer to Octavia and folded his arms. "That is, until last night."

"Are you accusing me? You're crazy!"

"Yes, I am crazy. I am crazy to care. I am crazy to believe that you are better than that. I am crazy to believe that beneath your love of power is the beating heart of a radiant, beautiful woman who wants to love and be loved."

"You've completely lost your mind."

"I know what you feel. I know what I feel. You can't hide it, nor can I. Octavia, I love you. Come with me. Leave this sordid world behind and take to heart the words of Mahatma Gandhi: 'Earth provides enough to satisfy every person's needs, but not every person's greed.'"

Octavia's eyes burned with anger. "Gandhi was weak!! That's why he was assassinated!!!"

Sharif swallowed hard and tried to remain calm. "Deep down you know that life is not about power. Life is not about oppression. Life is not about conquest. Life is about love. Octavia, don't you want love?" Sharif pulled her toward him and kissed her; she pushed him away.

"No! You fool! This is my world! Mine! I won't let you take it away." She growled as Sharif stood in silence. "Guards, come here!" Several armed men dressed in uniforms came into the room. "Seize him!"

"Prince Sharif?" asked one of them incredulously.

"You heard what I said," Octavia replied in a voice that was hypnotic yet seductive.

The guards seized Sharif and handcuffed him.

"Octavia, you have made your choice. You must live with the consequences."

"Then so be it. You have become a thorn in my side."

"Are you going to kill me, too? Like you killed Shahim?"

"No, Sharif. I'm going to banish you. You are hereby exiled from Babylon. I don't want to see you again. If I do, then you will be executed, just like your reformer friend."

As the guards dragged him away, Sharif's heart sank. He realized what a horrible mistake he had made, trusting and falling in love with the Queen of Babylon.

⋟

That was the last time she saw Prince Sharif. High above the clouds in her jet, Octavia wondered where he had gone. Her lust for him was as strong as ever. Maybe she had exiled him too hastily. If he was so infatuated with her, maybe she could have eventually gotten control over him.

CHAPTER 10
A STRANGER IN THE DESERT

THE SEAL TEAM slipped into Iran southeast of Qumi, a barren wasteland baking under the fierce desert sun. David, Chad, Frank and Flynn rode in the lead humvee. "So what's next, Frank?" David asked. "Is the next stop Tehran?"

"According to what we learned back in Jakarta, there are no terror cells in the capital. We should move westward toward the Iraqi border, where it might get rough."

They drove for several hours along dusty roads before stopping at Kavir National Park and Namak Lake. In the summer the lake isn't much more than a giant muddy spot in the middle of the desert. Except for passing an occasional nomad, they had yet to encounter any people in that part of Iran.

"Are we close, Frank?" David looked at Frank in the rear-view mirror.

Frank looked down at his tablet. "We need to go another 20 miles north/northwest from here. We'll go through Javadabad and then Varamin."

"Flynn, you know this area?" David asked, squinting behind his sunglasses.

"Like the hills of the Highlands."

"Where do we find the first cell?"

"Doesn't this eejit know?" Flynn pointed his crooked thumb at Frank.

"I know we're now about 20 miles from the cell."

"Well, lad, 'about' is not going to cut it. A mile off and we're all dead. Got it?"

"Well, where is it, Flynn?" Frank asked calmly.

"It's not twenty miles; it's seventeen."

"How do you know?"

"The whole road is open space. Sixteen miles up and there's brush. A mile further and we're in a place they call Ambush Alley, and for good reason. It can hide a cell and more."

"So what do we do?"

"Ah, we go maybe a dozen miles, perhaps a bit more. Assume they've got a lookout fifteen miles up and more of them at sixteen."

"And?"

"I say we split up at Javadabad. Some on foot, the rest in vehicles. Then we hit 'em both ways. Your call, David."

"I agree, Flynn. Okay, Gladiator, make sure you and your snipers are ready to go on foot when we get close. The rest of us will stay in the vehicles for at least another fourteen miles."

After a short break, the team moved thirteen more miles. From that point Chad and two other snipers proceeded on foot northwest, while David and the rest of the team kept moving north.

❦

Chad's voice crackled over David's radio. "Skip, I've spotted the targets."

"Where?"

"Over the hill, at ten o'clock from your position."

"Can they see us?"

"Not yet."

"Gladiator, any lookouts?"

"Yes, two, about a mile ahead."

"Can you take 'em out?"

"Should be no problem."

"Let me know and we'll come in from the east."

"Roger that."

Chad and his two snipers took positions high above the brush. They watched as the enemy lookouts drank from a jug that was passed back and forth. Blurry heat waves wobbled in the crosshairs as Chad looked through his rifle scope.

"I'll take the guy with the mustache; both of you take the other guy. Alright, on three…"

The sniper rifles fired, bringing both men down. Their jug broke into pieces as it smashed on a rock.

"Lookouts down, Skip," Chad said into his radio.

"Good work. Okay, guys, a few yards higher and we'll have a visual of the camp. Scott, take half the men and move further up the ridge. I'll spread out here with the rest."

"You got it."

When the SEALS were in position, David watched the enemy through binoculars. It was a cluster of nine white tents surrounding a small group of men sitting on crates and cleaning guns, mostly Kalashnikov AK-47's from the 1980's Soviet Union. The only form of transport were the six camels tied to posts on the outskirts of the camp. Large cargo sacks strapped to the camels indicated that these were primarily beasts of burden and few if any of the fighters rode atop the animals.

David talked to Scott over the radio. "We caught them unprepared. They're sitting ducks. The only question is how many more are in the tents."

"Shouldn't be a lot, the tents aren't real big. Hey, let's try not to hurt those camels. I'd like to cut them loose when the dust settles."

"I hear ya, man. I used to tell Sarah that after all the bad stuff I've seen, it would have been helpful if Noah and his family had jumped overboard after rescuing the animals."

Scott's roaring laugh was fuzzy over the radio. "I'm sure she had more than a few days on her own job when she agreed with that."

"Yeah Scotty, but she'd never admit it. She took the Bible way too seriously." David had to get back in the moment after getting choked up thinking of Sarah. "Alright, let's do this."

The SEALs blasted the camp with rifle fire and mortar shells. The fighters outside never had a chance. A few inside the tents managed to get out and return fire, but David's men were so spread out the terrorists couldn't get a good bead on the incoming rounds. It was a lopsided fight that was over in a New York minute.

Scott's half of the team carefully moved down the sandy hill, advancing on what was left of the camp. The only sound among the carnage were urgent voices speaking Arabic that came over radios in the shredded tents. Perfect, Scott thought, the enemy knows we're in the area.

"Flynn, take the cargo sacks off the camels, then cut them loose."

"Yer aff yer heid! Must be a thousand edible houghs on the bones of them beasties!"

"Flynn, I said cut 'em loose."

Flynn shook his head as he untethered the camels. "Aye, no need for kerfuffle. I expect you'll be celebrating World Camel Day on the 22nd of June."

The team salvaged any supplies they could use from the enemy before moving further northwest. David decided they should go no further north than Mamazand. He wanted to avoid Tehran and areas near the Caspian Sea, where according to Sarah, the Iranian military had a substantial presence. "How many more miles?"

Frank checked their location. "It's about four-point-seven,

Skip. Based on the coordinates, there should be fuel at that point."

"Now you're making sense, lad. That's Ambush Alley... been a supply depot for years."

Eventually the dusty road gave way to a stretch that was paved. A large building about the size of a typical Walmart came into view. As they approached, they could see a group of men wearing white thawbs in front of the building loading cargo onto trucks. About fifty yards short of the depot, David gave the order to stop.

Scott got out with four other SEALs and began to approach the men.

"Ah, let me handle this," whispered Flynn out the open door of the Humvee.

Scott nodded and backed away as Flynn stepped onto the road. Approaching the truckers, he began speaking to them in English but switched to Farsi. Seconds later, Flynn quickly pulled out his gun and shot the truckers dead. He calmly walked back to the convoy where Scott and David were waiting.

"Flynn, what was that about?" David asked.

"Skippy, they didn't have the password. They couldn't speak English; they were bloody imposters."

"So they were part of the cell we're hunting, and they ambushed our supply people?"

"That's right, lad."

"Gladiator and Scotty, get some men into those supply trucks," David ordered. "We'll stay a half-mile behind you in the Humvees after we refuel."

After a few minutes, the SEALs were moving again. The pavement ended about a mile past the supply depot. The convoy slowed as the vehicles went back onto a dusty, sandy road. The rolling terrain was completely desolate. Members of the terror cell emerged to welcome the trucks, which they thought their own people had hijacked.

"Now!" Scott yelled, as he, Gladiator, and the others in the trucks opened fire.

More fighters came out from the brush, shooting at the trucks.

Scott and his men took cover below the windows and were pinned down. David and the rest of the team moved up fast from behind, surprising the enemy with heavy gunfire, allowing Scott's team to go back on offense.

Three more terrorists ran out toward the road. Gladiator shot two of them dead. A third one tripped; his gun flew out of his hand. Scott killed him instantly. Flynn tossed a grenade into another bush and shot three more as they fled from it. The rest of David's team blasted the area, killing the remaining fighters. Once the threat had been eliminated, the team moved off the road to set up camp.

David retreated into his tent to consult HALO. This time the instructions were different; it was not about meeting a "friendly" or strategic advice. Sarah's image appeared, and without explanation, said he must immediately go alone to a place in the desert. He had no clue as to why she would want him to leave his men. However, once again trusting his wife's wisdom, he did so without hesitation.

After leaving the tent, he bumped into Frank. "Where are you going, Skip??"

"When your wife tells you to go somewhere, you do it. I'll be right back…hopefully."

David followed the coordinates on HALO, sending him along a narrow cart path. The rolling desert terrain was sparsely dotted with date palm trees, and an occasional Jericho rose or red yucca grew in the sand on both sides of the path.

About a mile from camp, the sky darkened, the wind began to blow, and a major sandstorm developed. HALO had been giving David verbal and visual directions but it suddenly went dead. Even with protective goggles, he was all but blinded. The wind was so strong, he could barely keep moving.

At a sharp curve in the path, David stumbled on a large stone and began falling fast down a sandy embankment. He tumbled over and over, clutching HALO while descending uncontrollably. The wind howled even stronger; he felt the goggles fly off his head. His face began to burn as the sand blasted him with tremendous force. David shut his eyes as tightly as possible.

Eventually he felt himself come to a stop on what felt like a bed of hay. The sand stopped blowing. He was suddenly lying in an eerily still place.

Opening his eyes, David saw a few yards ahead a bearded old man draped in a white cloak and red shawl. Blinking and wiping the sand from his eyes, David slowly rose to his feet. The man held a wooden staff as he stood at the opening to a large cavern in the hillside. The sky had cleared as the sun began to set behind the hill.

"David," said the man.

"Who are you?"

"Come with me…"

The man turned around and walked into the cavern. David followed, moving cautiously ahead with his hand on his holstered Beretta.

Once they were both inside, the man stopped and faced David. "Do you have it with you?"

"Have what?"

"HALO."

"How do you know about HALO?"

"David, I suggest you let Sarah answer." The man pointed his staff at the dusty HALO device, as David clutched it in his left hand. He raised HALO to his face and blew the sand off the screen; Sarah's image appeared.

"David, meet Elijah. Sometimes people keep secrets from their childhood to themselves. Let me tell you the only thing that I have ever kept to myself. Sit down David; I have a story to tell you. When I was twelve, my parents brought me on a tour of the Holy Land a year before my Bat-Mitzvah to learn about Jewish history. While on a tour of Jerusalem, I wandered off from my parents and entered a synagogue where a man wearing a cloak sat alone reading the Torah. I approached the man and introduced myself. This is where my story begins…"

"Hi."

"Hello, young lady. My name is Elijah. Do you know who Elijah is in the Bible?"

"Why yes, he never died."

"That's right, and if you truly follow God, you will never die. Sometimes when you wander into new lands, it's not by mistake, but by the intent of God…and today Sarah, is no mistake."

"How did you know my name?"

Elijah smiled. "You are about to become a young lady, and a prophetess of God."

Sarah raised her eyebrows. "What do you mean?"

"You will meet your basherter on a day of turmoil and destruction. Death will surround you, but he will save you. Let the Lord lead you in all you do." Elijah moved closer to Sarah and peered into her innocent brown eyes. "You will be a strong woman of God, just like Sarah of the Bible. But, I must tell you that your days will come to a close, in the year of 250. But do not fear. The Lord will redeem you and you will rise again." The front doors swung open.

Mel and Edith entered, frantically looking for Sarah, worried that she was lost. They were relieved to find her but concerned to find her with a stranger. "Your daughter is a woman to be used mightily by God. She is your treasure, and a treasure to the world." Elijah knelt down in front of Sarah. "Remember all I have told you today. It's yours, and yours alone, only to be revealed at the appointed time." Mel took Sarah by the hand and led her out of the synagogue. Sarah looked back and smiled at the man before the doors closed.

HALO powered down. David looked at Elijah in disbelief. "Where did you get this story?"

"This is Sarah's story, David…this is the design of God. On that day of death twenty-five years ago, people who were to bring life into this world met, but so did evil. All who met then…will meet again."

David shook his head. "Much of what you're telling me is available to anyone who chooses to access it. Are you trying to infiltrate and destroy my mission?"

"If I were, why would Sarah tell you to meet me here? David, you are just as much a part of this as Sarah is, but you haven't realized it yet. Your role in the salvation of humanity is just beginning."

"Listen, pal, you've made a mistake. I'm in no position to save the world. My mission is to help keep my country safe, for my daughter, my men, and others I care about."

"David, this is not a mistake; you have been chosen. You are part of a great plan. It is that plan that brought you here today. David, you've been chosen by God even though you don't want to be…and so shall be your son."

Irritated, David approached Elijah. "I don't have a son!" Elijah smiled at David. "You know, you're lucky I don't kill you."

"That's already been tried."

"How can I trust you?"

"You were sent to me by someone you *do* trust." David

turned away from Elijah and began to walk out of the cavern. Elijah called after him, "Petra."

David stopped and looked back. "What did you say?"

"Petra." The word had no special meaning to David, just a common name for women in Eastern Europe. As David began his trek back to camp, Elijah watched him. "Until our next meeting," he whispered.

✥

When David returned to the camp, Frank ran out to meet him. "David, what happened out there? You look banged up."

"Nothing...I fell down a hill."

"Did you see anything?"

David stopped and thought for a moment. "Just an old man with a staff." As David walked away, Frank noticed a different countenance about him and did not believe David had given him the whole story about his walk in the desert.

Continuing to follow Sarah's directions, the men moved westward, crossing over into Iraq not far from Basra. They finally reached a secluded dirt air strip in the desert. Making their way toward a makeshift hangar, they opened its doors and found a camouflage-painted jet, just as Raja had indicated.

Chad inspected every inch of the plane before giving the "OK" for boarding. The men filed onto the plane, stashing their gear in the overhead compartments while keeping their weapons close to their chests. Taking position in the cockpit, Chad checked the pre-flight systems and fuel gauge, then gave a thumbs-up sign to David. "Ready to roll, Skip." When the men heard the sound of turbines kick in, they settled in for takeoff.

Flynn was looking out the window with concern at the distant tree line. "Better move fast, Gladdy. That thick stand of palms is a perfect place for snipers to be hiding."

Frank frowned. "You're paranoid."

Flynn sneered back at him.

As they lifted off the runway and began gaining altitude, Flynn noticed tracer rounds being fired at the plane from two o'clock. He turned to Frank. "Paranoid? Those are not licorice pellets being shot at the plane, now are they, mate?!!" Flynn ran up to the cockpit. "They're in the bushes! Start climbing, fast!"

Chad pitched the airplane at a steep angle and climbed out of range of the incoming fire.

"Any damage, Gladiator?" asked David as he made his way up to the cockpit.

"We've apparently dodged them, but I don't think we're out of range yet." Chad checked the instruments.

Observing a worried Frank, Flynn exclaimed, "Looks like you need a sedative, junior."

"Scotty, can I have some of that chew?" Frank asked nervously. Scott opened the Skoal canister and held it up. Frank took a big pinch in his shaking hand and looked at it.

"It goes in the side of your mouth, laddy." All eyes were on Frank as he put the wad of tobacco in his mouth and started chewing. Within seconds, Frank was gagging and spitting. Flynn patted him on the back. "Sorry laddy, baccy is only for warriors."

Chad looked over his shoulder at the men. "Okay, we're at cruising altitude; we should get across Jordan safely and on to Israel."

"Ay, the Holy Land, David."

"Holy or not, Flynn, I'll be happy when we touch down at Ben Gurion."

≪

Corinthia summoned Wodan to his chambers. "Marcus, where is David Stein?"

"Prime Minister, our cells could not stop his advance. We've lost track of him."

"Marcus, where is Stein?"

"Prime Minister, I fear that Stein disabled many of our cells."

"Marcus, remember what I told you, Stein is not to make it to Israel. How could he, with his small group of bandits, not only make it this far but wipe out many of our forces?"

Marcus, fearing for his life, remained silent. He could not think of a safe answer.

"He must be getting help from someone. Get a full report, and I want Nigel on this immediately. Tell Nigel to find David. If we capture Stein alive, we'll let Octavia do what she wants with him before his demise."

"As you wish, Mr. Prime Minister. I will see to it."

❧

Several minutes into the flight, Frank looked out the window and saw what appeared to be liquid spewing from the wing. He nudged Flynn who was seated to his left. "You see that?"

"I do, laddy. That's fuel leaking from the tank." They looked at each other for a moment before heading up to the cockpit.

Chad looked over his shoulder when he felt their presence. "I know, I've been monitoring the fuel gauge. It's leaking at a pretty good clip. I didn't want to mention it unless it got more severe." Chad checked the fuel gauge. "It's more severe. The bullets must have pierced the tank and the pressure at 35K blew open a hole."

"Chad, will we make it to Israel?"

"No, we won't; but we're not just flying on a wing and a prayer. We're over Jordan now. That's where we'll land."

David came up front. "What's going on, guys?"

Chad looked back at David. "Trouble, we need to land, and soon. We've got maybe ten minutes of fuel left."

"Frank, contact Steve Dobson in Israel and bring him up to speed. Give him our coordinates; we'll need an extraction team. We're landing in hostile territory."

"I'm on it, Skip." David returned to the cabin and told his men to strap in and prepare for a rough landing. "Glad, do you know exactly where we'll be in Jordan when we touch down?" Frank asked nervously as he looked out the cockpit window.

"At this point, all I know is we're going down."

Chad spotted the flattest site he could from three thousand feet and lowered the landing gear, which could actually make things worse depending on the softness and depth of the sand. At about forty-five seconds before landing, he told everyone to strap in tight, prepare for a hard landing, and…pray.

A loud grating sound boomed through the fuselage as the plane's wheels ripped into the barren surface of the desert. The plane shook violently for a quarter mile before coming to rest with its nose stuck in a small embankment of sand. The nose landing gear had apparently collapsed, leaving the plane pitched forward by several feet. The impact knocked out the power but enough daylight came through the windows for the men to see.

David jumped out of his seat at the rear of the plane to check on the men. "Is anyone hurt?!" The answers were all negative as he went row by row down toward the cockpit. "Alright guys, sit tight until I can assess the situation. Gladiator, are you good?"

"Clocked my knee real hard bracing for impact. Nothing I can't handle."

"Great job getting us on the ground in one piece."

"That was the easy part. Now we need Dobson to find a way to slip his team into Jordan undetected."

"So where exactly are we?"

"A place called 'Petra.'"

"Petra??!" David was startled. He began to wish he got more information from that old man in the desert.

A loud bang came from outside the plane. Chad looked out the cockpit window.

"You see anything, Glad?"

"That explosion was the left engine. We've got trouble."

"What? The fuel tanks are almost bone dry. There's no chance of a major explosion."

Chad shook his head. "That engine was hit by incoming projectiles, I'm guessing 50-caliber rounds from a mile away. We could be under attack right now."

"Are you sure about that?"

"David, I hope I'm wrong but it's unlikely that engine would have blown just from our rough landing. The engines never touched the ground." David stepped back into the cabin.

"Guys, we have a potential combat situation. Let's lock & load to be safe. Frank, I need you up front." Frank followed David back into the cockpit. "Any response from Dobson?"

Frank checked his tablet. "He has our coordinates and communicated they'll be here ASAP. He wasn't sure if he would get us out by land, air, or some combination of both."

"Glad, what's your take on this?"

"The good news is we have one of the best planes for this situation. The cabin walls are plated with the most advanced military-grade armor. The windows are made from impact-resistant glass. We have three windows on either side of the cabin that can be opened manually."

"So, the fuel tank was punctured because the wings are not plated? That would make it too heavy to fly?"

"Exactly. We should be okay unless we're hit with the most sophisticated anti-tank shells, like depleted uranium. A direct hit from a bunker buster could also ruin our day."

Frank looked out the window through binoculars. "David, we've got company coming from the east, and lots of it." David faced his men on both sides of the aisle.

"Alright guys, be prepared for anything."

"Skip this doesn't look good. We are way outnumbered in weapons and men."

Seeing that Frank was a nervous wreck, David looked into his eyes. "Have faith, Frank." Frank reached into Flynn's stash and took a wad of tobacco, but this time he did not spit it out.

"Go easy on the chew, laddy."

Frank turned from the window to stare at David. "I should have faith!?"

"Yeah, faith in this." David nudged the butt of his rifle into Frank's shoulder.

In less than a minute the plane was surrounded by hundreds of heavily armed fighters arriving in a convoy of pick-ups, forming a circle roughly fifty yards out from the aircraft. Most of the truck beds held mounted high-caliber machine guns. Several more minutes went by before an armored personnel carrier came into view on the right side of the plane, just beyond the enemy line. A tall lean man with a heavy five o'clock shadow and thick dark grey-streaked hair stepped out of the vehicle wearing aviator shades and olive military fatigues. He was smiling and swinging a megaphone.

Chewing the tobacco rapidly, Frank peeked out the window. "Why aren't they doing anything?"

"You might be needing another helping of baccy, lad. That bloke who just arrived is Colonel Nigel Coles. To the commonality he's known just as 'Nigel,' one of the most notoriously ruthless mercenary leaders of our time. Seen a bit of his handiwork up close. Look at all that stonking weaponry. This bloody scene could go shambolic at any moment."

"We could try negotiating with Nigel and make him see reason." Frank nodded at Flynn with forced optimism.

"Aye, good luck with that, mate. That toe-rag Colonel is mad as a bag of ferrets. Isn't that right, David?"

"I'm afraid it's true. My team has fought against his people in Iraq and Afghanistan. They're a formidable group of warriors, and they'll do anything if they're paid enough."

"So, we'll just have to make them a better offer, right guys?" Frank looked from Flynn to David.

"If only it were that simple. Frank, take cover in the rear of the plane and stay as low as possible." Frank gave David the binoculars before walking back to the tail and crouching behind a service cart.

A loud voice erupted from outside. It continued in a pattern, repeating the same thing over and over. "Gladiator, can you get one of these windows open on the right side?"

Chad limped slightly as he came out of the cockpit, going to the window where Frank had been sitting. He removed a panel below the window and turned the hand crank inside. As the window came down, the voice on the megaphone grew loud and clear.

Guns in hand, the SEAL team watched through the windows as Nigel sauntered up to the airplane, kicking the tires on the rear landing gear. "...*Anyone need some roadside assistance here?! Looks like you guys got a couple a flats!*"

Frank's meek voice came from the back of the plane. "Maybe the Colonel is here to help us?"

"Frank, he's not exactly with Triple-A," David said, keeping a close eye on the Colonel's movements.

Nigel looked up at the cabin windows. "...*David Stein! You will surrender or you and your band of terrorists will be killed! You have two minutes to come outside before we destroy your little wrecked fuselage!*"

"Skip, I could probably take out the colonel pretty easily from this distance."

"Problem is, we're not in position to take out his whole force. I'll have to go out there and talk to him."

"Cor blimey! Nigel will die before giving you a fair deal! Tell the old mentaller to bugger off!"

"You're right Flynn, but I need to buy some time to figure all the angles. I'll go out there and stall as long as I can."

"You're a brave man, David Stein! So much bottle in you! If things turn all flitters, I swear to go after the Colonel with every breath I've got left. I'll strangle the skiver with my own hands, if need be."

"Thanks Flynn, I appreciate that. Alright guys, I'm going to put on as much body armor as I can in the next ninety seconds. Hold your fire, unless things get red-hot." David quickly clad himself from neck to toe with every conceivable type of armor.

Scott had been standing near the cockpit, lost in thoughts of Debbie. Seeing David suit up brought him back into the moment. "Man, I don't like you going out there alone. Let me go with you."

"Scotty, I need you in here. You're the most experienced man on the plane. Besides, if they're asking only for me, that's all they get."

"Okay, but only if you bring this." Scott reached into his equipment bag and pulled out his old riot shield. "Remember these bad boys?!"

"You kept yours?? That's vintage NYPD! Still has the American flag you painted-on after 9/11."

Scott handed David the shield. "I figured it might come in handy someday. Looks like today is the day."

"Yeah, supposedly it can stop just about any high-caliber round."

They heard three loud knocks on the outside of the fuselage. The megaphone squawked again. "*Anybody home?!! David Stein! You have exactly thirty seconds to come on out. Just in case you don't have a watch, let me count for you!*"

David ran his hand over the little window in the riot

shield. "Skip, you might really need that thing; the Colonel's crew ain't exactly carrying BB guns."

The colonel's voice came again. *"...Hey Davey! Are you going to make me count?! Alright, you're down to ten seconds!..."*

"Thanks Scotty, I guess it's better to have a shield and not need it than the other way around. Alright, Gladiator, you get the hatch."

"...You got three seconds! And two, And one! Time's up, Davey! I've got to go!" — The Colonel started walking back to his armored vehicle.

"You got it Skip, good luck." Chad bumped fists with David before opening the cabin door.

David stepped down into the sand that had piled up against the plane. As soon as he was outside, the ring of enemy combatants parted, giving David a view of the colonel's vehicle. There were more men surrounding the plane than David first thought. Nigel's mercenary force had to be at least two hundred.

The megaphone squawked. Nigel appeared in front of the vehicle. "Holy shit! It's Captain America! Commander Stein, nice of you to join us! Now, why don't you put down your little superhero shield and walk slowly away from the plane."

"I can hear you fine from where I stand! Tell me what you want, Colonel!"

"Didn't I make myself perfectly clear? I want you to get away from that aircraft!"

"And then what?!"

"You and I will have a nice little conversation. Just two kids shootin' the breeze in a desert sandbox."

"We're talking right now."

"Davey, I'm trying to start a relationship here! I am not here to kill you, but I will if you force me to. Someone of great importance would like to meet with you."

"Whoever it is, tell him I'll check my calendar but I think I'm booked solid for the foreseeable future."

Nigel shook his head. "Men from all over the world would give anything for a private meeting with such a distinguished leader. Your presence has been expressly requested, Commander."

"And who is this 'leader' that wants to meet with me, Colonel?"

Nigel shook his head. "You will attend the meeting… dead or alive. The choice is yours, Davey." Nigel spotted the barrel of a sniper rifle resting on the bottom of the open window. "You think your man is going to use that pea-shooter to kill hundreds of my men? You're in fantasy land, Davey!" David signaled Chad to hold back so they could buy as much time as possible.

"Why does this 'world leader' want to talk to me?"

"Your talents are well known. The two of you would accomplish great things if you joined forces."

"Under these conditions, Colonel, I'm afraid I'll have to take a rain check."

"This is not a good decision, Davey. It's not looking to be a good day for you. You will enter my armored vehicle or you, and all your men, will be killed."

In the plane, Scott prepared the men for immediate engagement.

"Commander Stein, this is your last chance! You think we're gonna let you and your little band of penguins get off scot-free after you were just about to nuke the whole world?! That's not the way it works, Davey! Don't be a fool! You're surrounded!"

A low murmur shook the desert. David looked toward the distant horizon and smiled. "No Colonel, you're surrounded!" Nine Apache helicopters in formation converged above the scene, with several Black Hawks following in the distance. David crouched low behind the shield as he squirmed backwards into the open door of the plane.

"Kill Stein!!" Those were the last two words David heard before all hell broke loose. Several hands grabbed his upper body, dragging him into the plane as projectiles slammed into the shield.

Heavy gunfire and missiles began to rein down from the choppers on the Colonel's men. Frank, still hiding behind the service cart, tried to look out the window. "Flynn, Steve's here."

"You don't say, mate."

Dobson's fierce attack quickly ripped apart Nigel's forces, leaving the enemy decimated. A few of the fighters managed to flee, following the Colonel's armored vehicle as it sped away across the desert.

As soon as the area was secure, the Blackhawks landed while the Apaches provided cover. David's men quickly filed off the plane. Dressed in desert fatigues, the leader of the IDF emerged from the closest Blackhawk followed by three of his men. "General Dobson, great to see you. Your timing is perfect."

"Please, call me 'Steve.' Glad I could help, Commander Stein. Hopefully this won't become an international incident."

"And you can call me 'David.' By the way, where exactly are we?"

"We're in Petra."

"What is Petra?"

"We're standing on it. It's a…significant place."

"We're standing on barren desert."

"Well, David, to many people it's more than just a barren desert."

David looked around at the landscape before he and Steve shook hands. "Steve, thanks for saving our lives."

"I'm sure you'd do the same for me. Now let's get out of here. We don't know if the enemy will try to regroup." David approached the first Blackhawk before signaling twelve of his men to board.

One of Dobson's men whispered, "General, are you going to tell David about Petra?"

"Not yet, Sergeant Barkai. It's not time."

Boarding the last of the men into the choppers, Steve said quietly to David, "This mission never happened; we are not supposed to enter Jordanian airspace." David nodded. The choppers took off, leaving the devastated battlefield behind.

CHAPTER 11
A MYSTERIOUS PAST

THE CHOPPERS LANDED at a base just outside of Jerusalem. A caravan of black Humvees pulled up on the tarmac to take the men to Steve's compound. Within the hour, they were passing through the iron gates that protected the house, a large stucco Mediterranean with a red barrel-tile roof. David noticed sharpshooters positioned on the second-floor balconies. Steve got out of the first Humvee and opened the front door for the men. The house staff directed most of the team to the lower level while ushering David, Scott, Frank and Chad into the main living room.

"You guys make yourselves at home. My staff will get whatever you need."

"Thanks Steve." David turned his attention to Scott. "Scotty, did you ever get any information on Corinthia?"

"It's one mystery after another, Skip. We have almost nothing revealing on him or his future motives until he showed up at the Sorbonne to study. In her research, Sarah discovered a thesis Corinthia wrote during his undergraduate studies. Then it was on to Italy. His thesis was about global governance, one-world government, that sort of stuff. He talks about how to subvert nations for that purpose. 'Doing it for their own good,' as he says."

"Frank, where's the paper?" David asked

"Sarah has a copy of it on her portal in New York. Hold on…I'm downloading it and I'll forward it to you right now."

David checked his tablet. "This is…let's see, about a hundred pages of his writings. Great job of Sarah to get some history on this guy."

"History on which guy, Skip?" Chad asked.

"Anno Corinthia. He seems to be gaining more power every time there's a terrorist attack."

"What does it say?"

"I'm going to read it, then I'll address everyone."

For the next couple of hours, David consumed Corinthia's thesis. He became more troubled with each page he read, as it gave more insight into Corinthia's psychology and blueprint for the world.

Frank found David reading Corinthia's thesis as the rest of the team relaxed in the lower level of the compound. "So what do you think, David?"

Leaning back in his chair, David seemed lost in thought. "Where do I begin? A college student, writing about how to save the world by taking it over. A college kid. Can you believe it? And then laying out a plan on how to do it."

"Like Hitler or something?"

"No....at least not at the beginning. He *sounds* like a humanitarian at first."

"A wolf in sheep's clothing."

"Right, Frank. I fear that's what he is, and a very believable sheep for many. Let's go downstairs and I'll fill in the men."

"They've had only about three hours of sleep."

"And I've had none. Get them up, Frank."

David waited a while before going to see the men, Corinthia's report in hand. "Okay, guys...I've got something to talk to you about." When he had garnered their attention, David began relating the contents of Corinthia's thesis.

When David was finished, Frank approached him. "So David, what does this all mean?"

"It fits with everything that's been happening up to now. What we have is Corinthia the mature adult beginning to fulfill the vision of the young student."

"So, who are we dealing with?"

"Someone who believes he has the answers to the world's problems. Someone who wants to abolish nations and concentrate all power in his hands by mobilizing the world against a common enemy. Corinthia promises to protect nations and people against that enemy if they completely surrender their freedom to his authority."

"But David, who is the common enemy?"

"Right now, it's terrorism...with a twist."

"What's the twist?"

"I believe the man who claims to be combating the terrorism is actually the one committing it."

"What are you saying, Skip?"

David looked intently at Frank. "What I'm saying is that Corinthia is secretly behind the terrorism, and now he's publicly going to rally the world against it."

"How can we warn the world?"

"We can't, Frank....no one would believe us....yet. We have his college thesis that is playing itself out as we speak, but that's not enough. I want to trace his birth place, family history, personal history, education, etc. Find out what sand box Corinthia played in when he was five. I want to know ALL about him. Frank, get our intelligence people on this. Also, call Robby and Mike back in New York."

"David, are they background research experts?"

"They might as well be. Those guys will figure out what rock he crawled out from under." David paced back and forth before approaching the window. He held up the file folder and looked intently at the photos of Corinthia contained in the report.

David quickly turned around. "Frank, contact Mel. I want him to order the surveillance videos from a building in New York."

"Sure, Skip. Which building?"

Lost in the past for a moment, he murmured, "the north tower of the World Trade Center."

"What?? I don't even know if those videos still exist. From which date?"

"September 11, 2001."

"Um…okay, I'll call Mel right now."

"Good. Where's HALO, Frank?"

"In your left pocket." David reached down and felt the front of his khakis.

"It's been a long day."

"Yes, it has."

David stepped into Steve's den and voice-activated HALO. Gazing at Sarah's image, he breathed a heavy sigh; then brightened up at the sight and sound of her.

"Welcome to Israel, David. As you know, I've been there countless times. Now, you are there…finally. Make yourself at home, darling. You're going to be there awhile.

"You might have already met Steve Dobson, head of the Israeli Defense Forces. A former U.S. Air Force pilot…he's the only non-Jew ever to head the IDF. He's behind all those victories a few years ago against Israel's enemies. His success is one reason the United States and the free world became so complacent these past few years.

"I will connect you to our traffic control people positioned at the airport. Once you and your flight are identified, ask them 'what's the good word?' If they say, 'Selah,' they're ours. Any other response means trouble. Once they reply with 'Selah,' they will tell you where to land safely. Once you land, they will have buses to drive you and the force to Dobson. The drivers will get off the buses and guard the plane."

David looked at Frank, raising his eyebrows as Sarah talked about the plane landing. "See Frank, you can't always predict the future."

"No Skip...just most of the time. We did make it to Israel just like Sarah said."

"Defending your co-worker, Frank?"

"No Skip, defending your lovely wife."

"Yes, my lovely intelligent wife..." David smiled wistfully, walking up to her holographic image. Looking into her eyes, he extended a hand out to Sarah. Frank observed David frozen next to Sarah's image. Saddened by David's loneliness, he looked down at the floor and quietly left the room.

CHAPTER 12
MORNING IN JERUSALEM

AFTER RISING AT dawn, David realized that the long trip Sarah planned for him had come to an end. He began to wonder what the future might hold. He and the SEALs arrived safely, but what was the ultimate purpose for his coming to Jerusalem? He thought about his home in Queens, the friends he left behind, his father-in-law, but most importantly, Rebecca.

As David walked out Steve's front door, he noticed several security officers patrolling the Dobson compound. In the distance, beyond the gates, he saw people beginning their daily routine. Turning back toward the house, he saw a familiar sight, a mezuzah on the front door frame.

"Good morning, Skip." David caught the scent of fresh coffee and looked up to see Scott in the doorway.

"Morning, Scott. How'd you sleep?"

"Pretty good. Some of the guys might still be asleep. You want me to wake 'em?"

"No buddy, let them sleep as long as they want. They've earned it."

Scott also noticed the mezuzah. "Hey, I thought Dobson was a holy roller?"

"He is. Sarah told me he's a Christian who loves the Jewish people. That's why he became an Israeli citizen."

Steve found Scott and David by the front door. "Hey guys, come on in." They followed Steve inside. "Today I'd like you and Scott to meet an important man who works in our government. Also, I've arranged for your team to tour some of our bases."

"Sure Steve, any time; we're not on a schedule," David said, looking at Scott.

"Great." Dobson surveyed the dozens of SEALs in his house. "Remember, my home is your home. I hope your men are enjoying the good food and hot showers after our little skirmish in the desert."

"They are. They were due for something better than military chow."

Steve ushered David to a corner of the living room to speak with him privately. "I have a message from your father-in-law."

"Good, I was hoping for that."

"Mel is fine, and of course he's taking great care of your daughter."

"Did Pop say how Becca is doing?"

"She misses her parents but she loves her grandpa. Mel is keeping her busy."

"My father-in-law is the ultimate Mensch."

"We should connect with them now before it gets too late in New York."

As Lorraine placed a small dish of chocolate-chip mint ice cream in front of Rebecca for her usual after-school treat, the doorbell rang. Rebecca knew who it was, and would usually run to the door to meet her grandfather but she was preoccupied enjoying her ice cream. Lorraine opened the door. "Hey Mel, come on in."

Just as Mel was about to kiss Rebecca on top of her head, his cell phone rang. "Cupcake, it's your father calling."

"Daddy! Daddy!"

Peering at his tablet, David beamed at his daughter. "Guess where I am, honey?"

"Israel!"

"How do you know that?"

"I see the flag behind you, with the star in the middle."

"The Star of *David*," said Steve. "How fitting."

"How is school? Are you taking good care of grandpa?"

"Grandpa's great. School is fine."

"Okay, honey, can you get Grandpa for me?"

"Sure Daddy."

David noticed a shadow standing behind Rebecca. "Hey is that Lorraine behind you?"

"Yes Daddy."

"Hi David, Rebecca was just having her after-school treat."

"Chocolate chip mint?"

"That's right, Daddy. See?" Rebecca giggled as she held her cup up to the camera. "Want a taste?"

"No thanks, honey. It's all yours."

"Lorraine, can you help me build my doll house."

"Gotta go David, the boss needs me!"

"Thanks a million, Lorraine."

A moment later, Mel appeared on the screen. "So, how are you doing, son? Bet you've got some stories to tell."

"Oh yeah. Tons."

"How's the mission coming?"

"Lots of action, some surprises, but nothing we couldn't handle. HALO and Sarah's planning got us safely to Israel."

Mel got closer to the camera and whispered. "David, things are getting dicey here in the states. Our major cities have been attacked and I assume you know what's going on elsewhere in the world."

"Yes, I do, Pop. Especially in Europe."

"Keep your eye on Europe, David. That's where I believe the trouble originates."

"Corinthia?"

"You got it. Great minds think alike."

"How did you figure out Corinthia was behind all this?"

"A combination of things. I reviewed Sarah's files back home."

"Which files are you talking about?"

"They're from a couple of years ago, well before all the

trouble. Corinthia's been on her radar for a while. Let me read you a few words from her notes:

'Last night I had a terrible dream about one of Italy's politicians – Anno Corinthia. I began to investigate Mr. Corinthia and found almost nothing on him before the age of eighteen, no residences, very little background.

'Strange, everyone has a history but Corinthia has almost nothing. That means he succeeded in hiding it and must have had lots of technical help concealing his past. I did come across a thesis he wrote in college, discussing how someone can methodically take over the world through seduction, intimidation, threats, and violence. He came across as megalomaniacal, and yet every word, every sentence, was deliberate and calculating. I read it through and then it vanished into cyber space. Vanished. And so I am left with a question. Who or what is this Anno Corinthia? Time will tell...'

"That's what Sarah wrote, son."

"Sarah's analysts confirmed the thesis as Corinthia's... that's when it disappeared on their end as well, but they had time to save it."

"Very interesting."

"Mel, could you send me whatever you have on this?"

"Absolutely David, I'll email it right away."

CHAPTER 13
CALEV

"DAVID, ARE YOU guys ready? My lieutenant, Ari Bock, will be here soon. He'll take most of your force on a tour of our bases, then on to the Negev. You, Scott and Chad are riding with me."

"Okay Steve, we're good to go."

❦

The four men arrived at a non-descript two-story Jerusalem-stone house on a dead-end street. Steve pointed to the house. "Welcome to Mossad."

"Headquarters?"

"No David, the living quarters of the man in charge."

"Is it still Calev?"

"Yes, Calev Silver." The four men exited the car and walked up an old rugged path.

Steve rang the bell; a young woman answered from the other side of the heavy wooden door. "May I help you?" she asked sweetly.

"It's Steve. Tell the boss I'm here with David and two of his friends."

"Steve, how are you? I'll be right back for you guys."

David looked at Steve. "Who was that?"

"That's Rachel, Calev's daughter...she's a nurse and hopes to go to med school."

The sweet voice came through the door again. "Okay gentlemen, just one question for you before I let you in."

"Please, go ahead," Steve replied.

"Whoever is David must answer the question."

"I'm right here; this is David."

"On which floor did you first meet your wife, in which building, and on which date?"

David glanced at Steve in disbelief. "How...how... did...?"

"How did Calev know? Sarah told him."

Still stunned, David paused before answering the question. "I...met my wife on the 77th floor, North Tower of the World Trade Center, on September 11, 2001."

"Thank you, Sir. And what a beautiful story on a very sad day."

Smiling, Rachel Silver opened the door and ushered the four men inside, greeting each of them warmly. "Please, make yourselves at home."

"Rachel, it's always a pleasure. Your dad raised a lovely young lady. Guys, I was there with my late wife, right outside the room, when Rachel was born."

"Steve, you know I never get tired of hearing you say that," she laughed.

"Rachel, allow me to introduce my guests. This is David Stein, United States Navy SEAL, and two of his men, Scott Miller and Chad 'Gladiator' Perry." The three SEALs nodded with respect. When David looked at Rachel, she unexpectedly gave him a quick hug. David saw a glowing young woman in the prime of her life, reminding him of Sarah when they were young. Rachel was about Sarah's height and had the same long brown hair and dark brown eyes.

"It is an honor to meet all of you. My father will join you soon. Please excuse me while I prepare some appetizers in the kitchen." Rachel left the room.

Moments later, a bearded, burly man came down the stairs, his bulky frame filling the narrow staircase. "Steve, I see you've brought us some special people."

"I have indeed, Calev."

"Well, your reputation precedes each of you. Gladiator, the best sniper in the world. Mr. Miller, the master tactician and strategist. And of course, the leader of the pack, Mr. Stein...husband of the greatest intelligence operative and analyst, bar none." Calev bowed slightly; his expression turned serious. "My condolences to both of you on the loss of your wives. It's perhaps little consolation to tell you that I, too, am a widower. My wife also died at the hands of terrorism, as did Steve's."

David looked Calev in the eye. "I'm sorry to hear that."

"It happened many years ago David, but it still feels

like yesterday. As we all know, life must go on. Our wives would want it to. Men are supposed to die before their women, loving and protecting them, but the world we live in is upside down, my friend." Calev gestured to the far end of the sparsely furnished living room. "Please...follow me. Rachel has set out food and drinks in the sunroom."

The four men followed Calev to a room in the back of the house, floor-to-ceiling windows on three sides provided a view of the lush garden. A round marble-top table surrounded by six chairs was the only furniture in the room. Calev filled five tall glasses from a pitcher of iced tea. "Please, sit down.

"There are two things you should know about this country. First, Israel is now extraordinarily complacent about threats to her safety and security. Second, she shouldn't be."

Scott shook his head. "I don't get it. Calev, how can Israel be complacent with rampant terrorism and assassinations in America, Europe and in Dubai? Not to mention the nuclear missile bound for Israel that Frank stopped."

"That's recent news that Israel has yet to fully digest. As you know, for the past few years, Israel has won a series of decisive victories over her opponents in the region. This has created a rare window of peace. Meanwhile, the engine of Israeli technology has created great wealth...and there is nothing that will make a nation more complacent than the cessation of war and the generation of wealth. And of course, there is the rebuilding of the Temple, just east of where we are now. We are rebuilding for the first time in

20 centuries, since the Romans burned it down and exiled our people."

"How close are you to completing the Temple?"

"It could be only a matter of months, David. But my point is that the rebuilding of the Temple is associated with peace, not war. It's another reason Israel is complacent. But there's a fourth factor here. We are cursed with an exceedingly weak prime minister. He has done nothing to bring us either prosperity or peace, but he is the beneficiary of both, like a prodigal son who inherited great wealth through an accident of birth...He is frankly a nothing, a nebbish, an empty suit, a politician's politician and a pitifully weak soul who refuses to be a man and say the unpopular thing – that we must prepare for trouble ahead."

"So what, in your opinion, is causing the trouble?"

"Two words: Anno Corinthia."

"So you know..."

"Yes, David."

"...That Corinthia is behind the terror."

"Yes. He wants to create crises, and then seduce the world into giving him absolute power to solve them."

"All for the good of humanity, of course," Scott chimed in.

"Yes. That's his big lie. But more on him later."

"I look forward to it, Calev."

"David, have you heard the news from Babylon and Dubai?"

"Yes Calev, we heard that Greater Babylon's governor was assassinated."

"Babylon has a new ruler."

"I presumed that. We were a little out of touch with world events for a while."

"David, I think you know who Babylon's new ruler is."

"I do?"

"Sarah knew her; she worked with her and never trusted her."

"The ruler is a woman?"

"Yes."

"An American?"

"Yes, and now allied with Corinthia."

"That makes her a traitor to my country. She worked with Sarah and was supposed to provide intel to help America, while she actually just helped herself?"

"Yes."

"Octavia Carlson?"

"Correct."

Taken aback for a second, David breathed a heavy sigh. "How did that all happen?"

"I'll give you the short version. As you probably know, Octavia Carlson came from a prominent family that had served your country well. Industrialists, bankers, diplomats, scientists, generals, and missionaries. Octavia inherited her family's brilliance, as well as their fortune. What she did not inherit is her family's moral rectitude. From day one, Octavia was only for Octavia." Calev paused for a moment before looking at David. "Sadly, her whole family was killed in a plane crash more than twenty years ago."

"So how did Octavia move from being an intelligence operative for the United States to…"

Calev finished David's sentence. "…Queen of Babylon?"

"She's calling herself 'queen'?"

"Actually, she favors the word, 'empress.'"

"Unbelievable. So how did it happen?" Calev proceeded to tell them the full story.

Chad sipped the last of his iced tea and put his glass on the old wooden table. "So the people of Dubai chose Octavia?"

"Yes Gladiator"

"But I still don't get it. Of all people, why her?"

"Partly looks, of course. But something else, too. She can have a hypnotic effect on people, especially men. One of my agents said Octavia has an uncanny ability to make the right people do her bidding. She has the power to make people surrender to her will and turns them into zealous servants who will do anything to please her. She wants to be adored and worshipped, and wants people to suffer as they pay her homage. Ms. Carlson is the kind of ruler who will capture and enslave rebels, parade them around as trophies, and then amuse herself by torturing them."

"In other words, she's a sadist and a sociopath!"

"Exactly, Scott. She was exiled by the Emir but was smuggled back into the country inside a basket aboard a cargo plane after the Emir was assassinated. A reformer named Prince Sharif was appointed interim governor. Good man, but he made an awful mistake when he turned over power to Octavia. For this favor she had him exiled."

David looked up at Calev. "Sharif. I believe I've met him. He's a Harvard alumnus and was well known for his abilities in the martial arts. We both trained at the same dojo in Cambridge. So, now Octavia runs the richest city and state in the world...Greater Babylon."

"Yes, and as Steve and your man Gladiator will tell you, the Bible predicts the rise of a new Babylon, symbolized by a depraved woman being smuggled there in a basket."

"Do you believe that, Calev?"

"Well, David, what's there is there. It is a striking coincidence. Of course, Octavia might have chosen the basket in an attempt to fulfill the prophecy. She is an avid devotee of the occult, which is what ancient Babylon was about. And to say that she hates Christians, as well as Israel, is the understatement of the century."

"So how does Corinthia benefit from her? What does he want from her?"

"Well, he isn't moved by her beauty or seductiveness."

"Why not?"

"Corinthia is one of those rare men who has no interest in the female body, no matter how alluring. And in case you're wondering, he's not interested in men, either."

"So what does Corinthia see in Octavia?"

"One word, David. Money. She's rich and she rules the richest city on earth. He needs money for the 'humanitarian' military campaigns he'll be launching as the new leader of the United Nations."

⤸

The rest of the SEALs, along with Flynn, reached the Negev after touring two military bases. Lieutenant Bock addressed the men. "We will stay here for the evening and leave for Steve's at daybreak. What all of you have seen and will see must remain with you, and is for your benefit alone. Are we all in agreement?"

"Yes."

"Alright, let's get a fire going. It's been a long day."

Throughout the night, Flynn regaled the men with accounts of his many battles waged and torments endured. As the men sat around the fire pit, the flickering light illuminated well-worn faces.

Frank looked at Flynn as he rubbed his hands together over the fire. "So, what was your worst moment?"

"Oh, that's an easy one, lad. It was long ago, near the turn of the century. We were gunning after the Lord's Resistance Army in East Africa, south of the Sudans. They were the worst ossified gowls on the planet. Their leader was a monster who snatched boys from their mums, raped them, and made them his soldiers. Then they in turn did the same thing to others.

"One day, they ambushed part of our force. I was among them. They chopped my mates to pieces with machetes and axes, then beat me into a dog's dinner before knocking me out.

"I woke entirely gobsmacked; I still had my gooter, but I was nailed to a cross in a field. Nothing around me but land and sky. Every nerve in my body was screaming out like a banshee; I felt myself fading as the vultures began to circle. I thought I was a dead man.

"Lucky for me, the rest of my force eventually came and took me down. I was there for maybe an hour, but it felt like an eternity. And being up there on that cross, it made me wonder what that fellow Jesus went through for hours. I can't even imagine the hell he endured. But if the tale about him is true, he had the last laugh three days later."

❧

Rachel returned from the kitchen. "Rachel, would you please get coffee for everyone?"

"Sure, Dad."

"Gladiator will have his black."

Surprised, David looked at Calev. "How did you know…?"

"Just part of what we do, information is everything."

Steve's phone rang. Seeing it was Ari, he walked outside to the back patio and took the call.

"So, you're finished, Ari?"

"Yes, we're headed back and will meet you at your home if that's alright."

"Sure. How did it go?"

"I showed them everything as you requested. Are you sure these men are trustworthy?"

"I would trust them with my life. Anyone David trusts, I trust, without question."

"All it takes is one rotten apple."

"There are no rotten apples on David's SEAL team."

"Alright, see you tomorrow."

"See you then, Ari."

Stepping back into the house, Steve approached Calev to shake his hand and embrace him. "We must go now; it's getting late."

"Yes it is, Steve. And I've got some work to attend to."

"Corinthia?"

"Correct. I'm still interviewing people for the job." Calev gestured to David, Scott, and Gladiator. As they walked over, he continued. "You need to know this, too. We are looking to infiltrate Corinthia. Let's discuss it soon."

"Will do, Calev. Thank you for today."

"My pleasure, David. Layla tov."

"Excuse me?"

"It means 'good night' in Hebrew."

"Then, Layla tov."

Rachel waved to the men. "Layla tov everyone!"

"Layla tov, Rachel."

After the men left, Rachel locked the door and turned to her father. "Dad, why didn't you tell David what caused the Carlson family plane crash?"

"I thought he knew, but if he doesn't, I don't think he needed to hear that today."

CHAPTER 14
GOG

CALEV HAD JUST fallen into a deep sleep when he was awakened by a sharp object pressing against his throat. The lights came on, temporarily blinding him. As his eyes adjusted, he saw three men dressed in black looking down at him. All three had pistols holstered at their sides. The man closest to him held a large Bowie knife and spoke with a Russian accent.

"Mr. Silver, if you want to see the sun rise again, you will do exactly as I say."

Calev raised his head off the pillow and looked across the room at the other two men before turning back to the man who spoke. "What do you want?"

"You will walk with us down the hall to your office. You will then give us the combination to your safe."

Calev nodded hesitantly and climbed out of bed wearing his old grey pajamas. As he led the men into the hall, they passed Rachel's open bedroom door. She was in bed, sleeping on her side in a blue night shirt.

One of the intruders pushed the door open wider and raised his eyebrows. "Your daughter is very beautiful; it would be a pity if something bad were to happen to her." Calev reflexively closed Rachel's bedroom door, making more noise than he intended.

"Father, is that you?" she murmured.

"Yes, dear," Calev responded through the door. "I am just finishing some work. Please go back to sleep."

"Okay Father, good night."

"Good night, Rachel."

It took every ounce of strength in Calev's body to refrain from yelling out a warning to his daughter. He continued on to his office while debating silently whether to provide the real combination to the safe. If they gained access, precious lives could be lost from classified information falling into the wrong hands. However, entering the wrong combination would be deadly for anyone near the safe if the code to disarm was not entered within sixty seconds.

The man with the knife rolled the desk chair toward the middle of the room and stood behind it.

"Sit here."

Calev sat down and looked across the room, while the other two assailants stood on either side of the safe. The third man ripped an electrical cord from the wall and tied Calev's hands behind him. Calev grimaced in pain. "What? Too tight?" Calev now knew that he would never reveal the correct combination.

"Tell us the numbers," one of the men demanded,

holding a pen and notepad. The barrel of a gun was pressed against the side of Calev's head.

Calev spoke slowly. "37, 22, 19, 48, 11, and…44."

The man jotted down the numbers before kneeling in front of the safe.

Calev heard a faint clicking sound as the man pulled the latch several times.

After a long moment the man with the notepad stood up and turned to make eye contact with the man behind Calev. "Mr. Silver, if you do not give us the right combination we will kill you slowly, while your daughter watches. Then we will kill her. Give it to us now."

Calev knew he had only a few seconds before the whole room blew. He swiveled in the chair, aiming the back of it toward the open door before pushing off with his legs as he tried to escape the impending explosion. As he rolled through the doorway, three bullets slammed into his upper body. Then came a loud flash, everything went blank.

Steve Dobson was relaxing in his den when the secure line rang. At such a late hour, that phone rarely brought good news. "Steve! Steve!"

"Rachel? Are you okay?"

"My father has been shot! He was in his office and they, they…" Rachel could barely get the words out between sobs. "…killed him."

"What?!! They killed Calev?!!"

"They killed my father while trying to get into the safe, but they couldn't do it. It blew up and killed them!"

"Rachel, where are you now?"

"I'm on the street in front of our house. There are police everywhere."

"I'm coming over. Wait there."

"Okay, okay." Rachel sobbed.

Steve strode quickly into the living room where David and some of his men were gathered. "David, Scott, Gladiator, come with me."

David stood up. "What's going on?"

"Calev's dead."

The four of them stepped outside just as Steve's car pulled up. "Get us to Calev's….and fast," Steve said to his driver before calling Rachel. When she answered, he heard chaos in the background.

"Steve?"

"Tell the police I'm coming now. Tell them to cordon off your father's office but not to disturb the crime scene."

"Okay."

"Rachel…I am so sorry."

Siren wailing, Steve's car hurdled eastward through Jerusalem's densely packed streets. Within five minutes they reached Calev's home.

Steve got out of the car while the media reported his arrival. He was met by Lieutenant Gottlieb, the scene commander. "Steve, we haven't touched anything."

"I appreciate it, Sid. As you know, this one's personal for me. The three men behind me are U.S. military. I brought them in case this has an international angle." The lieutenant nodded toward the SEALs.

"My gut tells me it's terrorism. We'll know soon enough if we can get a positive I.D. on the bodies upstairs. Let me get this crowd under control so you can get inside. I'm out here if you need me."

"Move away from the house!" bellowed one of the officers at the surging crowd. "Let them pass!" he added as David, Scott, and Gladiator headed for the door behind Steve. Rachel ran out of the house in tears and embraced Steve.

"Rachel, your father was a great man. Unfortunately, there's no time to mourn; we have to move quickly to find out who's behind this. I hate to ask, but, did you see the bodies?"

"Yes, Steve, they're next to the safe."

"Guys, come upstairs with me. You, too, Rachel."

From the top of the stairs they could see into the room where the charred bodies of three men lay slumped in front of Calev's safe. The force of the blast had blown out the windows. The wooden desk and file cabinets were torn apart.

"Rachel, do you have four pairs of latex gloves?"

"Sure, I'll be right back." Rachel left the room and returned in a moment, handing out the gloves.

"Okay, let's search the bodies." Steve took the body closest to the safe door and motioned for Scott and Gladiator to check the others. "Rachel, would you ask Lieutenant Gottlieb to come upstairs? He's in the police van parked at the curb."

"Sure, anything to keep me busy." Rachel left the scene

as the men pulled small items from the pockets of the perpetrators. They assembled a pile of cigarette packs, match books, chewing gum, bills and coins that were mostly Euros, along with a comb and a set of keys.

"Steve, what do you have?" The lieutenant entered the room carrying an electronics case.

"There's not much to go on. I'm hoping you can I.D. the killers. This first guy's hands are burnt pretty bad but maybe you can get some prints from the other two. That pack of Camels came from the guy with the black hands so it might give you something." The lieutenant looked around at the damaged room and shook his head.

"Alright, I'll get whatever prints I can. We can also try facial recognition. One of my female officers is trying to comfort Calev's daughter. That Rachel is a strong young woman. She's holding up better than I would have expected. Do you know if she has any family to stay with?"

"Calev has a brother in Miami; that's all the family I know of. If she wants to, Rachel can stay at my house as long as she needs."

"Okay, let's get this started." They watched as the lieutenant carefully cleaned the faces of the dead men before photographing them with an F.I.D. facial recognition device. He then used a scanner on the hands of the two bodies further from the safe. An officer came into the room carrying a plastic evidence bag. The lieutenant picked up the pack of Camels with a tweezer and placed it into the bag.

"I want that dusted immediately."

"Absolutely Lieutenant. I'll call you from the van when I have something." The officer left as the five men began the tedious task of going over every square inch of the room, combing through items large and small.

Almost an hour went by before the lieutenant's radio squawked. "Lieutenant Gottlieb?"

"I'm here."

"We have an I.D. on all three of them. They're from three different countries."

"Which countries?"

"Turkey, Iran and Russia."

Steve looked startled as he overheard those words.

"Good work; dig into their backgrounds; I want to know everything."

"I'm on it, Lieutenant."

The radio crackled before going quiet as Rachel appeared in the doorway with a blank expression on her face.

"Okay," Steve mumbled. "Turkey, Iran and Russia… The war has begun."

David, Scott, and Gladiator looked at each other.

"The war has begun? Steve, what war are you talking about?"

"Russia, Turkey, Iran. Gog and Magog, David. It was predicted long ago. Now, it looks like it could be happening."

"*What* could be happening?"

"I'll explain later, David."

Realizing that an attack against Israel was imminent,

Steve called Ari. "Ari, mobilize our troops, now! Call up every reservist in the country! And put the Navy on high alert!"

"Steve! I was about to call you…troops are massing outside of our borders! Should we call the Prime Minister before we move?"

"No, I'll call him later. The Knesset will back us up on that."

"Alright…" Steve hung up.

"David, I need you and your men."

"Of course, I'm with you Steve, and I'm sure my men will be, too."

"What's happening?" Scott asked Rachel.

Rachel could barely utter the words. "It could be the war that was prophesized."

"What war?"

"The war that is described in the Bible, Gog and Magog," Chad interjected. "It says that in the latter days, when Israel is living in peace and prosperity, there will be a sudden invasion, led by Russia. Turkey and Persia – Iran – will also be involved, as well as some of Israel's neighbors."

Scott glanced at David. "What do you think, Skip?"

"Israel is at war. All else is speculation."

�ै

Dobson was correct. Calev's assassination was the opening volley of a major war. Within an hour, Frank, Flynn and the rest of the SEAL team were reunited with David in Jerusalem. By that time, Israel was being attacked from land, sea, and air.

In Steve's living room, David spoke to his team:

"Gentlemen, we have two choices to make. First, do we fight for Israel or do we disengage? If we fight, then with General Dobson's permission, I will remain commander of our force and we will be free to make our own decisions in coordination with the IDF.

"Second, if we do fight for Israel, what is our strategy? If we are to fight for Israel, we need to decide now. I choose to fight for our host country. All who are with me, say, 'Ay.'"

"Ay!" responded the entire SEAL team, except one.

Scott stood up. "Are we going to fight as foreigners in a foreign land? Our homeland is being bombed daily. We're Americans, we should be back home defending our country, our family, our friends. What the hell are we fighting here for?"

David tried to remain calm. "This is our mission."

Scott stepped closer to David and pointed a finger in his face. "This is your mission! This is your wife's mission!"

David put his hands on Scott's shoulders. "Please, Scotty, you're my friend; trust me. We've come this far." David leaned in and whispered into Scott's ear, "I can't do this without you."

Scott scanned the room, looking at the other men while shaking his head. Walking away, he threw his hand up. "Ay."

David turned to Steve. "General Dobson, do I have

your permission to retain command of my men and do we have your permission to operate as an independent force in coordination with the IDF?"

"You do."

"Thank you, General. Where do you need us most?"

"Probably the northern front against Russia's forces, and Turkey's as well."

"Then the northern front it is."

Flynn smiled glumly. "Ahh, I know it well, like me second home."

❧

David and his men arrived at the front lines, taking position behind a ridge less than a mile from Lebanon. The enemy was massed near the border as Russian bombers circled overhead.

Flynn looked toward the northern sky. "They're dropping bombs to soften us up. Then the ground invasion will come, overwhelming us with numbers. Should make for quite a hooley."

Chad observed the enemy through binoculars. "They have lookouts all around. We can take them out with silencers while we have the high ground and can't be seen. That will buy time for the IDF to attain full strength on this front. Then we hang back and leverage their strength."

"Makes sense, Gladiator."

"Hey, David, wait…beyond the lookout…there's a large concentration of troops, packed into one area at ten o'clock."

"Let me have a look, Skip." David handed the binoculars to Scott.

"Whoa…that's a whole lot of Ruskies."

"Right. I say we take them out."

"I would not advise that," Scott said with concern. "There could be a thousand, maybe more."

"We need to move on them now, while we're invisible."

"Skip, are you serious?"

"Very… we move as soon as the bombers leave."

"But why? Why not listen to Gladiator? We'll take out the lookouts then wait for IDF to reach its strength."

"Scotty, if the enemy sees the IDF, our cover is blown. The Russians and Turks are all in one place, five hundred yards out. We have the element of surprise completely on our side. If we strike now, they won't know what hit them, and we'll halt their advance before it begins. We move in, we move quickly, we wipe them out, then we get out. By that time the IDF gets here and they take the lead."

"Skip, this is a suicide mission. We're not infantry. We don't have the numbers or equipment we need. What do you think, Flynn?"

"David's your commander, lad."

"That's not an answer." Scott glared at Flynn before facing David. "This is suicide!"

Frustrated at Scott's opposition, David leaned in close to his old friend and spoke in a tone Scott never heard before. "Let me make this clear, Miller. I'm your commander, and we're going to attack."

Scott spit tobacco on the ground between them. "Well,

Stein, then you can just count me out. I'm not having any part of you getting us senselessly killed. If you move ahead with this, you better order a big supply of body bags!"

David pointed at Scott's chest. "Miller, if you abandon the SEALs, that's desertion."

Scott looked to Flynn for backup. "Well?"

"Hold that chicken's neck. Like I said, laddy, he's your commander; do as he says." Scott turned his back on Flynn and David before storming away.

David prepped the men for battle while Scott remained in the distance.

A little later, David noticed Chad talking with Scott before both men returned. Scott hesitantly approached David; they silently stared at each other for an uncomfortable moment. "Commander Stein, I can't desert the men...what do you need me to do?" Both men still felt the tension between them, something that never existed before in their lifelong friendship.

"Alright — Gladiator, you and your snipers will drop the lookouts. Then we advance with smoke, grenades, the whole bit. We create a fog so they can't see us. They'll think we're a bigger force and fall back. Gladiator, get your crew in position."

"You got it, Skip." Chad and seven other snipers quickly took aim on top of the ridge. "Everyone locked on?"

"Locked."

"Now!" The sniper rifles made virtually no noise. Just

a few 'pffft' sounds were audible as Chad and his men neutralized the enemy lookouts.

"Let's go!" commanded David.

The SEAL team surged forward, launching smoke canisters and grenades while firing at the enemy.

Within minutes, hundreds of the enemy lay dead. Scott surveyed the area. "Mission accomplished! David, let's get out of here!"

"No, there are still hundreds left!"

"We decimated their front lines without any casualties of our own. Let's pull back and let the IDF mop up the rest!"

"Scott, the enemy is on the run. Keep moving, men!"

The SEALs advanced, still shrouded by the smoky cover. Unexpectedly, the desert wind picked up and the cover of fog began to dissipate, exposing the SEALs and making them visible to the enemy.

"Pull back!" David yelled, realizing that his men were now vulnerable. "Pull back!"

As the SEALs retreated, enemy fire intensified, striking and taking down several men.

Running for cover, Scott dove behind a large boulder and noticed a fellow SEAL who was still exposed. "Danny! Get over here!"

As Danny ran toward Scott, several bullets tore through his body; he dropped to the ground. Scott crawled to Danny and dragged him behind the boulder. Turning him over he saw several bloody exit wounds on Danny's torso.

Scott put pressure on Danny's wounds. "Hang on brother! Hang on!"

Danny looked down in shock at his bloody chest. "I'm not going to make it!"

Scott could see the color draining from Danny's face. "Don't say that! Every SEAL makes it! Medic! Medic!"

Scott looked around for help, but all he saw were the bodies of his fellow SEALs.

Danny's bloody hand reached into his vest; he pulled out a photo of him and his wife on their wedding day. Danny looked at the photo before handing it to Scott. "Tell Angie I love her." His lifeless eyes rolled back in his head; Scott carefully closed Danny's eyelids and wept.

Amid the gunfire, blood, and chaos, Gladiator and his snipers found some cover in an olive grove. They began picking off as many of the enemy as they could. The Russian and Turkish forces eventually retreated.

✍

The SEALs had killed hundreds of the enemy's troops before they could cross into Israel, but the cost was horrific. Watching the medics arrive, David knew that in the world of SEALs, one dead comrade was a terrible setback. This was a calamity, he thought to himself as much of his team lay dead while medics tried to save the wounded.

Walking past the dead and injured, Scott approached. Gazing over an unfathomable scene, he fought back tears and glared at David. "This is your responsibility! You killed our men! — Men with wives, children and families! I told you this would fail! You and your ghost wife just got our men killed!"

David stood numbly. Shaking with rage, Scott steadied himself before slamming his fist into David's jaw, knocking him to the ground.

As David wiped the blood from his lip, Scott looked down with contempt at his friend. "You damn fool! Was it worth it?!! I don't ever want to see your face again," he said through clenched teeth.

Scott stormed away, with eleven other SEALs following. David remained speechless as he watched his best friend and fellow SEALs disappear into the hills.

Chad approached David. "He's wrong, Skip."

"No Glad, he's not. How am I going to tell their families?"

Chad put his hand on David's shoulder. They watched as medivac helicopters landed on the scarred battlefield to remove the dead and wounded.

David and Chad saluted as the fallen SEALs were loaded into the choppers.

That night, David needed to be alone. He did not leave his tent at the makeshift camp the IDF had set up a few miles back from the Lebanese border. Sitting on a crate, with his head in his hands, he wondered how his seemingly perfect life turned into a total nightmare.

David took HALO from his pocket and stared at it while shaking his head. "You're not Sarah; you're just a damn machine!" He threw HALO across the tent. The device was activated by David verbalizing Sarah's name. In a few seconds her image was glowing larger than life in the small tent.

He stared at his wife while she began to speak. "David, there will be hard times on your mission, times when you'll swear you can't go on. But this is not just about you or your men. This is about freedom and the salvation of the world. I hope you hear these words just when you need them. I love you always."

Through the fog of anguish, David's anger turned to sorrow and his sorrow turned to tears, but not tears of surrender. Sarah's words had given him the strength to go on. Somehow it had become clear: completing this mission was his destiny.

✍

The remaining SEAL team was awake before dawn. They now numbered twenty-four, including David, Chad and Flynn.

Chad stuck his head into David's tent. "Skip, are you alright?"

Empowered by Sarah's words, he turned to Chad, "Gladiator, we have a mission to complete."

Soon, more IDF forces arrived at the camp, coinciding with more intense bombing by the enemy.

A somber David addressed the SEALs outside. "Men, we have another choice to make. Stay here and fight with the IDF or return to Jerusalem. I choose to stay here.

You are free to go. This is not your battle; this is not your country."

Flynn spat out a wad of tobacco. "You're our leader, David. I, for one, decide to stay and fight."

Chad stepped forward next to Flynn. "I'm staying, too. Our fallen brothers did not desert and neither will we."

The other SEALS responded likewise.

David looked up and down the line of his men. "Thank you for your loyalty. We may all die today, but we will die together."

≲

While David's battlefield maneuvers had gotten nearly half the SEAL team killed and triggered twelve desertions, it was a major victory for Israel. With hundreds of the enemy's force struck down, it slowed Russia's advance from the north and boosted Israel's morale. News of David's heroism and sacrifice spread as the IDF poured more troops into the region.

After the battle at the Lebanese border, David was given command of an IDF force, in addition to his remaining SEALs. Their mission was to continue holding the ground near the northern border.

In the ensuing battles, David and his forces continued to distinguish themselves on the northern front, but eventually, the Russian-led coalition brought in substantial reinforcements. Overwhelmed by the Russians, David's team and the IDF had their backs against the wall.

On the front lines, Steve Dobson's voice came over the radio. "David, get your SEALs out of there! Our satellites are showing a rapid enemy deployment in Syria, just beyond the Golan Heights."

"I'm staying put," growled Flynn. The others murmured their assent.

"General, we're staying."

"May God be with you David, and us all."

∽

On all fronts, enemy troops poured into Israel. In Jerusalem, Prime Minister Shaul Aretz sent out a worldwide appeal for help.

Hearing it on radio, David shook his head in dismay. "Who's going to help? Nobody. America is still recovering from being attacked. So, that leaves no one."

Across northern Israel, the enemy's forces gathered like locusts. David, his SEALs, and the IDF appeared to be trapped, with no chance of victory. The enemy was only a few hundred yards out and closing fast.

And then, everything changed.

Storm clouds rapidly moved in. The wind began to howl; the earth shook as the sky raged with intense thunder and lightning. Inexplicably, the enemy was literally unable to move forward.

Watching in amazement, David signaled Chad to open fire. As the snipers began picking off an immobile foe, the IDF infantry backed up the SEALs with artillery fire.

The sky blackened, illuminated only by lightning

streaks across the sky, followed by epic claps of thunder. Bolts of lightning struck the battlefield, killing many enemy troops. Some of the Russian bombers were also struck and crashed to the ground, exploding in balls of fire.

The rain began to fall, first a trickle, then a torrential downpour as though the sky had opened. Then the ground opened beneath the enemy, swallowing many troops. Dense fog descended, camouflaging the IDF while blinding the Russians and Turks.

As David watched in awe, General Dobson radioed in from IDF central command. "What's going on, David? We're picking up seismic activity near your location."

"I can't believe what I'm seeing. The elements are destroying the enemy!"

"I'm getting the same reports from the south and the east. It's all working against the other forces!"

"Amazing."

"Yes David, amazing, but predicted."

"Predicted?"

"Yes. Ezekiel…38 and 39."

"I'm a military man, not a preacher, Steve."

"And what do you think I am, David?"

"So what are you saying?"

"Remember what I told you…this war was predicted twenty-four centuries ago. A war against Israel, led by Russia to the north. A war in which Israel was about to be devoured, until God sent earthquakes, wind, rain, fog, hail stones, and lightning strikes against the enemy alone. Just like today."

"Okay Steve, Gladiator told me this earlier...so what comes next, fortune teller?"

"Well, Doubting Thomas, it's what we're seeing now – the crushing of these armies. And after that, look up at the skies and watch the birds gather."

"So why were you so worried before?"

"Because I lost hope and faith, David."

"If your God really exists, he understands."

"David, I know you've lost a lot of men, and paid a great price, but all in all you've done what God wanted you to do."

"Getting my men killed, turning wives into widows, causing children to lose their fathers, is that what your God wanted?"

"I'm sorry for your losses. Sometimes the will of God is hard to understand but maybe...someday we will."

Across the globe, the media reported how the war against Israel had taken a sudden and dramatic turn, resulting in a colossal defeat for the invading armies. Some were calling it a miracle. Others noted the aftermath of the war, including the grisly sight of vultures consuming the flesh and bones of Israel's fallen enemies, leaving an eerily empty battlefield.

CHAPTER 15
THE NEW TEMPLE

WHILE THE WAR ended in victory, in the weeks that followed, most Israelis blamed their prime minister, Shaul Aretz, for the prewar complacency and lack of preparedness. Determined to keep Aretz on a short leash, the Knesset voted to create an eight-person council to advise him. Because of David's heroism in the war, he became one of Israel's most prominent public figures and was selected to the council, as was Steve Dobson, who became its leader.

The upsurge in terrorism continued around the world. As the head of the United Nations, Anno Corinthia was granted unprecedented emergency powers. In a presentation at the U.N., Corinthia pledged to stand up against the onslaught of terror "as we stood against those who attacked Israel."

Back in Jerusalem, David and his men watched Corinthia's telecast in Steve's office.

Steve shook his head at David. "That pathological liar

is claiming credit for our victory when he had absolutely nothing to do with it."

"It was the elements, Steve."

"Yes David, initiated and directed by God in a strategic and timely way." David cast a skeptical glance toward Steve. "You still don't believe it was an act of God?"

"It was an act of Mother Nature, who occasionally has good timing."

"You're a hard agnostic to break, Mr. Stein."

Ari Bock entered the office. "General, here are the latest classified reports on U.N. military activity under Corinthia."

"Thank you, Ari."

Steve passed copies of the reports to David and his team. As they each read the horrific accounts, the room fell silent.

David finally spoke. "Soldiers bursting into houses. Gunning down women and children. Burning people alive. Reports of crucifixions. This is pure savagery!"

"And meanwhile, Corinthia makes pious declarations about peace and harmony, attempting to bring the world together under one ruler, himself," Steve said with disdain. "He is a liar and a deceiver."

In the immediate aftermath of the war, Israel poured its energy into completion of a rebuilt Temple in Jerusalem. Less than a year after peace had come, construction was complete. Dignitaries from across the globe flew in for the ribbon-cutting ceremony.

Octavia Carlson drew the lion's share of attention from the media, arriving in regal, opulent splendor. She exited from a golden Rolls Royce onto a long red carpet while members of her entourage bowed before her. Her form-fitting golden silk dress flashed in the bright sunlight along with her diamond-encrusted tiara.

But while most of the cameras were pointed at Octavia, it was Corinthia who made the biggest news.

Stepping up to the podium and facing the area where the Western Wall once stood alone, Corinthia spoke movingly about the history of the Jewish people and their travails. He went on to claim credit for Israel's victory in the war. Entranced by the Temple, he praised its beauty before proposing a U.N. security treaty with Israel to its "distinguished leader, Shaul Aretz." Clearly flattered by the proposal, Aretz said he would recommend to his advisory council that Israel approve it.

ॐ

Following Corinthia's offer, Israel's Knesset voted to give the Council of Eight the final say on whether to accept the treaty. The council was composed of David, Steve, Rabbi Yitzhak Ben Shalom, Rabbi Adam Cohen, and four members of the pro-Corinthia political party.

At the next council meeting, Steve addressed its members. "Friends and colleagues, thank you for coming here on this critical occasion for our country. As the council president, I urge that there be a full and candid debate on the draft treaty with the U.N. Following debate, we will have an informal show of hands on the vote. A day later, we will formally vote on the matter. A simple majority will be required for ratification or rejection. Any questions?"

The men in the room remained silent.

"We will now hear briefly from Commander David Stein and then from any others who wish to comment on his views or present us with views of their own. Mr. Stein?"

David stood up. "Thank you, General. Let me begin by saying that as much as anyone in this room, I want peace. I have spent most of my adult life in wars. During the past year, even before the latest war, my men and I were fighting terror cells throughout much of the world.

"I want to believe that the draft we have in our hands is our pathway to peace. But if I am to believe that, I also have to believe that the man who is proposing it will bring us true peace. I want to believe that." He looked down toward the floor, then looked up and raised his voice with firm resolution, gazing at the stoic council. "But I can't! Let me show you why. On the table in front of each of you is a report that I had prepared. I will give you a few minutes to read it alone, then I'll return."

Re-entering the chamber, David found the meeting in an uproar. "Mr. Stein, where did you get this information?!" demanded a member of the pro-Corinthia party.

"From our research and intel in America."

"This is impossible!" screamed another Council member. "You're defaming Secretary General Corinthia!

And it's all coming from a sinking nation that is no longer a world power."

"Corinthia is Israel's friend!" exclaimed another. "Where was America during the war?"

"America was crippled by terror attacks," Steve added. "We all know that. And we also know that there is no evidence that Corinthia did anything to help Israel during the war."

One of the Council members stood up in anger. "Well, if it was not him, then who?!"

"Hashem!…God!" exclaimed Rabbi Ben Shalom. "I am an IDF chaplain. I was there on the front lines. I saw it with my own eyes. Earthquakes, cloud bursts, thunder storms, hail stones, sand storms. And every one of them helped us and harmed our enemies. You, you say it's a coincidence, but I say it is Hashem! Corinthia? He was nowhere!"

"Shut up, old man!" shouted another council member.

Steve pounded his gavel twice. "That was uncalled for; we will debate civilly. Thank you, Rabbi, for your words. Commander Stein, you still have the floor; please continue."

"Thank you, General. So, now you've all seen evidence of the U.N. atrocities, and evidence that Corinthia had foreknowledge of them and may have even ordered them personally."

"But I repeat, Corinthia is our ally and friend," said another member. "He's one of the most powerful men in the world. He is good for Israel!"

"Let's accept for argument's sake that Corinthia is good for Israel," David replied. "If Adolf Hitler didn't kill us, but offered to help us, would we have accepted his help?"

"Comparing Anno Corinthia to Adolf Hitler! Despicable, Stein!" shouted a member.

"Whether you like it or not, this report on Anno Corinthia is accurate. All of you now have the facts, which speak for themselves."

With the room at a boiling point, Steve looked around the table at each man. "Alright everyone, please try to stay calm. Does anyone have anything to add?" The room fell silent. "Alright, it's time for an informal show of hands. Whoever is for the treaty, raise your hand." Hands went up for all four members of the pro-Corinthia party. "Who is against it?" Steve raised his own hand, followed by David and Rabbi Cohen.

"And what say you, Rabbi Ben Shalom?"

The rabbi, nearing 90, was silent for a moment. "I have not made up my mind."

"Does that mean you're abstaining?"

"General, I will make my decision tomorrow."

"Rabbi, if you don't decide now, that's an abstention. That means the initial vote is 4-3 in favor of the treaty."

The rabbi closed his eyes and his lips began to move in prayer while the rest of the council was quiet. He opened his eyes. "I want there to be peace, but I believe there can never be peace with a man like Corinthia. Only war. Only bloodshed. Only tears. Only death." The rabbi looked intently at each of his fellow Council members. "I vote 'no.'"

"You senile old man!" shouted a member. "Who gives you the right to deadlock this Council?! This is criminal!"

"Calm down," Steve said. "This is only an informal vote. If you think the rabbi is wrong, convince him with facts and logic, not screaming and yelling. If this behavior continues, I will have you ejected from the deliberations of this council. Am I clear?"

"Yes, my apologies."

"Thank you. We will all meet here tomorrow, same time, same rules, for a final vote on the treaty with the U.N." Steve pounded his gavel. "This meeting is adjourned."

The debate over the treaty and the outburst directed at him weighed heavily on Rabbi Ben Shalom as he trudged toward his home just a few blocks away. As the rabbi quickened his pace, he placed his hand over his chest as his heart beat faster and faster. Approaching his house, he began gasping for breath. Looking up toward the sky, the rabbi had a vision of the fall and destruction of Israel, the terrorizing of the Jewish people and the presence of evil encompassing the world. He cried out, "Messiah! Please come help us! God save Israel!" He stumbled before collapsing to the ground.

Quoting Scripture, he whispered, "Come, let us destroy them as a nation, so that Israel's name is remembered no more. Surely the Sovereign Lord does nothing without revealing it to his servants, the prophets."

Then, the sadness in his spirit started to leave as a smile crossed his face. "This is the covenant I will make with the people of Israel after that time," he recited. "I will put my law in their minds and write it on their hearts. I will be their God, and they will be my people."

Hearing her husband's voice, Emily, the Rabbi's wife, ran outside. Finding her husband's body sprawled across the front walk, she sat down and cradled her husband's head in her arms.

"Emmy, my sweet Ishah, the Messiah is coming, the Messiah is coming."

The rabbi held his wife's hand and looked into her eyes. "Ani ohev otah."

"Ani ohevet ot'h'a."

Emily sobbed as her husband's eyes turned lifeless.

❧

The rabbi's death pared the Council of Eight's numbers down to seven. The next morning, Steve Dobson brought the meeting to order. "As I'm sure you've all heard, Rabbi Ben Shalom died last night. May God rest his soul. I ask you all to observe a moment of silence in his memory."

The seven council members bowed their heads for a minute.

"I have called Rabbi Ben Shalom's wife and family to relay my deepest condolences and sympathy on behalf of this council. The funeral will be tomorrow and I will provide more information on the services after today's vote."

"General Dobson, are we still going to move ahead with the vote?" asked Rabbi Cohen.

"Yes, seven is enough for a quorum. All those against the treaty with the United Nations, raise your right hand."

David, Steve and Rabbi Cohen raised their hands.

"We now have three votes against the treaty. Whoever is in favor of the treaty, raise your hand now."

Three of the four members of the pro-Corinthia party raised their hands.

"I abstain," said the fourth member.

"Traitor!" yelled one of the three who voted 'yes.' "I demand an explanation for your change!"

"I don't like your attitude!" the fourth member shot back. "You killed Rabbi Ben Shalom by shouting at him. I abstain!"

"Are you sure you want to abstain?" asked Steve.

"I just said I abstain!"

"It looks like the Council is tied at 3-3," Steve announced.

"So what happens now?" asked the abstaining member.

"Under the rules governing this Council, the Prime Minister may vote to break the deadlock. I'll call him now and put him on speaker phone."

Steve called the prime minister's office and was put through to Aretz. "May I help you, General Dobson?"

"Sir, we are deadlocked. We're 3-3 on the treaty, with one abstention...and regrettably, one death."

"So I've heard...now you want me to break the deadlock, General?"

"Yes."

"And you want me to decide now?"

"That would be helpful. The council is awaiting your vote."

"Now isn't that wonderful, General? Because you people couldn't come to an agreement, it's all on me to decide for the nation. Do you realize what this means for me? Hmmm? You have now put me in the crosshairs of every religious fanatic in Israel for empowering their number-one villain!"

"If he's a villain, why vote for his treaty?"

"Because, General, Corinthia is NOT a villain! But your fanatical religious friends — evangelicals, messianics, and even Orthodox Jews – think he's the next Hitler."

"Shaul, if you wish to abstain, that's your right. If you do, we'll schedule another vote for tomorrow." Several seconds of silence passed as the council heard nothing from the Prime Minister.

"Alright! Alright! If you want me to vote, I'll vote! Anno Corinthia has been fighting terrorism and trying to unite the world from the moment he took power at the UN. Now this same man, the most powerful man in the world, wants to make a treaty with us. That's all I know and it's all I want to know. As Prime Minister, I vote in favor of Israel joining in treaty with the United Nations. That is my final word." The phone line went dead.

Steve sat down, deflated, and breathed a heavy sigh.

"So this is how it happens," he muttered, as if to himself. "Just as foretold."

David sat in stunned denial. "I cannot believe it."

David's disbelief turned quickly to indignation as he rose slowly from his chair. Clutching a copy of Corinthia's treaty, he shook it at his colleagues. "This vile document, this dictate of tyranny, is an abomination!"

David threw his copy of the treaty onto the table, his eyes flashing with white-hot anger. "You will rue the day you approved this treaty of death! You will look back on this day as a day of shame for Israel and the world. Here is what I think of your decision!" He tore his copy of the treaty in half and dropped it to the floor. "I will have nothing to do with this!" David slammed the door as he left the council chamber.

Dodging reporters who were waiting for news of the vote, David approached a taxi stand. He turned back toward the building that housed the council chamber. Looking up at the windows, he bellowed, "A treaty with Corinthia is a treaty with death!"

Turning around, he ran into two men wearing yarmulkas and sackcloth who were loudly preaching against the treaty. Both smiled at David and one of them nodded approvingly. "Who are those guys?" David asked one cabbie.

"Sir, they first came here last week. Some people say they're prophets."

"Have they been preaching against the treaty all week?"

"Yes and also against Corinthia. I gather you didn't sign the treaty, Mr. Stein. Thank you for taking a stand."

"How do you know my name?"

"Everyone in Israel knows David Stein. You're the hero of the war we just won."

David looked down at the ground before staring off into the distance, thinking of his men that were lost. "I'm no hero."

"Don't tell me you think it was Corinthia who was responsible for Israel's victory."

"No, never."

"Then it was you."

"No Sir, it was the elements."

"Mr. Stein, someone brought them all together. It was Hashem. It was God."

"Then your god is a hero. If it makes you happy to believe that, go right ahead..."

"So you really are an atheist, aren't you?"

"No, just agnostic."

"What's the difference? You won't admit there's a God?"

"No, I just don't know that there is a God."

"Do you want to know?" David didn't answer. "Well, you're going to find out soon enough."

"What do you mean?"

"It says in the Bible that two prophets will come to Jerusalem in the last days and preach on these streets for 3 ½ years. It also says they will proclaim and perform miracles."

"And if what they say comes to pass, that proves those two men are the two prophets?"

"Yes."

"Or it could just be a coincidence."

"So after all you've just seen, you still don't believe? Blessed are those who do not see and yet believe. The Bible also says you never know when you're in the presence of an angel....Do you need a ride home, Mr. Stein?"

"No, I can walk. I live right down the block from here, but thanks."

"God be with you, Mr. Stein." David departed. As he walked away, he twice turned around to see the cabbie smiling at him.

CHAPTER 16
THE PRIME MINISTER

As NEWS OF the decision to approve the treaty was broadcast throughout Israel that evening, most Israelis celebrated. However, the two prophets continued preaching on the streets of Jerusalem as they voiced their opposition to both the treaty and Corinthia.

From the balcony of his home, David could see the men on the busy sidewalk below thundering against the treaty, proclaiming it was not of God. Most people ignored them, but some people began heckling them in response.

A Corinthia supporter walked up to them and began to berate them savagely. "Look at them! The council just approved the Treaty and these imbeciles are still protesting it!" A large group surrounded the preachers and erupted in derisive, mocking laughter.

"Ridiculous fanatics!" yelled a man in the crowd. "Israel's had enough of people like you! God is dead. We're moving on!"

David had seen enough. He ran downstairs and pushed

open his front door. People stepped aside as he made his way over to the preachers. David heard his name being whispered through the crowd as he began to be recognized. "Leave these men alone. They have a right to say what they want. People have a right to free speech without being threatened. Now everybody go home."

The crowd slowly dispersed. David then faced the preachers. "If I were you guys, I'd go home, too."

The preachers were silent for a long moment before one of them responded assertively. "This is our home."

❧

While Israelis were overwhelmingly for Corinthia, they remained solidly against Prime Minister Aretz. Even when it was revealed that the PM had cast the deciding vote for the Treaty, they still despised him for leaving Israel unprepared for the war that had threatened their existence. Ironically, David was becoming the most popular man in Israel. Amid rising opposition to Aretz, the Knesset met and issued a vote of no-confidence in his government.

Shortly after the no-confidence vote, several Knesset leaders met with David privately at General Dobson's compound. "We have a proposition for you, Mr. Stein."

"What's on your mind?"

"You have become a tremendous asset to Israel. You are a great communicator and a natural leader." Pausing for a moment, the Knesset member leaned in closer. "So, David, would you consider running for prime minister of Israel?"

"What??"

"We need a strong and intelligent leader to deal with Anno Corinthia. And Aretz has shown himself to be neither."

David shook his head as he looked at each of the men intently. "You've got the wrong man," he protested. "I'm a military man, not a politician."

"David, some of Israel's best politicians were military heroes as well."

David looked down at the floor. "I'm not a hero."

"David, a true hero denies he's one. And besides, the people love you. If you run...you will win."

"But how can I run for PM if I'm not a sitting member of the Knesset?"

"We took the liberty of changing the law on that stipulation a while ago. Now that you have duel U.S.-Israeli citizenship, you can run without being an MK."

David looked around the room at the staring faces that seemed to have great confidence in him. He thought about this new call to mission and about Corinthia's menace to the world.

"So, David Stein, will you consider it? For the sake of Eretz Yisrael?"

David looked to Steve. "I recommend you do it. You can win, and yes, you can lead. We need you, Israel needs you...and the world needs you."

"I'll need time to think about it before I respond. If you'll excuse me, I need to discuss this with my team. Let's all meet here tomorrow at 8:00 am and I'll give you my answer." All who were in the room stood up and gave their ascent.

﹏

Since the War, David and the remnant of his SEAL team were living in a complex just west of General Dobson's compound. Each night, they would gather in Chad's apartment for dinner. That evening, David informed his men about the Knesset members' request that he run for Prime Minister.

Frank pulled David aside. "David, this may be the reason you were brought to Israel." The clicking of knives and forks stopped, along with the background conversations.

"Do it," said another SEAL.

"I'll drink to that," said another.

"Yeah!" another SEAL chimed in.

David looked across the table at Chad. "Gladiator, you've been silent. What say you?"

Chad quickly got up from his chair. "I second what everyone has said, but if we're right about Corinthia, we're going to have another war sooner or later. We're going to need you leading in battle."

David nodded in agreement. "Gladiator has a point."

"But David, you can do both."

"How so, Frank?"

"I'll tell you how so. What are you, anyway? You're guerrilla fighters. You move in, then you move out. You strike when and where nobody expects you. You are not always in the field. And if war comes, you will go out as a team and fight the enemy, right? David doesn't have to be with you every time. Steve runs the country's armed forces anyway. When and if David joins you in battle, Steve can run the country."

Flynn approached David and stood with him face to face. "Skippy, Aretz and his cronies… they're as useless as chocolate teapots! You're the best man for the job, mate! I know a leader when I see one. You were made for this." Flynn leaned in close and whispered in David's ear, "What do you think Sarah would want you to do, lad?"

David turned to the rest of his men. "Gentlemen, this is a tough call. And since all of you will be affected by my decision, it's yours to make as well as mine."

"David, are we going to vote?"

"Yes Gladiator, right now. All those in favor of my running for PM, say 'Ay.'"

"Ay!!!"

"All those against, say 'no.'"

The room was silent.

"Not one 'no'? Okay, the 'Ays' have it. I'll call General Dobson and inform him of my decision."

Steve, seeing David's number on his cell, anxiously picked up on the first ring. "David, have you made a decision?"

"Yes, I'm going to run."

"Great news…Mr. Prime Minister!"

After David hung up the phone, the men gave him a standing ovation. As he made the rounds shaking hands, David had his doubts about the task before him. The loss of his wife, his best friend, and the death of his men continued to weigh heavily upon him.

⤝

After the Knesset passed its 'no-confidence' vote against Prime Minister Aretz, the election campaign began. Replacing Aretz as the opposition candidate was Roni Gold, a longtime member of the Knesset and a close Aretz associate. Being identified with Aretz doomed her from the start. Running a simple campaign based on the need for Israel never to be as unprepared for war as it was before the Great War, David easily won the election.

His victory address was brief and simple:

"Israel and the world are now living in perilous times. Our victory in the Great War against Russia and her allies was magnificent, but the threat of war is not over. We need to rebuild our defenses and we need always to be ready for terrorist attacks and the unforeseen. I make two pledges to you tonight. First, as long as I am prime minister, Israel will never be unprepared. And second, as we will excel in preparedness for war, so will we excel in the arts of peace. Normal life will go on in Israel. Thank you for your confidence in me. I am humbled and will do my best to serve as your prime minister."

After David left the podium, his supporters lifted him off of the ground and began singing, "Duhveed, Melech Yisrael," meaning "David, King of Israel," but when David heard it, he shouted to the crowd:

"I'm not a king...but I will do my best!"

With that, the hall erupted in applause.

David went to his new office where he began receiving calls from leaders around the world. After several rounds of congratulations, David was getting tired. Frustrated, he turned to Steve. "Are we done now?"

"Just one more call, Mr. Prime Minister. We saved this one for last."

"Who is it?"

"Anno Corinthia."

"You've got to be kidding. I have to respond to *him*?"

"I'm afraid so, Mr. Prime Minister, protocol."

"Great," David murmured sarcastically. "Okay Steve, put him on."

David straightened his tie and posture before speaking with the U.N. leader. Corinthia's image appeared on the screen before them, strikingly charismatic and handsome, yet cold as stone. "Prime Minister Stein, congratulations on your victory tonight."

David glared at the screen for a few seconds before slowly and reluctantly responding, "Thank you, Mr. Secretary. I appreciate your call."

"Mr. Stein, I called to congratulate you tonight on your victory. I will let you do your…thing in Israel, to a degree." David's look grew intense. "But you will be watched. You will be working with Colonel Nigel Coles. He will be setting up my office in Jerusalem. You will meet with him each month to give him a report on how, ah… our people are progressing."

David grimaced, "They are not your people."

"Nor are they yours. You are an American. Stay put, do your job, and there will be no trouble."

"Are you threatening me?"

"Mr. Stein, you are the Prime Minister; you are not a king."

"And neither are you."

The two men stared at each other for an uncomfortable moment before Corinthia broke the silence. There was contempt in his voice, "Mr. Prime Minister, I hope you can do a better job protecting the State of Israel and its people, than you did with your family, your country, and your SEAL team." Corinthia smiled, "I wish you well." The screen went black as Corinthia cut the transmission.

David continued to stare at the screen; Steve put a hand on his shoulder. "I can feel the steam coming off of you."

"Yeah, I'm glad we didn't invite Corinthia to the celebration."

Dobson laughed. "Okay Mr. Prime Minister, let's get down to business."

&

In Babylon, Octavia heard the news of David's victory. "So, David Stein is the new Prime Minister of Israel," she chuckled. "His wife would be proud."

"I'm sure she would be," Corinthia said on the other end of the call in Rome.

"I have to admit; he is alluring. I'd love to...own him someday."

"Well, some day you will."

"But for now, he's untouchable; he's the Prime Minister of Israel," she sighed.

"Not for long…he's in for a surprise."

❧

Below the streets of Jerusalem, in a secluded basement apartment, Scott Miller and his rebel SEALs watched the news of David's victory. "So Stein is really prime minister. Unbelievable!"

"Looks that way, Scotty," said Tim O'Brien, one of the SEALs closest to Scott, as they stared at the TV.

"Of all the people in this crazy country to become prime minister, it had to be him. Good ole Skip…sonofabitch… always out for himself."

"He's got blood on his hands."

"You're damned right, Timmy! SEAL blood! Our blood, the blood of his brothers — now he's cashing in on it for power and fame! I told him he would get a lot of us killed! But he wouldn't listen! And the people elected that fool to be leader of their country?! Idiots! At least our passports will be ready soon, so we can finally go home. Yo, Tim, throw me another beer!"

Samantha entered the room. A short and sturdy woman of about thirty-five, she had been working as a housekeeper for the SEALs. "Scott, you're drinking too much," Samantha said as she started sweeping the floor.

"What are you Sam, my mother? My wife? Oh, that's

right. My mother died a decade ago and terrorists killed my wife! You're just another whore."

"Hey, come on Scotty, don't talk to Sam like that. She's been nice to us."

"Timmy, we pay her to be nice! She hangs around like a freakin' spider!"

Samantha blinked back tears.

"Scotty, don't make her cry!"

Scott got up out of his chair, knocking it over. "What? You're gonna stop me, Tim?"

"If you keep it up, yeah, I will! Leave her alone!"

Scott, realizing he was out of control, rubbed his head with both hands. "Tim, you're right...Samantha, I'm sorry; I'm just really drunk."

Scott's cell phone rang. He didn't recognize the number but answered it anyway. "Who the hell is this?!"

"Good evening, Mr. Miller."

Scott didn't recognize the voice. "I said, who is this!!?"

"That's not important; what is important is what I'm about to offer you."

"Is this a solicitation?"

"Yes, in a way."

Scott crushed his empty beer can and threw it against the wall. "Go ahead, pal. At this point...things can only get better."

"Very intuitive Mr. Miller, and that's how things will get if we work together. You see, you and I share a common enemy, an enemy who has gotten people we both care about killed. It takes a brave man, a smart man, a real leader to stand up to a deadly threat. Especially if it's from your…best friend."

"You must be talking about that bastard who just got elected."

"Exactly…David Stein. Mr. Miller, he will keep getting people killed if he's not stopped. As you have witnessed, this so-called hero got his own men killed. What do you think he'll do as Prime Minister?"

Both men were silent for a moment.

"I'll tell you what he'll do; he'll destroy Israel. We need a good man, a leader like you, a man who understands the havoc this careless fool will wreak."

Scott's hand went to his forehead, his bloodshot eyes looking around the room at his men. "Keep talking."

❧

The only sound at midnight in dark deserted Jerusalem was from the rain pounding on rooftops and streets. Scott chewed his tobacco in a covered doorway, waiting where the man on the phone instructed him to meet his contact.

A dark figure in a long trench coat emerged out of the shadows. The orange glow from a cigarillo partially revealed a man's face with a deep scar on the left cheek. "Miller."

Scott could barely see the man.

"Here's the deal. Our target dines regularly at Yashirs. Much of the time he has very little security, if any. It's the perfect place."

"It's the perfect place for what?" The man smiled at Scott. "You want me to take him out?"

"I want you to kill him."

"Look, I don't want the guy around. I don't want him leading Israel…but kill him?"

The man got closer. "Yeah, kill him. If you don't — thousands, maybe millions of people could die. People you care about will die, just as people you love have already died. You kill him, we both win, the world wins.

"Then, you get a well-deserved position as a leader in this new world." The man chuckled. "But, if you don't kill him — we will, and people you love, will die."

Scott puffed his chest and moved toward the stranger.

"Mr. Miller, before you get any ideas, think about it." Glaring at the man, Scott spat his chew into the small space between them. "Do it Miller. I know you have the tools to get the job done. We'll be watching, and we look forward to working with you on a more…permanent basis in the future."

Scott watched the man disappear into the rainy darkness. Standing alone, he could not believe he was considering what once would have been unthinkable.

Standing in the Prime Minister's official residence and celebrating his victory with Steve and the SEAL team, David pulled Steve aside. "I want to get in touch with Rachel Silver as soon as possible."

"David, she's working the night shift at the hospital. She said working helps keep her mind off of her father's death."

"She works at Hadassah?"

"That's right."

"I'll head over to the hospital now and talk with her. I wanted to go there anyway and visit my men who are still recovering from their battlefield injuries."

"That's a good idea."

⁖

Arriving at Hadassah, David told his two guards to wait in the car before he entered the hospital. He was immediately recognized as he approached the front desk.

The receptionist smiled broadly and straightened her posture while smoothing out her scrubs. "Mr. Prime Minister! Congratulations on your victory! How may I help you?"

"I'll be visiting my men in ICU, then I'd like to have a word with Ms. Rachel Silver."

"Of course, Mr. Prime Minister. Your men are all in unit 12, straight down the main corridor on the right."

"Thank you."

The typical hospital odors grew stronger as David neared the ICU. As the glass doors to the unit slid open, David stopped for a moment and took a heavy breath while scanning the room. Some of his men were conscious and in stable condition while others remained in comas. He went from bed to bed, assuring them that they and their families would be taken care of. In the corner of the room, David saw the youngest of the SEAL team, Charlie Johnson. He moved slowly across the room; Charlie's head was turned away as he looked out the window with a bedpan at his side.

David tapped Charlie on the shoulder. Tears streamed down Charlie's face; he began to cry. "Skip, I got no legs."

᠅

After witnessing the ravages of war, David pulled himself together while he made his way back to the reception desk.

"Is Rachel available now?"

"Mr. Prime Minister, please come back here into the office."

David was ushered into a room behind the reception desk where he found Rachel standing in her green scrubs with several other staff members.

"Mr. Prime Minister, what a nice surprise!" Rachel smiled across the room at David.

"Hi Rachel, sorry to come over unannounced, but I really needed to talk to you."

"I'm on my break, so your timing is perfect. What can I do for you?"

"I'd like you to come work for me as my assistant."

Rachel's eyes opened wide with surprise. "Oh my gosh! This is such an honor! But who would take my place here at the hospital?"

"Arrangements have just been made for your immediate

replacement. When you're prime minister, getting some things done takes only a simple phone call."

Rachel turned to Miriam, her supervisor.

"Rachel, we will really miss you, but if I were you, I'd say yes! Any day!"

Rachel looked at a beaming Miriam, and then back at David. When she nodded affirmatively, her coworkers erupted in applause.

"Rachel, tomorrow we will have dinner and discuss your new position. Please meet me at Yashir's, eight o'clock."

"Thank you, Mr. Stein."

David detected some doubt in her voice about accepting the position so suddenly. "Rachel, don't worry; you'll do great. See you tomorrow."

≪

With nervous anticipation, a somber Scott stared out the window into the twilight from his shared flat on the low-rent side of Jerusalem.

"Scott, you gonna shoot some pool with us tonight? Scott?"

"No Timmy, not pool... you guys have a good time."

After his fellow SEALs left, Scott locked the door behind them and began gathering his "tools" for the night's mission. His mind raced as he suited up. He remembered the best of times with David, the kind of moments only blood brothers can share.

Then he remembered how the July 4th celebration

turned into devastation because of David's faulty security plan. He thought about the slaughter of brother SEALs, the slaughter he warned David about, the slaughter that didn't have to happen, caused by a man he once called a brother.

Scott's face reddened, going from somber to angry. "He's a brother no more – he's a murderer."

Scott wore the sort of casual military attire that could be purchased at any Army/Navy store. He easily blended into the crowds in Jerusalem who were out for a late dinner, as he carried a long duffel bag. Unnoticed, Scott entered a seven-story building directly across the street from Yashir's restaurant. Walking up the access stairs at the rear of the building, he scoped several possible escape routes in case things got hairy.

Finally approaching the door to the roof, he turned the knob and found it was locked. Reaching into the duffel bag, he took out his old picking set, the same set he and David used to access rooftops in Queens when they were teenagers. Scott almost laughed as he recalled how the picks came in handy, especially when they needed a place to make-out with neighborhood girls.

He had the lock open in less than ten seconds. Walking to the edge of the roof, he looked down at the yellow and red neon lights of the restaurant. Scott had three semi-automatic pistols, one in each ankle holster, and the third in a shoulder holster. He set up a tripod and attached the M24 rife with silencer and night scope...and waited.

Pressing in a little chew transferred the butterflies in

his stomach to the corners of his mouth. He tried to focus and relax. Using the scope, he scanned the scene on the street. It was nearly ten o'clock and the crowds were starting to thin out. A parked vehicle caught his attention.

"Well imagine that," he thought to himself. "Two heroes just sitting in their car across from Yashir's. Hmm.... looks like my new friend there with one of his goons. Must be checking up on me..." Scott chuckled to himself, "If only they knew where I was."

∽

"So Rachel, did I explain enough about the position so that you feel comfortable?"

"Of course, Mr. Prime Minister."

David raised his eyebrows. "Please call me 'David.' I never liked titles."

"By the way, ah, David, I can be much more than an executive assistant. I was also trained by the Israeli military in special weapons and self-defense. My father wanted to make sure that I could take care of myself." She leaned in closer to David. "So don't let this girlish appearance fool you."

As they smiled at each other in the candlelight, David felt like he was sitting across from Sarah twenty years ago. "I'm sure Calev helped you to become quite capable, but you now have the whole nation of Israel to protect you." Reaching toward Rachel in a fatherly manner, he touched her hand.

Rachel's expression turned somber. "David, have

you had a chance to see the Holocaust Memorial...Yad Vashem?"

"No, but it's something I've been meaning to do. I almost went the other day after visiting the military cemetery; it's practically next door on Megadim Street."

"I'd be glad to go with you whenever you have time."

"I think I'll take you up on that. Now, let's get you home. We have a lot of work ahead of us tomorrow."

"Come on, come on; let's get this over with." Scott murmured as he looked through his scope at the front door of Yashir's.

He saw David and Rachel coming out onto the sidewalk; they stopped to chat. As he looked into David's face, he could hear his lifelong friend's voice in his head. He thought of the many successful missions they fought side by side.

Scott tried to remember why he accepted this assignment, but he could not forget the love for his brother. With David's head in the crosshairs of the rifle scope, the memories kept coming...playing stickball in Queens, driving to Shea Stadium in David's father's 1969 red Mustang convertible...

Scott looked to the sky. "God help me; I can't do it."

Readjusting the scope, he aimed the rifle at the two men in the car and fired.

Silent sniper shots pierced the car window, striking the man in the passenger seat, instantly killing him.

David heard the glass breaking and pulled Rachel to the ground. "Get down! That's gunfire!"

The driver looked over at his partner and saw the hole in his head. Before he realized what had happened, Scott put a bullet through his head as well. Seeing David and Rachel take cover, people on the street scattered. David slowly rose to his feet and told Rachel to stay down. He took a few steps toward the curb to check the scene. Out of the alley adjacent to the restaurant, a man dressed in black emerged. The man grabbed David around the neck and stuck a gun into his ribcage. "Don't move."

David froze. Rachel, still on the ground, saw her opening. She kicked the feet out from underneath the assailant, knocking him flat on his back. The gun fired, flew out of his hand, and slid across the sidewalk. David ran to grab the gun and quickly put it to the man's head. "Who are you?! Who's behind this?!!"

The man was silent for a moment. "You have great friends David, but I'm not one of them. Sooner or later, we'll get you!"

The gun still against his head, the assailant grabbed David's hand, putting pressure on David's trigger finger. A single bullet tore through the man's brain.

Knocking himself against the walls, Scott raced down the stairwell. Avoiding the lobby of the building, he was able to slip away into a back alley.

On the sidewalk, David called his two personal guards who were parked around the corner, telling them to investigate the crime scene and to get an I.D. on the deceased. "I want to know where those shots came from."

"Boss, it looks like they came from an elevated position. Probably up there."

The guard pointed across the street. David looked around at the building before turning to Rachel. "Rachel, you should…" David was about to say "go home," then he thought of how Rachel just saved his life. "Forget it; come with me."

David, Rachel, and the two guards entered the building, looking for the shooter's perch. They made their way up to the rooftop where they found the lock had apparently been picked.

David stared closely at the lock for a moment before moving on. The guards noticed several empty shell casings on the roof near the parapet wall.

"See, it's the perfect spot." The senior guard pointed over the side of the building. David looked down at the street and could see the bullet holes through the car windshield.

"Boss, I'm guessing you were the original target but the shooter decided to take out those two thugs instead. Or the perp was a real bad shot and missed you."

The police arrived on the street below and began to gather evidence.

"Mr. Prime Minister, see, over here, looks like a spot of tobacco, some kind of dip."

The guard slipped on a latex glove and pressed his

fingertip into the wet spot of tobacco, putting it to his nose. "Smells like fresh chew."

"Thanks, I'm going to check the stairs; you three stay here."

"Okay Boss."

David walked down from the roof in the darkened stairwell, moving his Maglite side to side. The light hit a small round object, a tobacco canister. He turned it over and looked at the label, 'Skoal.' David nodded before cracking a smile.

Putting the canister in his pocket before heading back to the roof, he heard one of his guards call out. "Hey Boss, find anything in the stairwell?"

David paused for a moment. "No...nothing."

∽

Scott burst into the apartment where he and his SEALs were staying. "Pack up! We gotta get out of here!"

"What are you talking about?" asked one of the men.

"What I'm talking about is, we are about to be hunted."

"Hunted....for what?"

"The attempted assassination of the Prime Minister."

"You tried to assassinate David?"

"No, but I probably should have. I gave him a better break then he gave our men, but I took out the two goons who were going to kill me if I didn't kill him."

"Holy smoke! What have you gotten into!?"

"I was hired by a mercenary group who wanted the creep dead. I was going to rid the world of our albatross......but, even though I hate his guts.…I couldn't do it. David is still a brother. And I'm sure my brother and those goons will be hunting down the 'unknown assassin.' So boys, we are going to be hunted by two groups of extremely dangerous people who want me, and probably all of you, dead."

"Who hired you?"

"It was just some low-level slime ball, probably linked to Corinthia in some way. You got to figure that megalomaniac wants David gone even more than I did."

"But Scott…"

"What?"

"You didn't kill him… You saved him."

Scott nodded his head and stared off into space for a few seconds.

"Alright guys, let's get the hell out of here."

≈

Just past dawn, the sun rose on the ornate building in Rome where Anno Corinthia's U.N. office was located. There was no usual pattern in Corinthia's personal habits as he did not eat or sleep much, and demanded the same of his subordinates. The sacrifice in following him was enormous, as were the rewards. It was the extremes of sacrifice and seduction that made people want to follow and serve him.

Corinthia spoke into the intercom on his desk. "Wodan, come give me the good word on last night's mission."

Moments later Marcus stepped into the office. "Come Marcus, let's break out the finest wine. We must celebrate the death of David and the impending death of his assassin, Scott Miller. You see how my methods work, Marcus? From friends to enemies, from enemies.....to killers. That is one relationship that evolved beautifully."

Corinthia happily walked to the wet bar on the far side of his palatial office.

As Corinthia poured the wine, Marcus struggled for the right words. "Secretary General, this is no time for celebration, not yet."

Corinthia looked up, glaring at Marcus. "What are you saying? Mr. Miller did not complete his task?"

"Unfortunately, he did not kill David but he killed two of our men, while David and the girl eliminated a third one."

Corinthia grabbed the wine bottle and smashed it on the bar. Blood-red wine sprayed onto his face and shirt. "Anyone, and I do mean anyone..." He glared at Marcus, "...who does not complete my assignment, pays the ultimate price!! I want this to be done right. Give this assignment to Nigel."

"But Nigel failed to kill David in the desert at Petra."

"Marcus, you should know..." Corinthia snickered.

"Know what?"

"...that I love giving people a second chance."

CHAPTER 17
REUNION

THE MORNING AFTER the assassination attempt, David met with Steve Dobson. "Steve, let's bury this sniper incident at Yashir's last night; I don't want any of it to get out in the press."

"I'll take care of it. How's Rachel doing?"

"You should be asking how I am. If not for her I'd be dead. Calev trained her well. Maybe she should join my SEAL team."

"So, do you think Corinthia was behind this attack?"

"I don't know, Steve, but if we're right about Corinthia, he will eventually come after us. We will be at war with him at some point."

"That's very likely."

"He will break the Treaty. And then, Israel will need all the people we can get."

"David, I'm glad you're saying 'we.' It sounds like you're bonding with your new countrymen."

"I am. Now, I would like the Knesset to consider and

pass a resolution. It is that the Israeli government from now on will encourage immigration to Israel, but not just Jews."

"You're not proposing changing the citizenship laws, are you?"

"Of course not. But we need a lot more people. I'm saying we should make it easier for any supporter of Israel, subject to vetting, to get permanent residency."

"Alright David, let me submit your proposal to the Speaker of the Knesset and get back to you."

⤳

Robby was just about to press 270 over his head for the fifth rep when the phone rang upstairs. "Can you get that, Dad?!!" Robby's voice strained to get the words out.

The sound of the broom handle thumped from above. "Robbaht! It's your friend David!!"

Robby racked the barbell and reached for the same black rotary phone that had been sitting in the wood-paneled basement for as long as he could remember. The cord attached to the receiver was tangled; the phone fell to the floor. After untangling the cord, Robby finally put the receiver to his ear. "Your dad never changes; he still thinks I'm working at White Castle on Rockaway Boulevard."

"David? Mr. Prime Minister, great to hear from you! We've been watching the events in Israel. I got a question for you, man. How does a New York City cop become a world leader?"

"Robby, I wish I knew. You guys still meeting at Tony's?"

"Oh yeah. The place had no power after a cyberattack on the grid but Tony paid Mike to hook up a generator, so we're back!"

"That's great! I really miss Tony's; it's the best bar in Queens."

"Yeah, despite world war, some things never change! Dave, hold on. Mike's right outside rewiring our electric panel."

Robby threw open the Bilco door. "Yo, Iron Mike, guess who's on the phone? King David! Here, talk to His Highness."

There was a scratchy sound as Robby handed the phone base and receiver to Mike.

"Hey man! How's it going, Mike?!"

"David Stein! My favorite prime minister! What an insane life you have!"

"You don't know the half of it. Mike, can you put Robby on the cordless? I want to talk to both of you together."

"Sure, hold on…" Robby pulled out the telescopic antenna.

"Okay guys, I'll make this quick. How would you two and the rest of the crew like to come to Israel and work for me? The legislature is passing a resolution welcoming everyone. And 'everyone' includes you guys."

"Wow, it's something to think about, but if we go, you're paying for the tickets, bro!" said Robby with a laugh.

"You got it, Robby. What do you think, Mike?"

"Uh, David, I think you forgot something."

"What did I forget?"

"I'm a married man, so I have to ask Lorraine. And Lorraine is helping Mel with Rebecca, plus Lorraine still has a few more follow-up treatments at Sloan. If I go to Israel, where does that leave my wife?"

"Talk to Mel; I'm sure you can work something out."

"Okay, we'll have a meeting at Tony's tonight."

"That's great Mike, let me know what happens."

Mel looked around at all of the friendly faces in Tony's Grille. "Alright, is everybody here?"

"I think so, Pops."

"Thanks, Robby. Tony, get me a beer. On second thought, bring a round for all the guys."

"So Mel, tell us what you think."

"About moving to Israel?"

"Yeah Pops."

"Well, Israel should be safe and prosperous for a while. Without a pretext, Corinthia will not invade so soon after signing the treaty. You guys will be working directly for David. He needs people around him he can trust. Leaving your families and acclimating to another country can be awkward, but I think you'll do just fine."

"Pops, will you be going, too?"

"Nah Carl, I can't."

"Why not?"

"Business. I've got to stay here. Plus, Rebecca's happy with her new school; I can't uproot her again."

"But what about me? I don't think Lorraine can go right now. She's helping you with Becca. And if she can't go, how can I leave her like that?"

"Mike, if Lorraine wants to go to Israel like you do, then both of you should go. She's been great with Becca, but I'm one step ahead of you. I have a niece in mind who can fill in."

"Ok Pops, if Lorraine doesn't want to go to Israel, I'm not going. But if she does, I can go first and let Lorraine get your niece up to speed with Rebecca before she joins me."

"Thanks Mike; sounds like a plan."

Entering their house in Ozone Park, Mike found Lorraine curled up on the couch nearly asleep. He kissed the top of Lorraine's head as she stretched like a cat. The house was dark except for the glow of the TV. Lorraine looked up at Mike, giving him a sleepy-eyed smile. "Hi honey. Did you have a good time at Tony's?" She slowly rose to a sitting position.

"Yeah, it's always good to see the crew," he said after a long pause. "Those guys are a bunch of clowns."

"Is everything okay?"

"Um, there's something I wanted to talk about." Mike sat on the couch and turned to face Lorraine, taking her hands in his.

Lorraine smiled suggestively. "Yeah?"

"Oh no, I'm not looking for that...yet," Mike laughed.

"I got a call from David. He invited the guys, including you and me, to come to Israel and work for him."

Mike saw Lorraine's big green eyes open wide in the dim light. "I know it sounds crazy, but the more I think about it, the more it kinda makes sense. A new life, a new place, a new beginning, and working for a lifelong buddy. It could be the best of all worlds."

Lorraine stared blankly at the TV. "I don't know Mike; our families are here. And after my battle with cancer, I'm afraid of everything. The Middle East scares me. I don't want to die."

"Honey, we'll be safe living in Israel. Remember, David is the Prime Minister. He can set us up in one of the safest homes available. Sure, there are no guarantees in life, but I think we'll be safer over there. We're probably more likely to be killed by a criminal in New York than a terrorist in Israel."

Lorraine exhaled heavily. "Look, if you really feel like you're being called to work with David, I'm okay with moving. I don't want you to be always wondering 'what if.' For me, I don't think I can leave for a few months; I'm not finished with my treatments."

"I know, and if the doctors thought there was even the slightest chance of your cancer coming back, there's no way we'd leave. But I feel I need to do this; we need to do this. If it doesn't work out, I can get my old job back."

Lorraine squeezed Mike's left hand before pinching his wedding ring as hard as she could; the gold wouldn't give.

"I love you, Michael."

"I love you, too."

❧

That night, Mel called David with the news that his lifelong friends were coming to Israel to be a part of his personal security team. "Pop, that's great, but I wish you were coming, too."

"Me, too, son, but I've got a job to do. At least with Robby, Mike, Carl and Johnny, you'll have people who will have your back each day…literally."

"Yeah, I can't wait to see those guys."

"That's great, son; you'll have everyone with you."

David's voice faltered. "Everyone but the one I want the most. I miss Sarah so much; I feel empty. I have to go."

Mel gazed at Sarah's college yearbook picture on the mantel in his living room as he choked back tears.

❧

Revived by the thought of old friends rejoining him, David thought of Sarah's old friend, the former First Lady and widow of President Daniel Thompson.

He called out to the adjoining office, "Rachel, could you get me Katy Thompson's contact information?"

"Sure, Mr. Prime Minister."

"Please, call me 'David.'"

Rachel appeared in the doorway. "Yes David, Mr. Prime Minister," she said with a smile.

"By the way Rachel, let's keep that incident at Yashir's between us."

"Sir, it never happened."

"Good. And by the way, thank you for saving my life."

❧

Following her husband's death after the Liberty Island attack, and her recovery from life-threatening injuries sustained that day, Katy Thompson withdrew to her home in McLean, Virginia. While she continued to receive a steady stream of old acquaintances and friends, the death of her husband and best friend remained devastating.

Returning from a drive to Old Town Alexandria, she heard her cell ring. "Hello?"

"Katy?"

"Yes, speaking."

"It's David."

"David! What a splendid surprise. And, congratulations, Mr. Prime Minister!"

"Thank you, Katy."

"Sarah would have been so proud….and Dan, too."

"You're too kind."

"No, David, not kind enough. It was my turn to call you, but…it's been rough."

"I understand. How are you feeling?"

"I'm doing well; I still have some aches and pains but my knees are pretty much back to normal."

"That's great Katy. By the way, have you heard the news from Israel?"

"About?"

"The Knesset passed a resolution opening Israel to anyone of good character who wants to live here."

"That's very cool."

"Katy, I would love for you to come."

"Oh, David...."

"If you wish to stay in Washington, I understand..."

"Oh, no, to the contrary. I would love to consider the offer. I would have to book a flight out of Dulles."

"I insist you fly in on a secure private plane."

Following a long pause, Katy responded. "Well, if the prime minister insists, what's a lady to do?"

"Great, I'll have a plane prepared when you're ready."

"David, I've missed you."

"I...I have missed you too, Katy."

David was just finishing up for the day when he sensed someone standing in the doorway. The green glow of hospital scrubs entered his peripheral vision. He looked up from his desk to see Rachel tentatively smiling at him from across the office. On her first day, he told her wearing scrubs in the office was fine as long as she was comfortable. He hoped that Rebecca would grow up to be like Rachel, a smart and capable woman. "Excuse me, Mr. David, just wanted to see if you need anything before I leave."

He smiled as he shook his head in mock exasperation. "As I told you, young lady, just 'David' will suffice, although 'Mister David' has a nice Alabama ring to it. But, no, thank you, I think you've done everything I needed for today."

"Okay, in that case I'll see you tomorrow morning."

He stood up as Rachel started to leave. "Hey, Rachel, is your offer to accompany me to Yad Vashem still good?"

"Of course. When do you want to go?"

"Is ten minutes too soon?"

"Not at all. Yad Vashem just closed for the day, but I think they'll bend the rules for you."

∽

David and Rachel were sitting in the backseat of an armored government SUV as it made the turn onto Ha-Zikaron Street. An identical decoy vehicle followed close behind with two motorcycle officers trailing the second vehicle. David stared out the window as they traveled up the long narrow road lined with tall cypress trees. "Rachel, I presume there's some archive that lists all of the people we know of who died in the Holocaust?"

"Well, David, there's a room here known as 'The Hall of Names' that holds a large list of Jews who were killed by the Nazis. Sadly, all six million may never be included. I think the database is close to five million names but after all of this time, it probably won't grow much more. Would you like to start by looking at the names?"

"Okay, sure."

David pressed a button; the divider separating the front seat from the passenger area slid open. Gideon, the driver, kept his eyes on the road.

The security officer in the passenger seat looked expectantly at David.

"Moshe, can we get access to the 'Hall of Names?'"

"Yes, Sir. The advance team is checking to make sure the building is secure. We can bypass the visitors' center and go directly into the Holocaust History Museum. There's a long corridor connecting the various rooms that lead to the Hall of Names. It will just be another minute."

David's car was waved through the gate leading to Yad Vashem's hilltop campus on Mount Herzl. They pulled up to a concrete building with large windows and a flat roof. The walls were pitched slightly outward, giving the building a very solid and stable appearance. Two of the bollards that protected the building from vehicles had been removed, and guards stood on either side of the opening. The small motorcade drove through the gap and continued to the rear of the building.

They stopped near a wide elevated walkway leading to the entrance of a long and narrow A-frame structure jutting out near the top of the hillside. Moshe and Gideon stepped out of the vehicle and opened the doors for Rachel and David.

"Sir, you can use the ramp to get directly into the museum. The guards will keep their distance unless you request otherwise."

"That's perfect. Thank you, Moshe."

"My pleasure, sir."

As David paused to take in the dramatic distant views in all directions, he experienced a feeling of dread over what he might see while inside. But with it came a realization that he was part of a people who overcame the worst tragedy in history, returned to their homeland after 20 centuries, and made its deserts bloom again.

"Beautiful, isn't it?"

He turned to look at Rachel. Her light green scrubs flapping in the breeze reminded David of Lady Liberty. "Yes, very beautiful. Shall we?"

He pointed toward the walkway. As soon as they reached the entrance, a uniformed security guard opened the door from inside. David returned the guard's salute as they passed. "Rachel, I assume you know your way around."

"I do...I've been here many times."

Inside, the concrete A-frame continued for several hundred feet, coming out on the other side of the hill where it widened into a large lookout area with spectacular views to the north. Skylights ran along much of the ridge, giving the corridor a feeling of openness. They couldn't walk straight to the Hall of Names. The museum was designed so that visitors would flow from one exhibit room to another on alternating sides of the corridor as they worked their way north.

David was shaken by some of the more disturbing exhibits as Rachel led him from room to room. "The Hall of Names is up there on the right," she said, pointing to the wide opening off the main corridor.

As David entered the Hall, he was overwhelmed as he tried to take in the surroundings. They crossed a small bridge leading to a circular viewing balcony at the center of the round room. The balcony was surrounded by clear glass railings and stood a few feet off the floor. A huge cone, its narrow end near the ceiling, hung directly above the balcony. The wide end of the cone was about two feet above David's head.

The inside of the cone was covered by hundreds of photos of Holocaust victims. Row after row, the faces of men, women and children stared down upon David and Rachel. Through the big hole in the center of the balcony, the same faces were reflected up from the water that filled a cone set into the floor. The curved wall of the room, about eight feet from the balcony, was lined with shelves that held small black boxes, similar to what once were used to hold VCR tapes.

David tried to speak after collecting his thoughts. "Rachel, what's in the black boxes with the white Hebrew letters? There must be thousands of them, maybe millions."

"Those are books containing the yizkor files."

David looked at her blankly. "Sorry David, I'd love to teach you Hebrew some time. Victims of the Shoah…"

He cut her off. "Wait, what does 'Shoah' mean?"

"Literally, Shoah means destruction. In the 1940's, many Jews began to refer to the Holocaust as 'the Shoah.'"

"And the yizkor files…?"

"Yizkor means 'remember.' Each book is a memorial to a victim of the Shoah. The files in the books include whatever could be gathered on each person. Often it's only a Page of Testimony."

"Testimony? As in trial?"

"The Pages of Testimony were created by people here at Yad Vashem. They wanted a standard form on which those who knew a victim could record basic information about the person. The forms might include date of birth, hometown, relatives, small photos, place of death, etc."

"It's a lot to take in. Now I know why my father-in-law wanted me to see this." David gripped the railing with both hands.

Rachel put a hand on his back as they stared at the millions of Hebrew names surrounding them.

"My paternal grandparents, the Silvers, were lucky. Their English friends helped them stow away on a boat to London in 1937. They stayed in England for eleven years before moving to Israel."

"My parents didn't talk to me about the Holocaust. I think they were waiting for the right time."

"So it never came up?"

"I always suspected that my dad's parents didn't make it. My own parents were killed right before I turned 18."

"Oh David, I'm so sorry." Rachel squeezed his shoulder.

"My mother's parents made it out of Germany but they died when I was a child. Hey, would it be possible to see if there's a file on my father's parents?"

"Yes, the records are now computerized so we don't have to physically check the files. Come…I'll show you."

Rachel led David into a large alcove adjacent to the round room. Several computer terminals were set up on a long table. "Do you know your grandparents' names?" She pulled out a chair and sat down in front of a keyboard.

"Harold and Rivka Stein."

Rachel's fingers moved quickly as she typed. David's

heart started to beat faster as he stared at the monitor from above her shoulder. A list of names filled the screen from top to bottom. Rachel began to scroll down, clicking on some of the names as she went.

On the third page, she stopped. "David, I think I found them." She pointed to a line near the bottom of the screen. "Do you want to sit here and click on this link? I can step out for a moment if you want to read it alone."

David felt his palms getting clammy. "Thank you but I think I'll feel better if you do it."

After a few clicks of the mouse, a man and woman looked back at them from separate black & white photos. David gasped and covered his mouth with his hand. The photos were attached to the left side of a form with several lines and a large header written in Hebrew. The lines were numbered on the right.

"Does he look as much like me as I think?"

"No question, David. Except your eyes are more like hers. Looks like they might be wearing restaurant aprons."

"My parents owned a deli in New York; maybe it ran in the family. What's written on that form?"

"Harold Jonathan Stein. Born in Frankfurt, November 10, 1908. Died April 17, 1944 at Majdanek concentration camp. Rivka Berman Stein. Born in Baden-Baden August 6, 1911. Died April 23, 1944 at Majdanek concentration camp. Harold and Rivka were married December 31, 1933. They were survived by a son, Arthur Adam Stein and Harold's two sisters, Esther and Rhea Stein."

"I remember my father talking about being raised by

his two aunts." Rachel looked back at David. His eyes were moist as he stared at the screen. He spoke carefully so his voice wouldn't crack. "It's a lot to process but it's probably good to finally know."

"That's basically everything on the Page of Testimony. It was a friend of Esther who provided the information."

"Thank you, Rachel. You've been a great help."

"We can dig further if you want."

"I'll think about it. But right now I need to leave."

"Do you have plans?"

"I'd like to see the Temple."

∽

David's discreet motorcade headed east, passing close to the Knesset on the way to the Old City. "Rachel, I don't mind stopping if you have to get home before I go on to the Temple."

"No, please, I'm looking forward to this."

"Are you sure?"

She nodded. "I still haven't seen the new Temple. I was supposed to attend the ribbon-cutting ceremony with my father."

David put a hand on Rachel's forearm. When Calev died, Rachel was not much older than David when his parents were killed. "Your father was a great man; it was an honor just to meet him."

"If only he had lived long enough to see the Temple completed…speaking of which, we should be there soon if your driver uses the Dung Gate to enter the old city."

David looked at her. "That's really what it's called? As in camel *dung*?"

"Well, in Hebrew the gate is called Sha'ar Ha'ashpot. Some believe it's the same gate that was used to bring ash from the Temple to the rubbish dump in the Hinnom Valley."

Dozens of soldiers lined either side of the road as the motorcade approached a nearly square opening in the stone wall surrounding East Jerusalem. Many of the soldiers waved to David's SUV. David waved back, thinking it was possible that he might have served with some of them in battle. After passing through the gate, David was struck by what he saw up ahead on the right. A massive retaining wall made of smooth cut-stone, standing at least thirty feet high, formed a giant rectangle the size of a city block. The wall appeared to be topped with a rampart behind embrasures. "Rachel, is that the Temple or a fortress?"

"It's both in some ways. It was designed to resemble Beit HaMikdash HaSheni, the Second Temple, built when our people returned from exile in Babylon and then expanded by Herod The Great hundreds of years later, only to be destroyed by the Romans in 70 C.E."

"I thought Herod was a madman."

"Indeed. He was so paranoid, he killed members of his family, including one of his wives. Herod came from a pagan tribe whose members converted to Judaism and the Romans made him King of the Jews. And you know the Christmas story about his killing countless Jewish infant males in Bethlehem...."

"I do."

"But as king, he was a great builder of monuments, and one of his projects involved expanding the Temple."

The motorcade stopped in front of wide stairs leading up to a grand entrance in the wall. Tall iron gates stood open at the top of the beige marble stairs.

David and Rachel looked up in awe as they stepped out of the SUV.

"Sir, there is no one inside these outer walls. Do you and Ms. Silver want security personnel to follow you into the Temple?"

"No, Moshe, that won't be necessary."

David looked at Rachel. "Let's go inside."

"Absolutely. I've got goosebumps just standing this close to the Beit HaMikdash HaShlishi."

"And that would be…"

"The Third Temple. David, you must learn Hebrew."

"You're not only a great secretary and fighter, but you're a great historian as well."

Rachel beamed in response to his compliment.

David stepped slowly up the stairs behind her. At the top they stepped into a huge open-air plaza. David thought it could hold several American football fields. The top of the massive retaining wall that rose up from street-level was flush with the top of the covered colonnade walkways surrounding the plaza. A relatively small rectangular compound stood at the plaza center, surrounded by an elaborate twenty-foot-high stone wall with taller square towers at the corners and midway along the north and south sides. A pair of brilliant golden doors shone from the middle of the eastern wall, about 50 yards directly in front of David and Rachel. Rising high inside the western wall of the compound, they saw the upper portion of a square stone building. White marble columns supported a porch cover wider than the rest of the building. "I assume we can pass through those golden doors?"

Rachel's hands cupped her face. "David, that's The Beautiful Gate."

"Is that significant?"

"In the Christian Bible, a disabled man sat by those golden doors every day for many years, begging for hand-outs from worshipers as they entered and exited the Temple."

"Did he eventually move on?"

"At some point, the beggar saw the Apostle Peter entering the Temple. Peter didn't have any food or gold, but he took hold of the man's right hand and helped him to his feet. Almost instantly, the man was cured and he could walk again."

David looked at Rachel with envy. Why hadn't he bothered to read the Bible at least once? If not for his own sake, he should have read it for Sarah. "That's a great story. Is it okay if we go through those doors?"

"I believe it would be fine to enter. David, do we really have a choice?"

"You feel it, too?"

"Yes, I do."

With Rachel at his side, David's legs started to move

forward, taking him straight across the plaza to The Beautiful Gate. As they drew closer, the glow of the golden doors intensified. Each door was made up of two rectangular recessed panels.

Upon reaching the gate, David and Rachel stared at the pair of large golden handles. "What if it's locked?"

"David, if it's locked, we are not destined to enter." With both hands, Rachel took hold of the handle on the right. David gripped the left handle. She nodded at him before they pushed.

The doors opened smoothly without a sound, exposing a large square courtyard paved in stone. Inlaid brown marble at the center formed a twelve-spoke circle. Covered colonnades ran along the left and right side of the courtyard; a heavy wooden gate was visible at the midpoint of either portico. Straight ahead, a rounded staircase led up to twin copper doors set into a twenty-foot-high stone wall. The wall was dwarfed by the much taller building standing beyond it. The setting sun cast surreal shadows as beams of light jutted through the crennels atop the building's parapet.

David pointed at the copper doors. "What's in there?"

"That's the Nicanor Gate. It leads to the Court of Israelites and the Court of Priests beyond."

"If the gate is not locked, should we continue in that direction?"

"David, you must go alone through the Nicanor Gate."

"Why?"

"Women are not supposed to go beyond this courtyard."

"Rachel, if you're not with me, how will I know what I'm looking at?"

"All I can tell you is what's most important."

"Please, enlighten me."

"You should be fine in the courts and chambers immediately beyond the Nicanor Gate. If you gain entry into the sacred Tabernacle, or 'mishkan' in Hebrew, you cannot go beyond the first room under any circumstances."

"Why is that?"

"It is Kodesh HaKodashim, the dwelling of Adonai. The first room is the Holy Place. The second room is the Holy of Holies, a place where God appears and where the Ark of the Covenant was kept after the Exodus from Egypt. Only the High Priest may enter the Holy of Holies once a year on Yom Kippur. There will not be a door or gate separating the Holy of Holies, only the Veil of the Temple. You must not pass the Veil."

As David looked at the copper doors of the Nicanor Gate, something continued to pull him in that direction. "Okay, if I can open that gate, I'll keep going. Will you be okay out here?"

Rachel smiled. "Don't worry. I'll be fine in The Court of Women."

David walked across the courtyard and up the stairs to the dark copper doors. Both doors bore identical raised relief patterns of a palm tree that seemed slightly windblown. The tree trunks were surrounded by swirls with what appeared to be a pineapple at the center of the trunks.

David pushed the door on the right. It didn't move at first, but then he watched both doors glide open.

The facade of the stone Tabernacle was a sight to behold. David's eyes took in the four white-marble columns topped in gold, soaring upward to the roof above the front porch. A pair of enormous golden doors at the center of the porch were unnaturally bright as dusk moved in over Jerusalem. The sound of the Nicanor Gate closing behind him brought David back into the moment. On either side of him was some kind of court or viewing area, separated by a low wall from another small court beyond. On the right side of the wide aisle from the Nicanor Gate to the front steps of the Tabernacle was a raised square pit with stairs along the near side. Across the aisle was a huge caldron with five smaller caldrons set up in a row along the aisle.

David continued moving forward, compelled to go further as the golden doors beckoned. He slowly ascended the steps to the front porch while focused on the two doors. Both were divided into six square panels with very clear designs embossed in each square. The two upper panels each had a cherub, the two middle panels each had a palm tree. In the lower panels was a type of flower that David could not identify. He pressed his hands firmly against the doors. When they didn't budge, he pushed harder.

After a long struggle, the doors opened a crack. Summoning all of his strength, David finally moved them far enough so that he could slip through the opening. The doors immediately closed behind him with a whisper.

Leaning over and breathing hard, he noticed the floor of blue Carrara marble. He knew it was blue Carrara because it was the same marble Sarah chose for the floor when they renovated their bathroom in 2023. He remembered her saying that the swirling bluish-white evoked a sense of looking at the ocean surf.

David stood up and looked around. He had never seen so much gold. The walls rose at least 40 feet and were completely covered in shiny gold, as was the ceiling. A row of large golden palm trees had been embossed along the walls on either side of the room. Five golden menorahs burned brightly in front of both rows of trees, bouncing magical flickers of light in every direction. At the far end of the room, a large curtain hung from wall to wall. "The Veil of the Temple," David thought as he recalled Rachel's words. The curtain colors were horizontal waves of purple, red, blue, and white with two golden cherubim set into the middle. In front of the curtain, a golden box sat on a gold pedestal. Smoke streamed from a small hole in the top of the box; David smelled incense. A small golden table sat just to the left of the pedestal; on top was a gold platter. Moving closer, he saw about a dozen round loaves of flat unleavened bread.

He was careful not to touch the curtain. Thinking of Sarah, he bowed his head. He still carried the guilt about her not being buried in a plain pine box in accordance with her wishes. David found himself silently asking for her forgiveness and for the strength to lead Israel in the way she would want.

"David Stein in prayer?"

David's head snapped back in shock. The curtain billowed slightly; a bearded old man stepped from behind the stream of smoky incense.

"Who the heck are you? How did you get in here?"

"Let's just say that I have special privileges." Amid the smoke, David stared more intently at the man. The white cloak, red shawl and wooden staff all looked oddly familiar.

"Elijah?"

The man stepped out of the shadows. "David, we meet again, and not by chance. On these grounds, Israel's ancient kings worshiped the King of Kings. On these grounds, King David's son, Solomon, dedicated the First Temple to God. This is the hall of your forefathers, your ancestry. This is where your destiny began. You are from the line of David. For such a time as this, you were meant to lead your people. Your grandparents' and your parents' deaths were to fulfill a purpose."

"What purpose?"

"To bring you here." Elijah stepped close to David, staring powerfully into his eyes. "You are from the line. You have been led here not only by Sarah, but by God."

Of one thing David was certain, it was this: Sarah would have wanted him to quell the anger and outrage he was feeling at that moment. Still he had to reply. "For what purpose does your God profit by having my grandparents live their final days in a Nazi concentration camp? What purpose did God have in my parents being shot to death and my wife being killed in a terrorist attack?"

Elijah held his hand up to David. "God's ways are not man's ways, David. And it is not for man to be the judge of the One who created him. Like ancient Israel, your nation - America - and humanity have abandoned God, have gone their own way, and brought tribulation upon themselves... because they want to be their own God. And so, evil men arise, seize nations, and unleash horror on the world. But what the enemy intends for evil, God will use for good."

David couldn't begin to imagine why his peaceful, generous, hardworking parents had to suffer at the hands of evil.

Elijah stepped closer to David, looming large above him. "When the time comes, lead the people of Israel from Jerusalem and out to the desert. Use the Golden Gate."

David shook his head. "Lead the people into the desert? Bring them into the barren, unforgiving desert?"

"In the desert...all of their needs will be provided for."

"Tell me why I should do that...and why should I believe you?"

"First, remember Petra. And second, on the day the towers fell, not only did you and Sarah meet, but so did good and evil."

David remained frozen for a moment, trying to process Elijah's confusing words. Elijah walked toward the front of the Tabernacle. David wheeled around in time to see the old man effortlessly pull open the huge golden doors and continue down the front steps. Looking back at the Veil, David shook his head at the two cherubim. He was tempted to move the Veil aside but Rachel's warning prevented him. He turned around and saw Elijah leaving through the Nicanor Gate, which closed behind him.

He felt the urge to go after Elijah; he didn't want the old man to startle Rachel. David sprinted past the open doors of the Tabernacle, hurling himself down the front steps in a single bound. He ran toward the heavy copper doors, throwing them open. Rachel stood expectantly in the center of the Women's Court. David looked around before closing the copper gate and walking down the rounded staircase.

As he approached, Rachel looked at him with concern. "David, what's wrong?"

"Did you see an old man in a white cloak come through here?"

"No, um, are you alright?" David looked around at the courtyard again. "David, was someone in there?"

"No, no, it's okay." He continued to look around in all directions. "We should get going."

Rachel looked at him skeptically. "Aren't you going to tell me about the Tabernacle? I can't wait to hear... everything."

David smiled and put an arm around her shoulders. "Rachel, it's been a long day. What if I tell you about it tomorrow?"

≈

"Knock! Knock! Knock! Knock! Knock!" came a familiar voice from outside David's office door. He smiled as he got up from his desk.

With the smile still plastered on his face, David made a fist and knocked back twice on his side before swinging the door open.

"There he is!" yelled Carl as he and the other guys from New York entered the Prime Minister's office.

Johnny high-fived David. "You da man!"

"So, Carl, what do you think?"

"Hey, nice spread! Harvard boy made good!"

"Here come da king of the Jews!" laughed Robby.

Mike looked at Robby. "So, who's the king of the Italians…? That gavone, what's his name?"

"You must be talking about Anal Corinthia," Robby blurted out.

His friends started cracking up while David tried hard not to smile. "Alright you guys, calm down," David laughed.

Robby walked over to David's desk and scooped up a handful of jelly beans out of a tray before sitting in David's chair and putting his feet up on the desk. Leaning back, he smiled from ear to ear. "I am calm." David shook his head.

The tone in the room changed as Mike put his hand on David's shoulder. "Hey, Dave, you hear anything from Scotty?"

David looked each of his four friends in the eye and thought for a moment before responding. "No, nothing." He quickly changed the subject. "Hey, let me introduce you guys to the man in the office right next to mine, the head of the IDF."

David led his friends to the adjacent office. "Meet General Steve Dobson."

Steve got up and approached the guys, shaking hands with each of them. "Ah, David's friends from home. It's always an honor to meet 9/11 heroes. Welcome to Eretz Yisrael."

"And welcome to the IDF," added David. "All able-bodied residents of Israel are required to serve in some manner."

"But, David, I'm a firefighter; I save people's lives," Robby said. "I'm not a military man."

"Well, you'll have the chance to save many lives here, but I can't promise you'll never have to take a life."

There was a light tap outside of David's open office door followed by a soft female voice. "David?"

David turned to see Katy Thompson standing in the doorway. He hurried over to her, they quickly embraced. David's friends looked at each other with raised eyebrows.

"Mr. Prime Minister, you're a sight for sore eyes."

"Katy! You look great; you certainly recovered well."

"Why thank you, David."

"Gentlemen, I'm sure you all recognize First Lady Katy Thompson." David's friends calmed down and were well-mannered around Katy, much to David's relief.

David took Katy aside. "I booked you at the American Colony Hotel, where we have a high security presence... Do you have any plans for tomorrow?"

Katy smiled at David. "No, I'm free as a bird, Mr. Prime Minister."

"Then, in that case, I'll show you around Jerusalem."

"That sounds delightful."

"Great. There's a staff lounge at the end of the hall. Please make yourself comfortable and I'll be with you soon."

∽

Robby, Mike, Johnny and Carl stood around the conference table in David's office. Robby pulled out a chair. "Listen Mr. PM, sit down for a minute. While you've been busy saving the world, we've been researching your buddy Anal. Oh, I mean 'Anno.'" Robbie smiled. "And let's just say, we can get more from a background check on Derek Jeter's dogs."

"What do you have?"

"We have some academic records. It seems he graduated from the Catholic University of the Sacred Heart in Milan. But when we made a few calls to some of his supposed classmates, they said they didn't remember him. He starts to come into the public spotlight around 2022. We did track down five of his professors."

"Well, what did they say about him?"

"Nothing much."

"Why's that?"

"They're all dead."

"All of them?"

"Yeah, three from car accidents and two suicides. What are the odds?"

"You have anything else?"

"Yeah David. We tried to research his family background. Nothing much on that either. Seems there were some family members who lived in the Scottish Highlands in the 1940's, but we need to look further into that. We found a Daniel Corinthia registering as a U.S. immigrant from Italy in 1903. Guess where he registered?"

David raised his eyebrows. "I have no idea."

"Ellis Island."

"Any further documentation?"

Robby opened a folder and placed it on the table. "Check out the passport photo from 1912. That's where the trail in the U.S. goes cold."

David studied the grainy black-and-white photo. "Wow, it looks like Corinthia. What do you think, maybe his great grandfather?"

"Who knows? We'll keep digging."

"Good. I want you to keep going on this. Mike, get a digitally remastered copy of the old photo over to Frank for facial recognition."

"Dave, we're on it." Mike followed Johnny, Robby and Carl out of the office.

Alone, David paced back and forth. Although the photo bore a striking resemblance to present-day Anno Corinthia, David felt that he had seen that face somewhere long ago but just couldn't remember exactly where or when.

∽

Corinthia looked across his desk at Marcus Wodan and General Vedirchi. "I never wanted David to make it to Israel, but maybe his becoming Prime Minister will fit with our 'Greater Plan.' His advancement can be used for our own gain. We have to reel in the...ahem, Doubting

Thomases of the world. They do not want any god unless that god is themselves. We will offer them exactly that. And make them realize my great plans for humanity."

"What are your plans?" General Vedirchi asked skeptically.

"People need to eat, people need to drink, and people need a roof over their heads. When basic human needs are threatened, people panic. When people panic, they gravitate to whomever or whatever is providing their means to live."

Corinthia confidently strolled to the window, gazing at the Vatican in the distance. He turned back to the general. "Vedirchi, do what we can to disrupt production and shipment of basic provisions. Do it slowly at first. Make sure you eliminate any large stockpiles of supplies under our control."

Vedirchi stood up. "You mean we are to destroy food, fuel, medicine and other staples of life?"

"I did not say 'destroy,' I merely suggested that we… minimize availability."

A smile grew across Wodan's face. "And then what, sire?"

"We sit back, and we wait. And as things get worse, I become the solution; I…become the source."

"When do we begin?"

"Immediately Marcus. That will be all."

Marcus and General Vedirchi stood up. Marcus joyfully pranced out of the room. The general remained still, looking Corinthia in the eye, shocked by what he just heard from the leader of the United Nations.

Corinthia approached Vedirchi and stood toe to toe. "I said, that will be all General."

Corinthia stared at Vedirchi's back as the general left the office. For the first time, he began to doubt Vedirchi's loyalty.

Corinthia pushed the intercom on his desk. "Contessa, get Nigel on the phone."

◆

Back in Jerusalem, David was enjoying a relatively peaceful time as Prime Minister. He felt increasingly secure now that he had his hometown boys around him, and having Katy as a companion helped him adjust to living without his wife. He appeared to be adapting to his new world.

David showed Katy much of his new country, starting with Jerusalem. In the months that followed, they were together frequently and talked of old times in the United States.

One evening, as part of a westward excursion from Jerusalem, they were walking along the Mediterranean near a row of cafes as the sun was setting. In a curiously sweet voice, Katy asked, "David, do you like me?"

Looking straight ahead, David answered matter-of-factly, "Of course I like you....you...you are...."

"No, I don't mean it that way. Yes, we've been friends for years...Dan and you....and Sarah and I since college. But I mean, you know...."

"Oh..."

"I mean, do you find me...attractive?"

"Well, yes Katy. Very."

"And I find you very handsome as well."

"I've enjoyed our time together. You're an amazing woman."

"David, I can't tell you how much I look forward to our...our..."

"Dates?"

"Yes. Dates." David looked down toward the ground sadly. "Sarah?"

"Yes."

"You still love her."

David stopped and looked forlornly into Katy's eyes. "I do."

Katy was disheartened. "I understand," she said quietly. They continued walking in silence, staring out to sea.

CHAPTER 18
CROSSING THE CHANNEL

WHILE KATY HAD become a constant part of David's life, nothing could compete with his love of his old country, the needs of his new one, and the mission placed before him. On the surface, much seemed well. Reflecting a stunning turn of events, Israel was at peace, and the guarantor of that peace was one of the most powerful men in the world, Anno Corinthia.

In contrast, David's daily briefings were filled with accounts of terrorist attacks elsewhere in the world and how U.N. forces responded brutally, often killing innocent civilians and inexplicably destroying valuable supplies. However, reports of these attacks were managed in Corinthia's favor, as he controlled the media, which gave glowing reviews of how the U.N. "heroes" were saving civilization from terrorism.

David's reports were filled with well-sourced accounts of atrocities, from rape and torture to murder. Meanwhile, Corinthia was accruing power. The financier of his activities was enriching and amusing herself in Babylon at the expense of others. In return for Octavia's money for his wars, Corinthia made sure that Babylon's queen received a steady supply of captured fighters to abuse and dominate and kidnapped young women that she could enslave and exploit.

As Israel's elected leader, David had to pretend he knew nothing about any of this, as the same Israeli people who had elected him still loved Corinthia as well. There were only two people in Israel willing to publicly vilify the U.N. leader. David kept a watchful eye on the two preachers who had railed against the Treaty with Corinthia and had set up shop just outside the Temple. They were now preaching a message of repentance for the nation and humanity.

One morning, after receiving reports of horrific atrocities committed against children, David's outrage reached its zenith. While in a meeting with Steve and other leaders, along with the remainder of his SEAL team, David was overcome with indignation and anger. "Innocent people everywhere being brutalized, and we just sit here and do nothing?! And worse, we are allied with the monster that's doing this, along with Octavia, that depraved witch on the Persian Gulf."

Steve put his hands up. "David, what can we do? We are the smallest country in the region. Our job is to protect Israel and its people. You are the prime minister of Israel. You are part of the fulfillment of God's prophecy and of His promise to Israel."

"So what.....prophecy? Fulfillment? We sit here in comfort while the atrocities continue. You're talking about fulfilling prophecies from an ancient book while I read reports about real people being killed or enslaved.

"What am I supposed to do...just sit here and wait until Corinthia comes after us, too? Steve, you know that famous saying, 'All it takes for evil to triumph is for good men to do nothing.' Well, I'm done with doing nothing!" Steve stared impassively. "No, we will not sit here anymore. The only questions are what should we do and how should we do it. We must find answers. We must do something."

Steve nodded slowly, the weight of David's words pierced his heart and soul. "You're right, my brother. We cannot sit idly by while the world is being raped. Corinthia must be stopped."

David was walking past the tech research lab near his office when he spotted Frank updating the HALO device. Sarah's life-size image was frozen in place. "David, she's on pause," Frank smiled. "I'll have HALO operational in a moment."

"Frank, just be gentle with that battery."

"With kid gloves, Skip." While Frank made his adjustments, a second image of Sarah appeared. "Sorry, David, it looks like my tinkering created two of her... I'll fix it."

"Wait a second. How many of her can you make?"

"I don't know. I never tried."

"Well, make a third one."

"That's easy enough......there you go." At that moment, a third image of Sarah appeared in the room.

"Frank, fill the room with Sarahs."

"It's about to get a bit crowded in here, but here it goes...." The room was instantly filled with 30 images of Sarah.

"Frank, I have an idea. Let's talk."

∽

Several hours later, David brought his friends from New York, along with Frank and Flynn, to Teddy Stadium. "What are we doing here, Dave? Don't tell me we're gonna play football."

"Not exactly, Robby."

Robby looked up at the scoreboard. "It ain't Giants Stadium but it's not too shabby, either."

Standing at the twenty yard line, David pointed toward the opposite end of the field. "Gentlemen, I have a surprise for you. Frank, introduce them to the new members of our team."

As Frank activated HALO, thousands of soldiers instantly materialized on the field and filled up the stands throughout the stadium.

Mike looked around in all directions. "Dave, we're surrounded."

"They're our new men. Let's go meet them."

Approaching the holograms, they all marveled at the detailed, life-like scale and appearance of the images. Reaching out to touch one of the 'soldiers,' Flynn found that his hand went through the hologram as though nothing were there. "These lads won't work too well in hand-to-hand combat, Skippy."

"We don't need them for that, Flynn. They're just a cover, a scare tactic. They'll make the enemy believe we outnumber them."

"These plonkers don't scare me much, laddy."

"Flynn, nothing scares you."

"Picture a video game from HALO," Frank interjected. "The operator can control the movements of the images, simulate an attack, and even introduce audio elements, from a cry of battle to the giving of orders. The enemy will see and hear what seems to be a genuine fighting force."

Wearing a skeptical look on his face, Flynn walked up to one of the holograms, drew back his fist, and swung through it. "James Street Stein! You think these ghosts will win a war against real fighters?" he sneered. "Never, David!"

"If we keep them at a proper distance from the enemy, this might just work. But if the enemy gets within a few feet of them, you're right, Flynn. We'll have serious trouble. Frank, dismiss our new recruits."

"You got it, Skip."

Frank powered-down HALO, emptying Teddy Stadium.

⌁

Later that night, David found Frank back in the lab. "So, how many holograms is HALO capable of producing?"

"Well, theoretically we can make an unlimited number,

but the more images we make, the lower the quality. A weakened operating signal, faltering transmission to the designated projection site, the presence of bad weather — any number of factors can degrade the images, making our 'soldiers' look less real, and more like Swiss cheese."

"Well, my friend, we'll just have to do the best we can." David immediately went to the conference room to meet with key members of his SEAL team.

David spoke with the kind of enthusiasm he hadn't felt in a long time. "Gentlemen, we are going to use HALO technology in battle. The question is what sort of battle. Remember Frank's words before you voted for me to run as prime minister. We're a guerrilla force. Well, that's what we are and we're going to fight again. But it will only be a few of us at a time. It will be mostly holograms…a war of illusions and shadows. We will hit Corinthia when we please, where we please, however we please. He will know and understand nothing. We will cut him a thousand times. We will make him bleed and we will make his empire bleed."

"Skip, may I speak?"

"Go ahead, Gladiator."

"All of our intel says Corinthia's headed for England next."

"Correct."

"And with some notable exceptions, Britain's political leadership has sold out to Corinthia. Therefore, Corinthia's forces will most likely take England with almost no opposition. Then they will cross the Tweed River to the north and do the same with Scotland."

"Go on."

"England's the big prize for Corinthia – fifty million people. Scotland has only five million. Once he conquers England, Scotland's easy. And much of Scotland is sparsely inhabited, especially all the way north into the Highlands. The last place in the world Corinthia will expect resistance is at the very end – in the Highlands."

"And so you're proposing…"

"A meeting in that old border cabin near the Tweed River…I can meet with the English and Scot fighters we know are secretly resisting Corinthia."

"You want to meet them in a miserable cabin, in the winter, in the middle of nowhere? Besides, these two groups hate each other, Gladiator. And haven't they told us they're not going to fight Corinthia but they'll be coming here to Jerusalem?"

"Yes, but with your permission, I will contact them tomorrow. They owe us one for Israel's offering to take them in, thanks to your change in the law. And so they will meet with me and I'll convince them to fight. Corinthia will take England and the cities and towns of Scotland. But once he gets to the Highlands, we will be there. We will unleash the holograms. His army will flee and we will cut it down."

The room fell silent. "You still haven't told us how you're going to convince the English and Scots to fight as a united team."

"Trust me on this, Skip. I have a plan."

"Oh, I trust you alright. But this is not some small guerrilla operation of sabotage you're talking about. This is the wipeout of an army."

"Do I have your permission?"

"Yes, at least for the meeting on the Tweed."

"Thanks Skip."

"Just one question, Gladiator. You really want to get to Scotland, don't you?"

"Well..." Chad grinned sheepishly.

"I think this is more than just business, my friend. And another thing, make sure Flynn will go with you."

"I couldn't stop him if I wanted to."

Flynn pointed at Chad. "You're darn right, mate."

᥊

Chad reached his English and Scottish contacts and they agreed to meet in the border cabin on the Scottish side of the Tweed. "So, Glad, when will you come?" asked Sean MacDougal, a leader of the Scots.

"If we have advance notice of Corinthia's invasion, we can meet before then. Do we still have a contact inside Corinthia's camp?"

"Yes, I was going to tell you about it. The contact says the invasion's expected in about a month."

"Are you sure?"

"Edward says he's as sure as can be."

"Alright, Sean. How about we all meet in the next day or two?"

"That's very little time, Glad."

"But enough time to do it, Sean. See what you can do."

"Aye, I'll try."

⋘

Twenty-four hours later, Chad got the call. The English and Scots agreed to meet the next day on the Tweed. David convened a quick meeting in his office with Steve, Gladiator, and Flynn. "Flynn, you're still in?"

"Aye Skippy, I'm not on holliers just yet."

"General Dobson, have you equipped them with what they need, just in case?"

"I have, David."

"Frank, how's HALO working?"

"Perfect."

"Great. Well, gentlemen, you need to get to Ben Gurion. Your IDF plane is ready. Gladiator, where will you land?"

"Edinburgh, then we trek south toward the cabin."

David shook hands with each of his men. "For the sake of this nation and world, and for your own sakes, may you succeed."

⋘

The flight from Ben Gurion to Scotland took about six hours as expected. After they landed in Edinburgh, Edward and Sean met them with a convoy of military transport trucks. It was an hour's drive south to the cabin by the Tweed and the English border.

When they arrived after dusk, the wind was howling and the rain relentlessly pounded, reflecting a mood of crisis and desperation. The cabin was packed with Edward's English and Sean's Scots, along with famed Scottish singer, Mary Black, who was there at Gladiator's request.

Edward Kelly was a born leader – smart, shrewd, and a positive motivator of men. But not even Edward had been able to break the hold that hatred held in his soldiers' hearts for Scots. And on the Scottish side, Sean had the same qualities and the same problem. The crowd fell quiet as Edward's charismatic presence loomed large over the room. He walked to the middle of the cabin and began to address the men. "The hatred of the past needs to end here, today, or we will all face certain annihilation. My Scottish brothers, my Irish brothers, my English brothers…we are all brothers. Real evil is upon us - religion, ethnic background, color, means nothing. All good men must join together, and it starts right here, right now. With that, I'd like to introduce you all to Chad Perry, U.S. Navy SEAL."

Before Chad addressed the crowd, he turned to Mary Black. "So good to see you again, Mary," Chad said, taking her aside. "Are you nervous?"

Mary laughed. "No Gladdy, I've sung before the Queen at Buckingham, so I'm just fine."

"Well, the fate of this mission might just depend on how you sing tonight."

"In that case, I'll have to give it my best."

There was still much tension in the air. While Sean and Edward were friends, their subordinates were not. This was reflected in the seating throughout the cabin. On one side were the English, on the other side were the Scots. Both groups sat separately, murmuring against each other, while giving each other the evil eye. Indeed the 'heat' in the room was percolating.

Clearly, there was no love lost between the Scot and English forces. While Britain remained a single nation, the Scots saw the English as past oppressors, while the English saw the Scots as perpetual secessionists, with vote after vote to secede being defeated by increasingly narrow margins. And as they met, England and Scotland were united in name only. Each was moving in a different direction, and there was no unified strategy on how to deal with Corinthia. Edward, Sean, Gladiator and Flynn were hoping to change that, and Mary Black's music was popular on both sides of the Tweed. Her angelic voice was the only thing that could avoid the start of an all-out brawl. Gladiator stepped up onto an old Bass Ale crate in the front of the room and began addressing the crowd.

"Thanks, Sean and Edward, for making this night possible. And thank you all for being here. You know why I called this meeting – to stand up to a common enemy who seeks to destroy us all. There is an old saying — the enemy of my enemy is my friend. For each of us here today, Corinthia is our enemy. And so, no matter what has happened between us in the past, we are now friends. I will say nothing more except this: Men, we are in desperate trouble. If we do not unite today, we will die tomorrow. There is no survival, not here, and not anywhere...not unless we surrender our liberty to a tyrant. But I'm not willing to do that, are you? Now, I'm sure you all know Mary Black. Please give her the welcome she deserves."

On both sides of the room, the men put down their beer mugs before standing up and giving Mary warm but restrained applause.

"Thank you, gents. Thank you." Mary clasped her hands and bowed her head before looking around the cabin, smiling graciously. "And now, let me sing a song that I have sung in Scotland and England. It's a poem from centuries ago, now a song that unites and honors the bravery of men from both Scotland and England. It's about you; it's about me. It's called, 'Both Sides the Tweed.'"

Mary picked up her accordion and sang her signature song, originally a song for Scottish pride, now an urgent plea for unity and freedom.

As Mary sang, the guarded personas of the warriors standing before her began to melt away. While she poured out her heart through the lyrics she sang and the music she played, several hardened men discreetly wiped away a tear from the corners of their eyes.

After finishing the song, Mary bowed her head and brushed a small tear away from her eye as well.

All was silent but the wind and rain that pounded the cabin.

Then, a giant of a man in the front stood up. And then another....and another. Soon everyone was on their feet and applauding. The applause grew louder and louder. In the back of the crowded room, Gladiator gave Mary a smile. Flynn scanned the room in amazement.

Standing with his English forces, Edward began walking to the other side of the cabin. When he reached Sean, the two men embraced, setting the place ablaze with shouts and cheers.

Men who several minutes ago were ready to kill each other, were now bear hugging like long-lost brothers, ready to join together in battle. Mary wiped away another tear and whispered to Chad, "thank you."

He whispered back, "Your voice has soothed the savage beasts."

Sean and Edward gathered their now-united force around Chad, who introduced Flynn as co-leader of the operation.

The next day, when the weather improved, they all traveled north to Sean's base outside of Edinburgh. Soon after arriving, Gladiator received a call from Jerusalem. "Hey, Skip."

"How'd it go, Glad?"

"Great. Everyone's now on board and they've decided our SEAL team should take the lead."

"Excellent work. So, you're battle-ready?"

"We're ready for anything."

"That's what I like to hear. We received intel that Corinthia plans to invade England in less than a week."

"David, are you sure?"

"Positive. Where are you now?"

"Edinburgh."

"Okay, get everybody to the Highlands quickly before Corinthia arrives. Glad, I wouldn't want anyone other than you to lead this mission."

"Thanks Skip; we're ready to move out. Flynn told me about a property on Loch Ness that's been abandoned for decades, a good spot for us to lay low until the time comes."

CHAPTER 19
THE HIGHLANDS

MOVING NORTH ON the badly deteriorated M90, Flynn and Chad were in the lead vehicle of an eleven-truck convoy. They crept along, maneuvering around potholes and cracks, many of which had become large craters with time. In the last hour Chad counted only three vehicles traveling southbound on the other side of the highway. The convoy had yet to encounter any other traffic in the northbound lanes. Looking out at the small farms and villages of central Scotland, Chad could see how world conditions had hit the country hard. Many houses were boarded up and surrounded by overgrown yards while weeds had taken over many of the local roads. Chad thought of a special young lady living in western Scotland. He hoped her area had fared better. "Gladdy, we're nearing Perth. I've made arrangements to take on supplies there before we reach Loch Ness. I suppose there remains a few quid out of what David has given you?"

Chad squeezed his thick wallet.

"Yes, but not many pounds; most of it's in Euros. In these hard times, I guess the merchants won't tell us to bugger off."

"That they won't, Gladdy. Seems listening to Edward has rubbed off on your American tongue." Flynn gave Chad a crooked smile before exiting onto the A912. "There was a time when I might have chosen M90 to span the River Tay to A85, but I don't believe the Friarton Bridge is in any condition to withstand eleven lorries. The old Edina Road will bring us right to the heart of Perth."

They crossed over railroad tracks before the road cut through a large park. Tall evergreen trees lining the road were the only thing in the park taller than the grass. The fields had turned into wild meadows. For the first time in many miles, the road surface was relatively smooth.

"Were these fields once used for things like rugby and cricket?"

Flynn looked out the driver's side window and shook his head. "The old South Inch, pains me to see her like she is. Many a game has been played on these grounds, for myself it was always fitba."

At the far end of the park, they entered the heart of Perth. The sidewalks were virtually deserted, as were the roads. Turning onto Marshall Place, Chad felt eyes following them. He looked up to see people peering out of old stone and stucco buildings.

"It's a short way to St. John's Shopping Centre. Angus Montieth has been fiddling with their rubbish for years. He sells anything that slips through the cracks."

As the convoy moved up Scott Street, it occurred to Chad that the pedestrians they passed were virtually all men and the few women he saw were very old. After three more turns, the trucks moved down a side street, stopping in a large paved area surrounded by loading docks. A steel door on the loading dock immediately to Flynn's right rolled up with a loud screech. A tall man in a plaid shirt and denim overalls stepped out into the grey daylight, his thick grey hair and full beard matching the color of the sky. Flynn jumped out of the truck and hurried up the steps to shake hands with the man.

"Flynn! Hoo's it gaun? Are you here to chorie me once again or would you be paying this time?" The man grinned.

"Angus, I haven't come to swick anyone. My mates possess hard currency, and I'm certain Sean's credit is fine with you." Flynn pointed toward Sean who sat in the driver's seat of the second truck. Angus smiled in recognition.

"Aye, there's no need for Sean to bring me poppy. If there's any man who can save Scotland, it's Sean MacDougal."

Flynn leaned in closer. "Angus, we've seen hardly a wummin as we came through town. Was a time when there was a bonnie lass, or two, on every corner in Perth showing a bit of leg." Angus's face froze; his eyes went from light blue to nearly black.

"These are dark times; feels as if Satan himself has taken up residence. Young wummin have been vanishing without a trace. It all started months ago, and now all the biddies are afraid to walk the streets, even with their faithers. My Brenda has moved her five quinies. They're lying low in Dundee. And my son Derek is on the run too. He hid his quinie in Balhousie Castle before fleeing toward Tibbermore."

"Aye right?"

"One of Logan Burnett's quinies was sent back in a small box for her faither to bury."

"Did the kidnappers cremate her?"

"No, Flynn." Angus looked at his feet.

"So, what was in the box?"

"Only her head."

Flynn's eyes flew open wide with anger. "Any idea who's responsible for this madness?"

"The Chief Constable has no answers, and even Scotland Yard is stumped. If you and Sean cross paths with the evil hooligans, I trust you'll do what is needed."

"That we will, Angus; that we will."

"Good to hear. Now, let's get these lorries filled. The pallets are heavy; have your strongest keelies step forward."

᷍

Less than two days and nearly 200 miles later, the convoy stopped as it arrived in the Highlands. Chad, Flynn, Sean and Edward stepped out onto the country road. The four commanders gathered in front of the lead vehicle before the final approach to Loch Ness.

Sean looked intently at Chad. "Let's hope these ghost soldiers work, Gladdy."

"I'll second that," Edward added.

Flynn stepped between Sean and Edward. "HALO definitely works, mates. I saw her work back in Jerusalem."

Chad checked the GPS. "Okay, let's scout our positions, and then Flynn will lead us to our place for the night."

"How much food and supplies do we have, Sean?"

"We've got plenty, Edward. Should be enough for two weeks here, and two weeks west of the mountains. These men can live off the land if need be."

Flynn assured both men. "That's right Sean. These SEALs can eat the bark off trees. And Angus made sure to give me a special care package in the last palate, so we won't be surviving on army food alone."

David's intel was accurate. Corinthia's army landed in southern England and quickly swept north, encountering no resistance. Soon the invading forces had crossed the Tweed into Scotland. From there, they overtook Glasgow and Edinburgh with similar ease.

Back in Rome, Corinthia received the news from his general on the ground. "England is ours. So are Glasgow and Edinburgh."

"Excellent, General. Keep moving north."

"How far should we go? Soon we'll reach the Highlands and there's only desolation there. Shouldn't we stop now?"

"I told you before; I want the Highlands." Vedirchi remained silent. "You will move into the Highlands, General. Am I clear?"

"Yes, Mr. Secretary."

❧

As Flynn drove the lead vehicle on the approach to Loch Ness, Sean, now riding shotgun, looked up in alarm. "Flynn, are you taking us where I think?" Flynn glanced briefly at Sean without comment. "You know there's been nothing but trouble at Boleskine House. At least turn on the headlights; it's getting dark in this wicked place."

"Have no fear Sean. I know these roads like the back of me gnarled hand."

Flynn turned into an overgrown driveway blocked by a pair of tall rusted gates secured by an old chain. The left gate had an elaborate 'A' centered at the top; the gate on the right had a 'C'. "I'll get out and see if I can get those gates open."

"No need, laddy."

Flynn stomped on the accelerator. The truck smashed through, ripping the gates off the hinges. "Gates open."

The convoy proceeded through stone pillars, moving slowly up the rutted driveway. A large weather-beaten house came into view as the last bit of daylight faded.

Flynn stopped the truck by the gothic front door. Sean got out and gave orders to his men. "Give this house a thorough check. Sweep every room; we don't want any surprises. Clancy, get the door!" A big lug stepped down from the back of the truck and slammed his shoulder into the wide front door; it opened with a loud creek. "Good… let's go in."

A little later Sean came out front where Flynn, Chad and Edward waited with their men. "The place is a real hames inside but we've got a fire started. Now let's get some grub and some sleep." The men filed through the door and found places to bunk down while the leaders gathered around the fireplace in the main hall.

Chad looked around at cobwebs hanging from the ancient chandeliers and wall sconces. "Sean, what is this place?" The walls were deeply cracked. Chunks of plaster were missing in many spots, exposing old wooden lath. There was abundant evidence as well of the fire that had nearly destroyed most of the interior back in December 2015.

"This is what's left of the great Boleskine House. Time and the elements have made a real hash of it, but she still stands after hundreds of years, evil and all."

"What evil?"

Flynn leaned in close to Chad. "It's much more than just a house, Gladdy. Do you really want to know?"

"Yes, I do."

"Back when I was a young lad, me brothers, me faither and me grandfaither used to camp near the loch. Me and me brothers, we'd sneak up to Boleskine House, trying to get a peek of that old rocker Jimmy Page. He once owned the place, you know. But before that, the house had a dark past, a history of evil, sacrifices, black magic and death. It was in the tenth century when a church standing on this very spot burned to the ground with the entire congregation inside."

All eyes were on Flynn as more men gathered around.

"For centuries after that, there was no good that happened here. In 1899, the wickedest man in the world took possession of this house. His name, was Aleister Crowley, but some called him the Great Beast. Rumor has it that it's not the Boleskine House that's evil, but what's buried beneath her."

Flynn paused to spit a wad of chew into the fire; it burst into a strip of golden dust and disappeared. His gaze swept across the nervous faces of the men.

"It's the black onyx, the six mystical and sacred stones of Samhain. Crowley once told of how he used those six black stones to summon the twelve Kings and Dukes from hell. The stones are waiting for the right time to be found, waiting to be possessed by their rightful heir. Legend is that the stones can give power over life, power over death. I've heard that Hitler himself thought he was heir to the stones but he was defeated before he had a chance to overrun Scotland. As far as we know, the stones have never been found. Maybe it's mankind's pardon that these evil stones always remain buried, buried here, buried beneath us tonight."

Flynn slowly got up.

"Have a peaceful sleep, gents." He grinned and walked away from the fireplace. The men remained, quietly staring into the fire, mesmerized by Flynn's tale.

After leaving Boleskine House at dawn, Chad had split the joint force into two. On his end of Loch Ness were

Edward and the English. On the other end, led by Flynn, were Sean and the Scots. Chad was the first to spot the approach of Corinthia's army; he radioed Flynn. "They're coming. I have Frank on HALO ready to materialize our hologram force."

"Affirmative, Gladdy."

Chad picked up his binoculars. "We have a visual on the approaching forces. There are approximately five square miles of open country for the projections where the enemy will not see them materialize. Frank, I'll give you the coordinates. I have a clear transmission route and satellite connection."

"Thanks Gladiator. Alright, let's do it." Frank established connection with the satellite which began transmission of the hologram soldiers to the ground coordinates.

The hologram forces suddenly appeared under the ridge, beyond Vedirchi's sight as Frank had planned. From the heights of the Highlands they came by the thousands.

Shocked by their sheer number and by the sudden piercing blare of bagpipes, Vedirchi's army broke ranks and fled in terror through the valley below.

Chad yelled into his radio, "Open fire!"

"Take 'em, lads!" roared Flynn.

Sean's men launched dozens of shoulder rockets, mortar rounds and heavy rifle fire, quickly devastating Corinthia's forces. Scores of dead and injured covered the ground; screaming and moaning echoed eerily through the air.

Chad turned to Flynn with the inevitable silent question. Flynn answered immediately. "There's no more Geneva Convention, Gladdy. Corinthia's men are some of the worst mercenaries ever to walk the earth. Rape and torture are their way; they're completely radge. Leave no one alive."

Chad nodded before he and his men walked through the field. With pistols in hand, they put the wicked to rest.

❧

When Corinthia learned of his army's rout in the Highlands, he flew into a rage. "How did this happen, Marcus?!! How did my army lose to a handful of outlaws?!!"

"Vedirchi reported that the enemy numbered in the tens of thousands; they seemed to come out of nowhere, they overwhelmed us."

"Then Stein must have recruited fighters from other lands." Trying to contain his fury, he lowered his voice to a near whisper. "Tell our generals this will not happen again or they will pay the ultimate price."

"We lost hundreds of men. If Vedirchi did not order the retreat, all of our men could have been killed."

"I don't care how many died!! Marcus...did we achieve our goal?!!"

Marcus looked at the floor. "There was one missing. Vedirchi found only the five lesser stones in the crypt."

"The sixth stone has the power! It draws the energy from the others. Without it, the other five are useless. Who might have taken the sacred stone?" Marcus stared blankly. "Find out, get my treasure, and kill the thief. He who brings to me my sixth stone of power will receive a great reward."

"What will that be?"

"They will be allowed to live."

Chad stepped up onto the back of a flatbed truck and addressed the men after their victory. "For the first time, Corinthia's army has been soundly defeated, and we are the ones who did it. We have cut him down to size, proving he is just a man."

"Now we break out the Windswept Wolf! A beer fit for warriors!" Flynn opened several cases of beer and tossed ice cold bottles into the crowd.

"To the two peoples of England and Scotland, who are finally now one, a toast to our new allies and our new brothers! We have united, and we have prevailed without any injury or death among us!"

After Chad stepped down, Flynn quickly pulled him aside. "Well, laddy, we head south from here. I'll take over. Now, go do your business."

"Thanks Flynn; see you in Edinburgh."

"Now, don't you come back by your lonesome."

"I won't," Chad vowed. Wearing his white Navy dress uniform, he adjusted his hat and jumped into his Jeep.

Flynn led the victorious force south. With the enemy destroyed, there was nothing but daylight between them and Edinburgh.

In town after town, as word spread of the defeat of Corinthia's army in the Highlands, many Scots poured onto the streets to greet Flynn and the victors, waving both British and Scottish flags.

❧

Chad headed west, along roads that wound through an idyllic countryside. Whirling around a mountainous bend, he prepared for a steep, upward climb to his destination. As he drove through the mist and fog, it was like entering a dream while his anticipation grew.

On top of the hill stood Elsie, a stout elderly woman beaming with pride, as a beautiful dark-haired young woman sat on the schoolhouse lawn teaching Gaelic to her students, the mother tongue from the land's Celtic past.

Reaching the top of the ridge, Chad approached the schoolyard. His eyes met hers. "Colleen," he whispered to himself. Reaching into the back seat, he grabbed a dozen long-stemmed roses and jumped out of the Jeep.

It had been more than two years since he first met her on a visit to Scotland. They quickly fell in love, and Chad had remained in Scotland to be with her, leaving behind his home on Cape Cod. Then came the call from David in New York after the Liberty Island attack. Chad left Scotland, promising Colleen he would one day return.

As Chad approached, seeing her love, Colleen's heart began to race. The pen and pad fell from her hand; she squeezed the locket that held his picture. Frozen with passion, they stared wide-eyed at each other in rapt silence.

Elsie whispered to Colleen, "Well, must I tell you two what to do?"

Lost in each other's gaze, Chad and Colleen ran toward each other, embraced, and kissed as Colleen's students giggled nearby. Still looking into her eyes, Chad got down on one knee and removed a small box from his pocket. He opened the box facing Colleen. Her hands went to her heart and her eyes opened wide.

"Colleen Anjelica Shea, will you do me the honor of being my wife? Will you marry me, Colleen?"

Tears of joy streamed down her face. "Yes. Yes, Chad Worthington Perry, I will marry you." Chad gently took her left hand and slowly slipped a diamond ring onto Colleen's finger.

Elsie smiled at the group of children. "Well, it looks like you girls will need a new Gaelic teacher."

Chad carried Colleen and set her down in the passenger side of the Jeep. "Where are we going?"

"My darling, we are going to the promised land."

"I'll go with you anywhere; my home is wherever you are."

With Colleen's head on Chad's shoulder and his arm around her, they drove southeast through the countryside. They joined the victory party in Edinburgh, where they were immediately spotted by Flynn standing on George Street near St. Andrew's Square. He was loading his Rattray's Scottish Thistle.

"Darn Calabash, good for nothin'! Never gets in there

quite right!" Chad's Jeep came to a screeching halt at the edge of the square. Flynn, noticing the auburn-haired lassie in a long white dress gliding out of the passenger seat, quickly forgot about his pipe troubles. "Ohhhh, lucky man you are, laddy!"

"It's a pleasure to meet you, Mr. Flynn; I heard so much about you on the drive over."

"Oh, just call me 'Flynn,' lass. Now, come with me. We'll talk later about what still remains to be done at Rosslyn. But first, they're about to sing 'Flower of Scotland.'"

Moments later, the crowd began to sing Scotland's still-unofficial anthem, changing the song's villain from the centuries old English King Edward to Anno Corinthia, and a tone of lament to one of unrestrained glee.

CHAPTER 20
RETURN TO JERUSALEM

WHEN FLYNN AND Chad made it back to Israel, they were accorded a heroes' welcome. Soon after, David called a meeting in his office with General Dobson and his commanders. "Steve, I understand your staff has an update on Corinthia."

"Yes, Corinthia is still humiliated by the defeat in the Highlands. He is seething about it and relieved General Vedirchi of his command."

"Vedirchi? Are you sure?"

"Positive. Vedirchi started to question Corinthia's motives. It was reported that Corinthia was going to execute him, but guess who stopped it?"

"I have no idea."

"The Empress of Babylon."

"Octavia?"

"Yes. She said she wanted him delivered to her in Babylon...alive."

"To be added to her man collection, no doubt. So Corinthia sent him to Octavia?"

"Yes, but something happened on the way to the empress. Vedirchi escaped. Octavia has offered a bounty of several million dollars for his capture."

"How did he escape?"

"Remember Prince Sharif? Calev mentioned him when we all met."

"Yes, he's a good man."

"Well, Sharif formed a guerrilla force that's been attacking Corinthia's troops near Turkey. One of the guerrilla fighters had a contact in Corinthia's camp. He found out about Verdirchi and that he was being transported to Babylon."

"So then what happened?"

"Sharif's men hijacked the plane and killed Vedirchi's captors. They landed with him in Turkey, and reportedly fled to the mountains."

"So, Vedirchi is now working with Sharif's men?"

"That's right, David. Our intel revealed that General Vedirchi's questioning of Corinthia's methods and motives had been going on for some time."

"So, Sharif and Vedirchi are both on our side?"

"It looks that way. A prince who's now a warrior like his legendary father, and Corinthia's finest general."

"Great, but one question, Steve. Do they know which side *we're* on?"

"What do you mean, David?"

"Officially, Israel remains allied with Corinthia but it

may not be widely known that many of us want nothing to do with him."

"Sharif knows our position; Calev told him."

"So let's contact Sharif and bring him on board."

"I don't know, David. It's a risky proposition. Corinthia has his spies, too. It could blow our cover and violate the treaty."

"I'd still like to find a way to reach out to Sharif."

"Okay, I'll look into it."

∽

The two preachers were gaining notoriety and continued to stir things up in the heart of Jerusalem. Near the Temple, they were still preaching against the Treaty with Corinthia. They were not intimidated by the many threats directed at them and would not go away. Since taking to the streets, they had continued to deliver a spiritual message of repentance that was taking hold with many Israelis.

After Corinthia's defeat in Scotland, it seemed their sermonizing had entered a dramatic new phase. They began to call out other nations and governments for their crimes against humanity and declared that these regions would be hot, dry, and receive no rain for predicted periods of time. Their rhetoric especially caught the attention of Corinthia, as these "fanatics" were beginning to stir up zealots against him. While Corinthia's forces disposed of these zealots easily, either by executing them or by delivering them as "gifts" to Babylon's depraved ruler, he was clearly worried. From almost the moment they appeared on Jerusalem's streets, they had spoken about natural disasters to come to the countries that were committing atrocities. It was as if they were in command of the weather. They would proclaim an end to rain, and it would stop. They would call out to God for scorching heat or devastating cold and it would occur. They would declare an earthquake, and cities would shake violently. They would predict a tornado would strike a town in two days, and two days later, that town would be devastated.

What had once been sporadic was now commonplace. Their warnings became more strident and frequent, and every time, as before, they came to pass.

One day, the prophets spoke out against Rome and Babylon. "Hear the word of the Lord, Rome, the seat of power, is forecast to receive drenching rain tomorrow. But there will be no rain in Rome tomorrow or the next day or the day after that. For the next 180 days, not a drop of rain will fall on the home city of Anno Corinthia. There will be scorching heat and shortages of water.

"Hear the word of God, Babylon, the seat of wealth, is in its dry season. But tomorrow, the rain will begin. There will be floods the next day and the day after. For the next 180 days, streets will become rivers in the home city of Octavia."

The next day, the rains stopped in Rome but came to Babylon. And as the preachers foretold, the pattern continued, day after day, for the next six months.

∾

"Steve, what should we do about those preachers?"

"There's nothing we can do, David."

"Many people are concerned with those two, mostly because they've been denouncing Corinthia. We have had peace in Israel since his reign. If they keep preaching against him, what's to stop Corinthia from marching in here and seizing control of our country?"

"He can't do that."

"Why not, Steve?"

"Two reasons. He made a treaty with us. He will not break it in front of the world – at least not yet."

"And what's the other reason?"

"I don't know how to say it in a way that you'll believe it."

"Well, say it anyway."

"The Bible says that two preachers will have power to do as they please for three-and-a-half years."

"Yes, that may be your belief, but it's not mine."

"With all due respect, David, what you or I believe about them is irrelevant. They will preach until they are done. The smart thing is to stay out of their way and keep telling Israel that you will honor their freedom to speak."

"But what if you're wrong? What if Corinthia loses his patience and invades us?"

"He won't."

"But Steve, didn't you say that he wants Jerusalem?"

"Yes."

"Well, now he has his excuse for invading Israel."

"Wrong, David. If these preachers can turn on or shut off rainfall at will, they can stop Corinthia from invading."

"Do you really believe that, Steve?"

"What I believe does not matter. If these two men are the prophets spoken of in the Book of Revelation, Corinthia is not coming for us until they've completed their mission."

"So, what you're saying is that these preachers could be protecting the whole nation from Corinthia."

"Yes, and we should enjoy the relative calm while it lasts."

David and Steve turned their heads. Through the door to David's office, the sound of heavy boots could be heard coming down the hallway. There was also the vague sound of someone whistling Dixie.

The door slammed against the wall after it was kicked open with a loud thud. David and Steve drew their guns.

"Well howdy, neighbor! Man! You two guys are really on edge! I thought getting elected prime minister would have a calming effect on you, Davey…obviously not."

The tall lean man dressed in military camos marched confidently toward David's desk. "Not too long ago we were all playing together in the same desert sandbox." Nigel smiled broadly. "Put your guns down, boys. I'm just here with my welcome wagon."

Steve lowered his gun. However, David kept his pointed at Nigel, recalling their recent encounter in Jordan. "Colonel, you better have a good explanation for storming into my office unannounced."

"I guess Anno forgot to tell you boys. He just signed a deal to put his new consulate in that little building right next door." Nigel went to the window and peered out.

"Why was I not informed of this?"

"Gee Davey, I guess you forgot to read the fine print in that treaty y'all made with the U.N."

David looked at Steve while keeping his gun on Nigel. "Can Corinthia do that?"

Steve shook his head. "I'm afraid so."

"So, my boys and I will be stopping by every now and then, just to say 'hello.'" Grabbing an apple from the fruit basket on David's desk, Nigel took a bite and smiled. "Hey, maybe we can grab lunch sometime." Walking out the door, Nigel turned around and threw the bitten apple into the garbage can across the room. "Three points! Damn I'm good!" Nigel left the office, slamming the door behind him.

Steve walked to the window and pulled the curtain aside. "We've got a problem."

"No Steve, Nigel's got a problem."

"What's his problem?"

"Me."

Back in Rome, the drought brought severe hardship, as water had to be rationed, and hundreds died. But in Babylon, hundreds died in floods, and food riots ravaged impoverished neighborhoods.

Octavia's moral compass continued to point ever lower.

She had no concern or compassion for the victims in her country, only for herself. Fuming in her palace, Octavia watched out the window as the bodies of men, women and children were swept away by the raging rivers. "Those fanatical soothsayers in Jerusalem, I'll have them beheaded one day!" she said to Hussein, one of her aides.

"Do you believe that those two preachers caused the floods, Your Highness?"

"Of course not! That's superstitious nonsense!"

"So what exactly did the preachers do if they didn't cause the floods?"

"You dare question your queen?!" she shouted menacingly.

"No, no, Your Majesty, never!"

Octavia clapped her hands twice, summoning the guards who stood at attention near the door. "Arrest him for treason! Bind him and tell Ali to come at once." They put Hussein in handcuffs and held him until Ali appeared. Octavia sashayed closer to her terrified aide. "Hussein, I will ask you again. Do you think the preachers caused the rain?"

"My queen, I know you are the wisest in all the land and you have that answer. I yield to you."

"Of course you yield to me! You are an insignificant little pawn!"

The guards forced Hussein to his knees and held his head down. In the corner of his eye, Hussein saw Ali holding a large executioner's sword. "Noooo!" he yelled, squirming as the guards pressed his head onto a large marble pedestal. Ali unsheathed his sword, raising it high. In a flash he brought the sword down on Hussein's neck, instantly decapitating him.

The severed head toppled off the pedestal, coming to rest at Octavia's feet. She bent down and picked up the head by the hair. With his eyes still open, she kissed his lips. "I am so going to miss you Hussein." She tossed Hussein's head to Ali. "Clean up this mess."

Octavia sauntered to the far side of the elaborate room where she reclined on a velvet couch. A servant handed her a golden goblet filled with red wine. "I'm feeling much better now. Bring me my nymphs."

The guards escorted twelve teenage girls into the room; they were in tattered clothes and chained together. Octavia put down her wine and approached the girls. "Why would you little nymphs not service the men of Babylon, as I ordered?"

"We're innocent; we've done nothing," one of the girls pleaded.

"Exactly. You've done nothing for me, after I've brought you here at great expense. I selected each of you based on your appealing beauty and sexual magnetism."

"Queen Octavia, we are Christian women, women of God. We choose to wait for the Lord to provide us with husbands before we give ourselves over."

Throwing her hair back, Octavia laughed hysterically. "You have a choice. Either give your bodies over to my will, or, I can guarantee you will never meet your future husbands. I'm sure your…Jesus…will forgive you."

The girls were silent as Octavia walked back and forth in front of them like a drill sergeant. "I've had enough. We've been playing patty-cake for too long. Any of you girls who want to work for me...and live, step forward." Trembling, the girls pulled closer together. They held hands and stayed put.

Octavia looked at the floor and shook her head. "What a shame, you're all so pretty. You will not be my slaves in life, but you will be my slaves in death." Octavia picked up her goblet and toasted the girls as they began to sob.

"Ali, put an end to their tears. Take them away and bring me back some gifts."

The girls cried as they were led from the room.

In a fury of power and lust Octavia immediately summoned Corinthia. He appeared on the screen in front of her. "Empress Octavia, to what do I owe the honor?"

"Anno, I want David Stein. If you capture him, you will give him to me. And in return, I have something that is of great value to you."

"What could you possibly have that would interest me?"

"You will see tomorrow when I arrive at your compound in Rome. Make sure to have your finest royal accommodations available."

"Very well, Octavia. I will see to the arrangements personally, while anxiously awaiting your mysterious gift."

"Anno, you will not be disappointed."

"Let's hope not."

Octavia stroked the large stone held in her necklace after Corinthia's image faded from the screen.

The doors to Octavia's chamber swung open. The guards entered with a large platter of heads. Smiling triumphantly, Octavia tipped her goblet sideways, pouring wine onto her twelve grisly trophies.

"Ali, now that the virgin followers of Jesus have been baptized, send their remains back to their families."

CHAPTER 21
STEAL HIS HEART

CORINTHIA AND MARCUS Wodan were discussing plans to deal with the two preachers in Jerusalem when the intercom buzzed on Corinthia's desk.

"Yes?"

"Mr. Secretary, Her Highness Octavia has arrived."

"Send in the Empress." Octavia made her grand entrance, wearing her signature skin-tight gold sequin dress with matching cape and diamond-encrusted gold tiara.

"Anno, is there any news on Vedirchi?"

"It appears he is on the run, but when he is found, he will pay dearly for his defeat in Scotland."

Octavia laughed mockingly. "Shouldn't your wrath be focused on David Stein? For it was he who defeated you, not Vedirchi."

"My wrath is focused on whom I choose it to be. Stein will pay too…in time."

"We both want David Stein for our own reasons,

but I have something with me today that you may want even more."

Octavia strutted seductively across the office while wrapping a finger around the stone set in her choker. "Have you been searching for something?"

"Indeed, I have."

"Sometimes, my dear Anno, we fail to see what's right in front of us."

Corinthia opened his hands wide. "My Empress, please, enlighten me."

Octavia began toying with the single black stone held in a gold setting on her necklace. Wodan's eyes opened wide when he noticed the black onyx stone just below Octavia's neck. He got up and approached her for a better look. "Not too close, weasel. I inherited this jewel after my entire family died in an 'unfortunate' plane crash...a long time ago." Octavia chuckled, "Fortunately, I refused to go on the trip." Octavia moved closer and whispered into Corinthia's ear. "But you already knew that."

Corinthia's eyebrows rose as Octavia stepped back. "This family heirloom has much sentimental value attached, since it was the last thing I took...I mean, inherited from my mother. Mystics say that this stone has been sought after by kings, princes and emperors for centuries."

Corinthia suddenly realized that around Octavia's neck hung the missing Stone of Power from the Six Stones of Samhain, the stone he had been searching for his whole life.

"What do you want?" Corinthia was barely able to contain himself after finally setting his eyes upon the stone.

"It would appear that I have your attention."

Corinthia nodded. "Yes, you do."

"I thought so. The stone could be yours, but what I want in return is David Stein...alive. Then Anno, we will each have one."

"It will be difficult to get to Stein in Israel."

"You don't have to go to Israel...I want his heart."

"If you want his heart, I can get you his heart. Then, he will give us anything we want."

"Well, Anno, you do have an insurance policy on David."

"Precisely...and I will cash it in at the right time."

"Of course, it couldn't hurt to have some additional coverage."

"Empress, what do you mean?"

"I'll be leaving Babylon on a 'business' trip, to capture David's heart."

"Do you mean, the Empress of Babylon is about to descend from her throne for a mere insurance transaction?"

"Precisely."

"And why, if I might ask, is Her Royal Highness so suddenly eager to transact this business?"

"Anno, this is personal. Let it be decreed, the Empress of Babylon will descend from her throne and steal David Stein's heart."

"Your Highness, you're one of the most recognizable women in the world."

"Lest you forget, agent Carlson is a master in the art of disguise."

"Well, I will await the outcome with…baited breath. And now, to seal our agreement, kindly hand over the stone to Marcus." Marcus inched closer to Octavia with his hands out.

"On your knees, Marcus." Marcus knelt down before Octavia. She unclasped the black Stone of Power, placing it into Marcus' cupped hands.

"Thank you, Queen Octavia, Empress of Babylon."

Shaking her head, Octavia glared down at Marcus. "You pathetic little man."

Planting her golden stiletto into Wodan's chest, she pushed him forcefully. He fell backwards, landing flat on the floor. "Corinthia, why do you put up with this circus midget?" Octavia turned on her heel. Strutting out of the office, she laughed at Wodan. "Now crawl to your master, little weasel."

Marcus obediently crawled across the floor and handed Corinthia the stone.

Mesmerized by desire, Corinthia held the stone high in front of him. "After decades, my quest to obtain the Stone of Power has been realized. Marcus, I almost had possession of the stone once before."

"When was that, Master?"

"You see Wodan, I am well aware of how and where Octavia's family perished."

"How, Master?"

"I was there, Marcus. Now, take the stone and put it in my chambers with the other five, until the right time."

"When will be the right time?"

Corinthia looked down at Marcus with a vacant stare. "You will know."

✧

The pilot entered the cabin. "Are you ready, Your Majesty?"

"Yes, I am." Octavia took a seat in her private jet.

"Very good, Your Highness, it should be approximately noon local time when we reach our destination. And Your Majesty, may I say, you look ravishing."

She looked at him accusingly. "You mean I don't look good as a brunette?"

"No, no, Your Highness," he stammered. "Your new look makes you shine in a new and different way."

"Now that sounds better."

"Yes, my Lady. You are as brilliant as you are beautiful."

"Marvelous. I assume our flight plans will not be tracked?"

"That's correct, Your Highness. All has been arranged; our driver will be waiting for you in the terminal."

✧

Lorraine was taking a cookie sheet out of the oven when her phone rang. "Hi, Lorraine, it's Mel. I have an unexpected meeting in an hour in Manhattan, so I'll pick up Becca around four instead of three-thirty. Is that okay with you?"

"Sure, Mel. I like having her around, especially with Mike away in Israel. Becca's a treat; she gets me through the loneliness."

"There is some good news, Lorraine. My sister says she can take over for you if necessary. I've already bought your ticket to Israel, so you can join Mike when you're ready. Being away from the people we love in this new world of ours is tough, tough on all of us."

"Thanks for understanding, Mel. I can't wait to see Mike again. I'll pick up Becca from school at the usual time."

"That's great Lorraine; I really appreciate it."

At that moment, a car pulled up in front of Lorraine's house. A beautiful, tall, tan, long-haired blond woman, wearing Gucci sunglasses and a form fitting, above-the-knee pink cotton dress, slipped out of the rear door of the sedan. Her Manolo Blahnik heels clicked seductively as she confidently glided up the stone pathway toward the front door. Holding a case of cosmetic products with her left hand, the woman adjusted her Avon I.D. With a bored sigh, she puckered her lips while refreshing her lipstick. Her slender white-gloved index finger pressed the doorbell.

"Mel, I have to go; someone's at the door."

"Lorraine, you're a sweetheart; see you at four."

Lorraine crossed the living room and looked through the peep hole. A strikingly beautiful woman holding a cosmetics case stood outside. Lorraine thought it couldn't hurt to see what the woman was selling. She opened the door slightly. "Can I help you?"

"Why yes, my name is Veronica Styles." The woman smiled broadly. "I'm a representative with Avon and I would appreciate the opportunity to show you our new line of beauty products."

Lorraine looked at her watch; it was almost time to pick up Rebecca. "I'm sorry, but I'm really busy."

"Well, today honey, we're offering several high-quality free samples that will make your skin just radiate and look years younger."

Lorraine noticed the woman's youthful radiant skin. "Okay, but I have only a few minutes."

"Thank you, a few minutes is all it will take."

"Good, come in. I'm Lorraine, by the way."

"Well, Lorraine, do you have a makeup mirror we can sit in front of while I demonstrate how great our products will make you look?"

"Sure, I have a vanity in the bedroom."

As they walked through the living room, Ms. Styles noticed several family photos hanging on the wall. "Is that handsome man your husband?" Veronica gestured to one of the photos.

"Yes, that's my husband."

"Pretty hot guy, Lorraine; you're a lucky woman."

"Yes, I am."

"Looks like he's in the service."

Lorraine, frustrated with the direction of the conversation, motioned Veronica toward the bedroom. "Um, about your makeup line, I'm anxious to apply your foundation and blush. You look stunning!"

"Yes, I know."

Lorraine raised her eyebrows at Veronica's vain

response before escorting her guest into the bedroom. A large mirror was displayed on the vanity.

Veronica pulled out the chair. "Now sit down, honey, and face the mirror so we can both witness the beautiful change in your complexion while I apply our life-changing products."

Lorraine sat facing the mirror; Veronica slowly tugged off her white gloves one finger at a time. "How long have you been working for Avon, Ms. Styles?"

"Oh, I've been a cosmetologist for as long as I can remember." Standing behind Lorraine, Veronica began gently applying the natural color foundation onto Lorraine's face.

"Ms. Styles, this shade looks perfect."

"It does look good, honey, but I think we need to go with a bit more, hmm, red blush…indulge me." Veronica gently added the blush.

"Oooh, that feels nice."

"Doesn't it, honey? When you massage it in correctly, it's very energizing; it's virtually orgasmic. You're already glowing. There is nothing more stimulating than watching yourself become beautiful."

Becoming more comfortable with Ms. Styles, Lorraine joked, "Well, I could think of a few other things, but my husband is not home right now; he's, uh, in the service."

Both women chuckled, their eyes meeting in the mirror.

"And you're here…all alone? Do you two have any children?"

"No, it's just me and Mike. We never had a chance to have kids with our busy work schedules."

As Veronica continued applying the makeup to Lorraine's face, she slightly repositioned the chair, reaching past Lorraine's blouse while seductively grazing her left breast.

Lorraine's expression changed to one of unease. "Oh, I'm sorry, just a slip of the hand. Honey, you need to relax; you're so tense."

Veronica began to massage Lorraine's shoulders, putting Lorraine back at ease. "Now Lorraine, I thought you had a daughter."

"No, Ms. Styles, why would you have thought that?"

"Well, don't you have to pick up Becca from school today?"

A lightning bolt of fear struck Lorraine. She tried to get up from her chair but Veronica pulled her back down by her hair. "Lorraine, let me correct what I just said. The one thing that is more stimulating than watching yourself become more beautiful....is watching yourself die."

Lorraine's face grew flush in horror as she was held down in the chair.

"See, I told you the red blush would look perfect."

Lorraine squirmed as she struggled to get up, but couldn't.

In a flash, Veronica pulled a switchblade knife from her thigh holster and slashed Lorraine's throat from ear to ear. Facing the mirror, Lorraine watched in horror as her blood poured out and the life drained from her.

As her lifeless body slumped forward, the beaming saleswoman whispered in her ear, "Yes, red is definitely your color."

Octavia wiped the blade clean on Lorraine's blouse and put it back in the holster. As she walked through the living room, she turned to smile at the photo of Mike, blowing him a kiss before snatching Lorraine's car keys from the coffee table.

It was time to pick up Becca.

Rebecca, waiting in front of the school with her classmates, spotted Lorraine's car. Rebecca waved and approached the open passenger-side window of the red Grand Cherokee. Seeing that the driver wasn't Lorraine, Rebecca peered at her quizzically. "Hi Becca, I'm Lorraine's friend, Ms. Styles. But you can call me Veronica."

Rebecca noticed Veronica's Avon badge and smiled. "Where's Lorraine? I don't know you."

"Lorraine and I were shopping, and she wasn't feeling well. She asked me to take her car, pick you up and bring you to your grandfather's house."

Octavia pointed toward a children's makeup case on the floor. "See, I have some pretty pink lipstick and makeup for you to try."

Rebecca smiled and got into the car. Octavia reached over, grabbed the passenger seat belt, and buckled Rebecca in. "Just for safety, honey."

Rebecca smiled as they drove away. She sat happily exploring the contents of the makeup case for a few moments. "Can I call my grandfather and tell him I'm with you, Ms. Styles?"

"Honey, I'll call him and let him know." Octavia dialed the phone. "Hello Mel, I have Becca with me. We'll see you at 6:00 PM."

"Understood," answered Anno Corinthia on the other end of the phone.

Frustrated, Rebecca looked at Octavia. "My grandfather said he would pick me up at four. I want to talk to my grandpa."

Rebecca reached over to grab the phone; Octavia quickly pulled it away. "I can see you're daddy's girl." Octavia leaned over face to face with Rebecca. "Listen you little bitch, I suggest you sit back and shut up, if you ever want to see your father alive again." Rebecca glared at Octavia, triggering a sinister smile on Octavia's face.

Rebecca threw herself back in the seat; her face went blank with fear as they sped up the ramp onto the Van Wyck Expressway.

◈

It had just turned four o'clock when Mel arrived at Lorraine's house. After parking in her driveway, he got out of his Mercedes and turned back to click the remote to lock his car. Heading up the front walk, he shouted his usual greeting to Rebecca. "Cupcake, Grandpa's here!" Usually Rebecca would rush out to greet her grandfather. "Cupcake! It's time to go home! Cupcake?"

As Mel called out repeatedly in his usual manner,

his jovial mood turned to one of concern by the time he reached the front door. The former prosecutor began to process a string of curious signs – a small makeup case sitting by the front door, Lorraine's car not in the driveway, and his shouts to Rebecca unanswered.

Mel then noticed another ominous detail. The front door was slightly ajar. Reaching under his jacket, he drew the silver-plated Bren Ten pistol from its holster. Stepping carefully through the door, he felt an eerie silence in the living room.

Reaching the bedroom, he slowly pushed open the door and saw Lorraine's body face-down on her vanity. A large pool of blood had collected under the chair. Fear, anger, and terror coursed through his veins, momentarily paralyzing him.

Yelling out Rebecca's name, Mel raced through each room in the house and into the backyard. After calling the school and learning that Rebecca was picked up in Lorraine's car, he called the police. "911, what's your emergency?"

"My name is Mel Goodman. I'm at my granddaughter's babysitter's house. The babysitter has been murdered in her home and my granddaughter, Rebecca Stein, is missing."

"Mr. Goodman, we will dispatch a unit right to your location."

"Send the k-9 unit and your best crime scene techs. Contact Commissioner Gorman, and make sure he knows that it's Mel Goodman's granddaughter who's missing."

"Stay at the scene, sir. The police are on their way."

"Negative, I'm going over to P.S. 146 to look for my granddaughter."

❧

Back in Jerusalem, Frank Robbin's cell phone rang as he prepared to leave the office after another long day. Seeing the number, Frank answered on the first ring. "Mel, what's up?"

"Frank, get David...I need to talk to him...immediately!"

Alarmed, Frank opened the door to David's office. "Have you ever heard of knocking before entering?" David asked with a smile.

"David, Mel's on the phone. It sounds important."

David grabbed Frank's phone. "Mel, what's going on?"

"Son, there's no other way to say this, so I'll give it to you straight." David felt a lump in his throat upon hearing a tone in Mel's voice he'd never heard before. "Lorraine has been murdered; Becca is missing. NYPD is looking for her; we've got an APB out."

There was a prolonged silence. "David? David?"

David rose from his desk. "What?? Lorraine dead... Becca missing?!"

Steve Dobson came in from his adjoining office. "What's going on?" Ignoring Steve, David continued speaking to Mel.

David's face went cold and blank. "I will get on a plane for New York in one hour. Call General Joe right now and get him on this. I'm coming home."

"David, you don't have to leave Israel. I will handle this. I'm here. I don't need my son-in-law to risk his life, especially now that you're prime minister. If the media finds out, the extra attention could hamper the search efforts."

"Mel, I'm coming home."

David hung up and tossed the phone back to Frank.

Steve looked at David. "I heard every word. This is terrible, but Mel can handle it. We need you here."

David stared at the floor shaking his head. "The President of the United States is dead because my detail failed to protect against terrorism. My wife is dead because I couldn't protect her. Scores of my men were killed in battle because I was reckless. My homeland is in turmoil because I failed to protect it, and my parents are dead because I wasn't there for them." David pounded his desk. "I will not lose the last thing I have left! I will not lose my daughter! I'm going to New York!"

David did not notice Katy standing in the doorway. "David, you did everything you could to protect Dan; it wasn't your fault."

David quickly looked up. "Katy! So you heard everything?"

"Yes. I came here to surprise you, but I had no idea…"

"It's okay."

President Thompson's widow hugged David and looked him squarely in the eyes, "I want to go to America with you. I want to help you find Rebecca."

Steve stepped between them. "As IDF commander, I can guarantee neither your safety nor David's."

"We understand," Katy replied with authority in her voice, as if she were First Lady once again.

CHAPTER 22
NOW IT BEGINS

NOT FAR FROM Istanbul, Sharif and his band of guerrillas from old Dubai were discussing their next raid against Corinthia with their new ally, General Vedirchi. Sharif looked across the room at the General. "You know Vedirchi, with Babylon and Rome reeling from six months of tumultuous weather, we can strike Corinthia now."

"You may be right."

"We can take him out in his capital city."

"You want to kill him in Rome?"

"Yes."

"That would be difficult, Sharif. He moves in and out of Rome with little notice. He could be anywhere. He spends a lot more of his time at his operational command center in the desert."

"Let me ask you something, General."

"What is it?"

"If we can get to Corinthia, and kill him, how will that

affect his realm? I mean, if I cut off the head of the snake, will the rest of the body die?"

"I don't know, Sharif, but I'll let you in on a secret. We had discussed doing it ourselves."

"Who's 'we'?"

"I and another one of Corinthia's commanders. Let me tell you something. We are Italians and Romans first. We love our country and our city. At first, we were proud that under Corinthia, Rome and Italy were taking the lead in the world. But then we heard about his plans. The idea of forcing Europe into a new Roman Empire betrayed our belief in freedom and democracy. But Corinthia won the support of the majority, so our hands were tied. We couldn't betray our own principles and go against the people. But once he made it clear that his ambitions were to conquer the world, he began ordering us to commit terrible atrocities and it also became clear that it was he who was stirring up terrorism in order to defeat it. We finally considered plans to kill him."

"General, are you implying we still have allies inside Corinthia's camp?"

"Yes, I am, because we do."

"So what happened to your plans to eliminate Corinthia?"

"Calev wanted us to strike immediately, but I told him to wait. Corinthia was too strong. But after several defeats, Corinthia's hold on the world has weakened, though he doesn't want to believe it. The plans were derailed when

Calev was killed. Should we heed Calev's advice and kill Corinthia?"

"If you had the chance to kill Hitler before World War II, would you?"

"Yes, I would."

"Then you know what we have to do."

"So Sharif, what's your plan?"

"General, you know where Corinthia's compound is. Keep him under surveillance, then have your sources contact us when he's there."

"Alright, Prince, I concur. Let's terminate this monster before it's too late."

❦

Rebecca, her stomach feeling like it was tied in a not, had been nervously staring out the window of the Grand Cherokee as they drove further and further from Queens. Now headed north on Interstate 95, she was trying to imagine what her father would tell her. That's when she saw the sign at Exit 19: PLAYLAND PARKWAY RYE-HARRISON. Grandpa Mel had taken her to Playland last summer; she won a Mini Mouse tee shirt in the bean bag toss.

Octavia noticed Rebecca looking closely at her watch. "Don't bother checking your watch, spoiled brat. There's no way you're getting home on-time tonight." Rebecca looked at Octavia. "And wipe that smile off your little face, before I smack it off."

Rebecca squeaked, "Yes, ma'am."

Instantly, the tip of a long finger with a perfectly manicured red nail was an inch from Rebecca's face. "You will address me as 'Empress Octavia.' Ma'am is a title for dried-up old spinsters!!!"

Rebecca pushed the button on the side of her watch. She couldn't stop the half-smile that came to her lips when Mini Mouse's face turned green.

⁓

Sharif selected his six best fighters to join him and Vedirchi on their covert mission. A plane would fly them to a remote landing strip, then a stealth chopper would place them within striking distance of Corinthia's compound.

The plan was set in motion immediately. Sharif's men had loaded the plane with tactical supplies. The initial leg of the journey was the easy part.

Once they deplaned and transferred to the helicopter, Vedirchi addressed Sharif and his fighters on what was to come. "Corinthia is slippery and unpredictable. He knows there are many who love him, but others desperately want him dead. Gentlemen, we will soon be approaching the belly of the beast, the heart of the wolf's lair. This is where the real Corinthia lives. We are heading to a place where he plans and commits his worst atrocities. It is here where his chosen few and his inner circle see who he really is."

Vedirchi looked intently at Sharif. "Be prepared, my friend. Be prepared to do battle. Be ready to die for your cause."

"I'm ready, general…I'm ready."

The chopper ride was rough, they were pummeled by wind and sandstorms while flying above the desert terrain. Navigating through the elements, the helicopter eventually set down in a desolate area where Sharif and Vedirchi exited the craft.

Surveying the forbidding landscape through protective goggles, Sharif cast a bewildered glance at Vedirchi. "Where is Corinthia's compound? I don't see anything but barren desert."

"Of course you don't see it. It isn't here."

"Then where is it?"

"Its entrance is about 200 yards southeast."

"General, why can't I see it from here?"

"Follow me, and you will find out."

Sharif looked at the general with heightened skepticism and then back at the helicopter.

As the two men walked further away from the chopper carrying the other five fighters, it began its ascent and headed toward a mountainous area for cover. As it disappeared over the horizon, Sharif radioed the pilot. "I will contact you when we're ready for pick-up."

"May God be with you," came the fuzzy reply through the howling winds.

Vedirchi shook his head. "Sharif, there will be no pick-up."

Sharif understood that the odds were against their getting out alive. "General, everybody has to die sometime... let's move."

They trudged on for what seemed like miles as sand blasted their faces.

Soon Vedirchi stopped walking and checked his watch. It displayed 0558.

"What is it?" Sharif asked.

"It is scheduled for every day, at 0600. Two men emerge from the compound to retrieve supplies that have been dropped off the night before. They should be coming out any minute."

"General, you keep mentioning a complex or compound. We've walked a long way and I still see nothing but sand and dark sky."

Vedirchi nodded before pointing straight ahead. Suddenly, out of the desert floor rose a small concrete building.

Sharif raised his eyebrows.

"You see, Corinthia's compound is completely underground. It's supported by a hydraulic foundation. It can be raised at any time and is otherwise undetectable from land or air. Sharif, give me your radio and ankle pistol. I'll bury them here for our escape, should we be lucky enough to make it out."

As Vedirchi expected, two men clothed in sand-storm gear walked out the door pushing large cargo bins. One of the men pressed a button on a handheld remote. The ground on one side of the small building began to shake; a mound of sand crumbled away revealing the tops of several storage containers.

Vedirchi gripped his pistol and signaled Sharif; they approached the men from behind. Sharif tapped one of the men on the shoulder. "You dropped this."

Startled, both men whirled around.

Before they knew what was happening, Vedirchi and Sharif snapped their necks. As they lay on the ground, Vedirchi saw they were still alive. He shot both men. "Sharif, help me remove their uniforms. We'll need them."

The sandstorm continued to pound as they dragged the empty bins into the small concrete building. Vedirchi shut the door and entered the code to initiate the descent into Corinthia's compound. They continued wearing their masks as the hydraulic system lowered them deep underground.

Dressed in the uniforms of the maintenance men, they were able to pass by several guards undetected. Vedirchi led the way as they rushed to the area of the compound where the general believed he would find Corinthia. Entering a conference room with multiple doorways, they attempted to pass through the room to reach a large corridor on the other side.

Without warning, the doors to the room slammed shut. Corinthia knew they were coming. Trapped, Sharif and Vedirchi drew their weapons.

A moment later, a large monitor descended from the ceiling. They looked up at the screen just as Anno Corinthia's face appeared. "General Vedirchi, it's nice to see you, and I see you've brought a guest. And what is your name? Not that I need ask, Prince Sharif of Dubai. I'm surprised a man of your lineage and stature would associate with such a traitor and coward as Vedirchi."

Several doors opened, heavily armed guards entered, their automatic weapons aimed at Sharif and Vedirchi. "Gentlemen, I think it would be in your best interest to put your guns down." Sharif followed Vedirchi's lead and laid his pistol on the floor.

Pointing at Vedirchi, Corinthia nodded, "take their weapons, and take this renegade away. Leave Prince Sharif and me alone."

As soon as Vedirchi was removed, Corinthia entered the room. He confidently walked over to Sharif and put his arm around the Prince's shoulders. "Let's take a stroll, shall we?"

Corinthia led Sharif through the compound, placing his hand in front of the scanners that opened each door they approached. They finally ended up in a grand chamber reminiscent of a royal throne room. "Prince Sharif, it is a pleasure to meet you at last. I have heard very much about you as a gallant leader, a man of great power, and an earnest reformer. Even with Vedirchi's help, I am impressed how you made it this far into my compound. Come with me."

"Do I have a choice?"

Corinthia tightened his grip on Sharif's shoulder. "No."

An entryway opened onto a room fashioned in the style of a traditional Japanese dojo of the mid-Edo period.

Two place settings and a platter of food sat on a low table in the center of the room. Sharif's eyes immediately went to the sword rack and trophy case on the far wall. He recognized the eight swords, or katana, as being from the Shinshinto period. "Sharif, please feel free to admire my trophies. I've had so many victories, I've lost count. I hear you were also quite a swordsman in your time. In this room, Prince Sharif, it is just you and I. There are no cameras, no security devices. Everything we discuss and do here will be private. Please sit, and have something to eat."

Corinthia waved his hand over the generous platter of exotic foods.

Sharif stared at Corinthia. "I did not come here for the buffet."

"So, what are you here for?"

"I've come here to kill you."

Corinthia looked up at the swords on the wall. "Well Prince, I commend your honesty, and…maybe you'll get your chance. But in the meantime, let's talk business."

"What have you done with General Vedirchi?"

"Let's just say, the general has been relieved of his command and should no longer be your concern. Prince Sharif, I've brought you here to ask you to join with me. Together, we can transform not just Dubai but the world. We can bring peace and oneness to humanity in these times of terror and turmoil. I am told that these are your goals as well."

"And who told you that?"

"Oh, come now Prince, surely you must know. Our

mutual friend, and your love interest. As I'm sure you already know, the Empress has joined forces with me, and you would make an excellent addition as well."

Corinthia, shaking his head, approached Sharif. "Prince, how do you resist a woman as ravishing as Octavia? She's the most beautiful woman a man could ever dream of. With her, you will not only rule Dubai and Greater Babylon, but much of the world, if you desire. How could you resist the power that all men such as us desire? Sharif, Octavia will be your Queen and you will be a King."

Sharif grasped the small wooden cross that hung from his neck. "There is only one King."

Corinthia's eyes narrowed; his countenance became more severe. "This King of yours has been dead a very long time. You and the rest of the world need to understand that I am the answer to the world's problems. I am the way, I am the truth, I am the light and I am the source."

Sharif shook his head. "You are nothing. You are a deception, a shadow. Funny, I once thought you controlled Octavia, but maybe it is she who controls you. Without her wealth, you are powerless. The truth is that she rides you like I ride one of my horses. I do not seek the material things and power of this world. Truth is what I seek. Power can be gained quickly, and lost just as fast. However, Corinthia, truth is eternal."

Corinthia glared at Sharif. "I will choose to ignore your feeble attempt to degrade me. As for Babylon's Queen and Rome's leader, we shall see one day who rides whom. But as for the truth, Prince Sharif, I am the truth."

"I've seen your 'truth.' I've seen how your thugs kidnap underage girls, enslaving them as prostitutes, while you take a share of the profits. I know of your plans to ration food and other staples of life. I know about the many atrocities you've committed in the name of fighting the terrorism that you yourself have created. I am well aware of your 'truth.' You kill and destroy while claiming to be the savior the world is looking for. You say you want to free the world when actually you are its slave master. I'd rather die than join with someone like you."

Corinthia smiled cynically, clapping his hands. "Bravo, Prince. Right out of Hollywood central casting. A dashing young idealist bravely confronting overwhelming power, armed with just the power his words. But, I am a fair man. I will give you until tomorrow morning to consider my offer; your self-righteous monologue was all that I can endure for one day."

Corinthia clapped twice; several men entered the dojo. "Guards, take the prince to his quarters for the evening. He appears delusional after his difficult journey through the desert." Sharif did not resist as he was led away.

The guards forced Sharif into an elevator that went down deep below the compound. When the elevator finally stopped, the doors opened into darkness. He was dragged a short distance before being shoved into a dimly lit cell with a concrete floor and steel bed. It took his eyes a moment to fully adjust to the lack of light. The sound of a heavy door closing and then locking was followed by that of boots walking away.

Sharif sat on the edge of the bed and began to think of Octavia's role in all of this. How could he have misjudged her so completely? Did her beauty initially make him see only what he wanted to see? The United States government had apparently been fooled by her as well.

Sharif was replaying moments from his relationship with Octavia in his mind, when he heard a low groaning sound that brought him back into the present. He heard it again, this time slightly louder.

"Sharif...." The voice was hoarse, barely more than a whisper, but Sharif recognized it.

It was Vedirchi in the adjacent cell. "General, I hear you. Are you hurt?"

"The guards beat me badly but I'll survive for now. Did they do anything to you?"

"No, but I'm supposed to stay here overnight and think about Corinthia's offer."

"What offer?"

"He wants me to join with him. Maybe if I make a tentative deal with him, I can convince him to let you go."

A hacking cough came from the general's cell as he tried to speak. "Sharif, don't do it. Forget about me; I'm not important. If you get the chance, you must stop Corinthia...at any cost." The general gasped as he struggled to clear his throat. "That's our mission."

"General, are you okay? General?"

There was no response.

❧

"Hmmmm! Hmmmmm! Hmmmmm!"

Vinny, Joe's spotter, yelled to his buddy Gino, "Yo, check it out! General Joe's benching serious reps with more than 600 lbs.! Holy moly Joe, it looks like your chest is gonna explode!"

The barbell bent slightly as Joe slammed it back onto the rack and sat up. "Ain't so much, Vinny. In the Army I was benching over 750, on a bad day." Joe gave Vinny a thumbs-up sign. "Put an extra forty-five on each side." Joe laid back on the weight bench and prepped to push his max for the day. At first he was going to ignore the vibrating phone in his pocket. Breathing heavily, he pulled it out and saw a familiar number.

"Grandpa Mel, how you doin' today? Mel…?"

There was a little more time than usual before Mel responded, and it was not in his typically confident tone. "Joe, Lorraine was murdered; Becca's been kidnapped."

Joe's face went blank. He jumped off the bench, looked at his watch, and walked straight out the front door of the gym. "Mel, you and I both know, we have only 48 hours."

"Hey, Joe! Where you goin'? You forgot your gear!"

Joe didn't hear Vinny calling after him. In the parking lot, he stopped and took a deep breath.

"Joe, the K-9 Team is looking all over! They issued an Amber Alert, and there's an APB out on Lorraine's car! Nobody's been able to come up with anything."

Joe pushed the button to activate the GPS display on his watch. He waited for a moment in silence… finally, a beeping sound was followed by a blinking green light on the face of his Mickey Mouse watch. Joe climbed into his Hummer. "I know where to find Becca; I'm going to get her."

"How do you know where she is?" Joe slammed his truck into gear, smoke shot from all four tires as he crushed the accelerator to the floor. "Joe?! How could you know?"

"Mini Mouse."

CHAPTER 23
IT IS ONLY THE BEGINNING

AFTER AN UNCOMFORTABLE night on the cold metal bed, Sharif was jarred awake by the slamming of a heavy steel door. Four guards stood at the open door to his cell, one of them mockingly bowed before him. "Did you enjoy your sleep…Prince?"

The other guards laughed as they grabbed Sharif by the arms and dragged him out. They escorted him back to the room adjoining Corinthia's private chambers, dumping him on the floor before leaving him alone.

Sharif looked toward the swords on display that he had seen the day before. After rising to his feet, he approached the sword rack and inspected the assorted katana with a discriminating eye. These were the real deal alright, an impressive collection that must have cost a fortune. Each sword contained the soul and essence of its maker. Sharif carefully removed the second katana from the bottom, finding himself drawn to its white lacquer finish with blue and green ornamentation. He slowly unsheathed the blade, holding the ghostly saya out in front of him while examining it closely. The hara was beautiful and appeared unaffected by age. He imagined the sword had been used on only a few occasions during its long life.

Returning the blade to its saya, Sharif took the ancient katana in both hands and slowly turned to face the kamiza and sit seiza, the formal kneeling/sitting position of the Samurai. He laid the glowing white katana in front of him and bowed to it in deep reverence.

Sharif heard the distinctive gentle scraping sound of the shoji door sliding open behind and to the left of him. In his peripheral vision he saw a dark robed figure enter the room, slide the door shut, and kneel in the seiza position about ten feet away. Sharif knew enough of traditional Japanese duels to recognize he was being challenged. His opponent was well-versed in Samurai edict and decorum, normally indicative of a warrior who valued the virtues of honor and respect for one's enemies. But Sharif knew better. Corinthia was nothing more than a sophisticated narcissist. This elaborate production was a charade, a cynical mockery of what the Samurai call Bushido.

With katana now back in his left hand, Sharif's suspicions were confirmed as he slowly turned 180 degrees to face his opponent. It was now obvious that Corinthia had been schooled in Kogen Itto Rye style of Japanese swordsmanship. It was the style of the dreaded Shinsengumi special forces who were tasked with the protection of the Kyoto Shogun in the late 1800's, the very style that Sharif had dedicated years of his life to in a warrior's quest for mastery. He had long wondered how he would perform in a duel to the death. He sensed that this question would soon be answered.

"Sharif, I have given you ample time to reconsider my offer. It is my sincere hope that you have come to your senses. Accept my invitation to join forces with me, so we might spend these next moments drinking sake while celebrating our new and powerful alliance. I can assure you, the alternative will be far less pleasant."

"I made my choice last night, Corinthia. I will not reconsider."

"That is most unfortunate for you. However, I must confess, the warrior within me is pleased with the opportunity to advance my skills in mortal combat. As you may be aware, there are twelve men from my elite guard behind the walls of this dojo. With a casual wave of my hand, I could end your life instantly. But since I am a man of virtue and honor, I will give you the chance to decide your fate in a duel. You will surely lose, but out of respect, I have chosen to give you a warrior's death."

Corinthia's face revealed his hubris. Sharif considered ways in which to exploit this weakness as he locked eyes with his opponent. Time seemed to freeze as both men stood in eerie silence, waiting for the other to present even the slightest opening.

Corinthia's eyes finally betrayed his growing impatience.

With lightning speed, Sharif drew his katana in an upward motion, implying a bold attack from above. Corinthia instantly drew his blade.

Sharif moved at the last possible moment, letting his sword fall into a watershed block to protect his left side from three feet of razor-sharp blade that would have sliced through his abdomen. Sharif spun 180 degrees to attack Corinthia from behind as he passed with a flawless Kesagiri cut.

Corinthia mirrored Sharif's spin move, utilizing the Gyaku Kesa Giri diagonal upward cut.

Their swords clashed and for a moment seemed to be stuck together by some unnatural force. Sharif allowed Corinthia's katana to follow its initial upward path as he raised his own sword into Jodan No Kamai.

Taking the bait, Corinthia again focused his attack on Sharif's abdomen. Sharif retreated back and to the right, sustaining only a minor flesh wound across his stomach instead of the disembowelment Corinthia sought.

Corinthia was so focused on delivering his killing blow that it took him a second to realize that Sharif had, amid his retreat, delivered a kote strike that had taken Corinthia's left hand clean off.

The physical and emotional pain that followed threw Corinthia into an animalistic rage. With his katana still in his right hand, he bound wildly toward Sharif, forgetting his years of training and acting purely on rabid instinct. Sharif deflected the strikes of this unorthodox attack long enough to allow Corinthia to expend the rush of adrenaline.

As Corinthia paused to draw a revitalizing breath,

Sharif delivered a Tsuki strike that passed through Corinthia's core. Corinthia stood in motionless shock as he watched the sword withdraw from his body in sickening slow motion. Sharif raised his katana and brought it down on the top of Corinthia's forehead, slicing a deep gash that ended at the bridge of the nose. He performed the traditional chiburi, shaking the blood and guts of his enemy off of his sword in one swift motion and returning the sword to its scabbard with ritualistic finesse.

Corinthia lingered for a brief moment before falling into a heap at Sharif's feet. More out of habit than a true feeling of respect, Sharif bowed slowly to his fallen enemy before scooping up Corinthia's severed bloody hand.

Where were the guards that Corinthia warned him about? Was it all a bluff? He swiftly headed for the sliding door, knowing it would not open without a scan of Corinthia's left hand.

After finding his way through a maze of short hallways, Sharif ran down a long corridor.

He stopped short in horror.

Peering into an enclosed glass room, he got closer and pressed his face to the glass, cupping his hands around his eyes for a better look.

In the room were dozens of ten-foot-tall glass cylinders containing motionless people who appeared to be frozen in a gaseous cloud. He saw several oxygen tanks and flashing vital-sign monitors. It was as if they were in suspended animation. Many had their eyes shut tightly while others' eyes were wide-open with looks of terror on their faces.

Shocked by what he saw, Sharif stood motionless. A blaring alarm sounded, followed by rapidly approaching footsteps and loud voices shouting commands. Sharif continued running down the corridor until he found the elevator that was used to take him to the holding cell the day before. Still using Corinthia's bloody hand as a passkey, he quickly brought the elevator down to the level of the holding cells. He made it through a security door that led into the dimly lit area where prisoners were kept.

All of the cells were empty except for Vedirchi's. "General, wake up! We must leave now!"

Sharif entered the cell and shook Vedirchi as he slept. He winced when he saw the general's badly bruised face. The general stirred on the bed and could barely open his swollen eyes. "We have very little time to get to the rendezvous point."

Sharif unlocked and opened the cell door. "The whole world will be hunting us soon."

Vedirchi looked at Sharif in dazed confusion. "Why would the whole world be hunting us?"

"I just killed Anno Corinthia."

Vedirchi excitedly grabbed Sharif's forearm. "My friend, you have completed our mission!"

"Now we have a second mission."

"What's that?"

"Getting out of here alive."

"Sharif, you go, save yourself. In my condition, I will only slow you down."

"We came in together and we will leave together."

Nodding his head, Vedirchi slowly got to his feet. "Okay. What is that you are carrying?!"

"This hand is our ticket out of here. Let me help you." The general put an arm around Sharif's neck as he hobbled out of the cell.

As they found their way through the compound, the alarms continued to blare. They made it undetected back to the above-ground maintenance building where they first entered.

Stumbling out into the unforgiving sandstorm, Sharif tossed Corinthia's severed hand onto the desert floor. They located the drop-off point before radioing the chopper to pick them up. Struggling to fly in the difficult conditions, the stealth craft approached with its hoist cable lowered. Sharif and Vedirchi hooked themselves on and gave an 'OK' sign.

The chopper hovered as they began to ascend. Suddenly, the desert floor opened. Rising out of the ground on a platform was a rocket launcher; it fired a missile into the tail rotor. The impact knocked Sharif and Vedirchi off the hoist, causing them to fall more than thirty feet onto the sand.

The helicopter struggled to stay airborne, twisting and turning for some distance. Sharif and Vedirchi watched helplessly as the chopper crashed to the ground, exploding in a ball of fire. Running to the wreckage, Sharif plainly saw that none had survived. He was able to salvage a gun and a few supplies from the crash site, pulling a rifle from beneath the charred body of one of his men.

Sharif ran back to Vedirchi, whose left leg was severely

twisted. "Let me splint your leg, general. We need to get moving."

Vedirchi grabbed Sharif's collar. "There's no time! They're coming!"

"I can't leave you."

"Leave me here! I can't walk!"

Unable to see clearly, Sharif shielded his eyes. He didn't want to leave the general behind but he knew he'd never make it out of the desert carrying Vedirchi. "General, I'll make it to my people and send a rescue team for you. I'll be back."

"I won't be here."

"I said, I'll be back."

Sharif turned to look at Vedirchi one last time before running off alone into the blinding cyclones of sand.

⌁

The alarms in the compound continued to blare as Marcus Wodan ran into Corinthia's dojo. Corinthia lay motionless; his severed wrist and head wound were bleeding profusely.

Corinthia's loyal servant was in shock. Wodan leaned down near Corinthia's body and found no evidence of breathing or a pulse. He immediately summoned the compound's medical team, which arrived in seconds.

The mortally wounded Corinthia was taken on a stretcher to the medical unit where doctors and nurses had assembled. The chief ER physician examined the body. "He's suffered massive blood loss and has no vital signs."

Working feverishly, doctors succeeded in suturing

Corinthia's wounds, but with no vital signs, the situation remained grim. "Defibrillator! We need paddles!" the ER doctor yelled.

The nurse placed the paddles on Corinthia's chest.

"Clear!" Corinthia's eyes burst open as his whole body was jolted.

The doctor checked the monitor. "Not good. Still no sign of life."

A nurse cried, wiping away a tear. "He's not going to make it."

"Clear!" Corinthia's eyes remained open as the screeching heart monitor remained flat-lined. After several more attempts, the doctor halted his efforts. The room fell silent.

The doctor turned to Wodan. "We've done everything we can; he's dead."

Wodan glared at the medical staff. "Everyone leave at once! I need to be alone with him!" The chief physician pulled a sheet over Corinthia's body, covering his face.

When he was alone, Wodan proceeded to push the gurney back to Corinthia's private chambers.

What first was reported to the media as an attack that severely wounded Anno Corinthia, was now officially declared a homicide. The prime suspect was identified as Prince Sharif of Dubai.

Corinthia's staff in Rome appealed to the world for help in finding Sharif, offering a fifty-million-dollar reward for his capture — dead or alive.

Back in Jerusalem, Steve Dobson received word of Corinthia's assassination and informed David, who was preparing to leave for America with Katy.

"What?! Are you sure?!"

"All of our sources have confirmed."

"You know...right now, Steve, I just want Becca back. Get the stealth fueled, armed, and ready for takeoff in an hour. No one is to know that I'm gone."

"Of course."

Frank entered David's office. "David, I wish you would stay. The people of Israel need their prime minister now more than ever. Corinthia is dead, and the treaty may be considered shaky at best. But I know Becca is most important, and I know you can't be in two places at the same time." Frank squinted and scratched his head. "Or can you?"

Frank and David paused for a moment before smiling at each other. David removed HALO from his pocket and waved it at Frank before handing it to him. "Frank, for now...HALO is yours."

"Be safe, please keep us informed about Becca." Frank left the office fiddling with HALO.

David turned to Steve. "Listen, when I'm gone, you're filling in for me."

"How in the world do I tell that to the Knesset?"

"Quite simply, you don't. As far as anyone knows, I never left."

"How long will you be gone?"

"However long it takes to find Becca."

David and Steve embraced. "Take care, my friend."

Steve then hugged Katy. "You take care of David, and yourself as well."

"And you take care of Israel, as I know you will, Steve. And one more thing, call Mike in Tel Aviv and tell him to meet us at the airport."

"God be with you both."

&

As David and Katy waited for a car to take them to Ben-Gurion Airport, they saw the two preachers in front of the building. The preachers began speaking in the street to passers-by.

Approaching them, David greeted them with a nod of his head. "Gentlemen, if reports are correct, you may no longer have much to preach about. Anno Corinthia has been assassinated."

"Mr. Prime Minister," one of them replied, "our mission is not complete. Until it is, we must continue."

"Will nothing satisfy you? Do you have such a thirst for attention that even Corinthia's death will not bring you peace?"

Katy gently tugged on David's sleeve. "David, I have heard these two many times; they have said and done nothing wrong."

"It is not a time for peace, David, but war, a war for the hearts and souls of men," the prophet responded. "Send out a call to all those in the world who stand for freedom, truth, and justice. Invite them to Israel to follow the God of Abraham, Isaac, and Jacob."

The other preacher stepped close to David and placed his hands on David's shoulders. "You must prepare for the coming of the great and dreadful day of the Lord."

David shook his head in disbelief. "But Israel is very small. How will all of those people fit into this country?"

"Because while many are called, few are chosen. For wide is the gate, and broad is the road that leads to destruction, and many enter through it. But small is the gate, and narrow the road that leads to life, and only a few find it." David wondered if the prophet meant that even if sanctuary were offered to the people of the world, not many would accept it.

The prophet leaned in closer to David. "The heart of the fathers will turn to their children, and the heart of the children to their fathers. Go, to America…for your daughter's sake."

"How, how did you know…?" David stammered.

"The Lord reveals what He will to whomever He will for His own good purposes. Go in peace, David. Shalom."

David and Katy watched the two prophets walk back to where they were preaching. They resumed their message that the final days of tribulation had arrived and that every human being must repent.

David was bewildered. How could the prophets have known about his daughter?

The car pulling up to the curb brought David back into the moment. The driver stepped out. "Mr. Prime Minister, are you ready to go?"

"Yes, let's get to Ben-Gurion."

"Will Ms. Thompson be accompanying you?"
"Yes, she will."

❧

When they reached Ben-Gurion, Katy and David spotted Mike waiting near the plane. Frank had already told Mike about Lorraine's murder, along with the apparent kidnapping of Rebecca. Somberly, he greeted David and Katy with a hug, agreeing to go with them to the States. "David, I want Lorraine's killer."

David looked into Mike's bloodshot eyes.

"And I want Rebecca's kidnapper. My brother, we'll get whoever did it; Lorraine's death will be avenged."

As they boarded the plane, reports of Corinthia's death kept coming in on international news outlets. Prince Sharif was still being named as the alleged assassin. Interpol reported that UN authorities had put out a worldwide APB for Sharif. David shut off his phone.

Deep in thought, David stared out the cabin window at the runway. "Sharif is now a marked man. With the whole world after him, we're the only people who can help him."

The pilot's voice came over the PA system, announcing it was time for takeoff. The turbines rumbled as the plane began to pull away from the terminal.

As the Gulfstream taxied toward the runway, something way out on the tarmac caught David's eye. A man was running toward the plane, wildly waving his arms over his head. As the man got closer, David did a double-take.

"Robby?" He pushed the call button in his armrest. "Stop the plane!"

The pilot immediately powered down the engines; the plane soon came to a halt. "Open the cabin door!"

Katy looked out the window. "What's going on?"

"I don't know; I need to get out there and see what Robby wants."

David quickly opened the cabin door and ran onto the tarmac where Robby was breathing heavily with his hands on his knees; a file folder was on the ground at his feet. "Robby, this better be important."

"It is." Robby bent down to pick up the folder. "David, your instincts were right on. You gotta see what we pulled off those security tapes from the World Trade Center."

"You found something?"

Robby pulled the toothpick from his mouth. "I got three things. First, here's a picture of you carrying Sarah out of the lobby of the North Tower."

Stunned, David gazed at the picture for a moment. "What else?"

"Look at the passenger manifest from American flight 11. On page three, look at the names circled halfway down." David spotted the names of John, Alexandra, Martin and Cindy Carlson. "All of Octavia's family died on the flight that crashed into the North Tower. The only Carlson not on flight 11 was their eight-year-old daughter, Octavia.

"Octavia's biological mother died giving birth; the baby was adopted by the Carlson family. Take a look at the birth certificate." Robby handed David the document. "Look where she was born."

"Foyers, Scotland?"

"Now look at her birth name."

"Octavia.... Crowley?"

"Aleister Crowley, the evil occultist, had many great-grandchildren. One of them was a girl named 'Octavia.' And that's not all. Here's an 8x10 glossy of what looks just like your nemesis entering the stairwell of the North Tower, 22 minutes after you entered that same stairwell."

"Corinthia?"

"It looks like you were all destined to meet that day." David grabbed the folder out of Robby's hands and quickly headed back to the plane. "Skip! This is no coincidence."

Before boarding, David turned around. He looked at Robby. "I'm going back to New York to get my daughter."

Mike was sitting alone in the rear of the plane, sobbing quietly. David sat down next to Katy. She looked at him and took his hand in hers; he squeezed her hand tightly. She kissed his cheek and rested her head on his shoulder. "Don't worry, David; we'll find her."

"Yes, and I will also find the kidnappers, and I will kill them."

As the plane ascended through the clouds above Jerusalem, David was contemplating his return to America where Sarah's mission for him began long ago.

But this time, the mission was his. He pulled out the picture of Sarah and him escaping the World Trade Center.

David peered out the cabin window as Katy began to fall asleep. Taking a deep breath, he remembered what Sarah said to him underneath his shirt when they first looked into each other's eyes.

As he watched the clouds whisk by the wing of the plane, he whispered, "Elijah."

꿍

In the room where Corinthia's body lay motionless, Marcus Wodan closed the door. Cautiously approaching the covered body, Wodan could not believe that the leader of the world, Secretary General Anno Corinthia, was truly dead. He closed his eyes for a moment and meditated, remembering the commands that Corinthia gave him.

Marcus looked up and realized: Now is the time.

Wodan removed the black onyx box from the wall safe and placed it on a table next to Corinthia's body. He slowly pulled back the sheet, revealing the fatal head wound and bloody stump where a left hand used to be. Wodan took five black stones from the box, placing them on the center of Corinthia's torso in the pattern of an upside-down crucifix. He placed the sixth stone of power over Corinthia's heart.

Marcus opened the Codex Gigas.

He closed his eyes and spread his arms wide. "I invoke thee, the terrible and invisible god: Who dwellest in the void place of the spirit. Thou spiritual Sun! Satan! Ar, o, go, go, ru, abrao. Sotou, thou the savior!"

After he chanted the Satanic mantra for several

minutes, Corinthia's body remained motionless, pale, and drained of life. Dejected, Wodan turned away and started to leave the chamber.

In an instant, the lights in the chamber began to blink. The floor shook and the gurney that held Corinthia began to rumble. Marcus whirled around; he shielded his eyes from the blinding white light and smoke streaming from the black stones. A wave of energy shot through the room, knocking him to the floor.

Staggering to his feet, he put his hand over his mouth and gagged as the odor of burning flesh surrounded him. The stones of Samhain turned bright hot orange and sunk deeply into Corinthia's body, absorbed by his flesh.

Marcus stood in shock as the mortal wound in Corinthia's head healed, and a hand appeared where there was none. Coughing from inhaling the smoke, Marcus approached cautiously. Corinthia's eyes opened before he slowly rose from the gurney. Marcus could see that this was not the same man that he knew. Looking into his eyes, Marcus now saw something different, something powerful, something eternal.

Corinthia placed his hand on his forehead and stroked the area where Sharif's sword had killed him. Smiling at his new left hand, he moved it back and forth.

Marcus, trembling, was barely able to speak. "Master."

"Well done, Marcus," Corinthia uttered in an ominously deep tone that echoed through the chamber.

Marcus gazed in awe at the risen Corinthia. "Master, how may I serve you?"

"You must have Ali prepare for the rationing of food, water, medicine, and all other necessities of life, to go only..." Smiling, Corinthia looked at Marcus, "...to the approved. Have Octavia capture David Stein, and exterminate him. Nigel will prepare my seat in Jerusalem...and kill the prophets."

Corinthia arose from the gurney and glided across the room; reaching down, he picked up the katana that Sharif had used to slay him. The blade was stained with his blood. Examining it, he laughed before dropping it to the floor.

Marcus bowed down before lowering himself to his knees. He then looked up at Corinthia. "Master, you're alive. I thought, I thought, it was the end."

Corinthia stood erect, his arms were folded across his chest; his burning eyes looked through his loyal servant. "No, Marcus...it is only the beginning."

A sequel to "Freedom's Last Stand – The Rise of Evil"
is scheduled for release in 2021

Made in the USA
Monee, IL
17 May 2021

68817303R00207